OBSESSION MINE

Anna Zaires

♠ Mozaika Publications ♠

Copyright © 2017 Anna Zaires & Dima Zales
www.annazaires.com

Published by Mozaika Publications, an imprint of Mozaika LLC.
www.mozaikallc.com

Cover by Najla Qamber Designs
www.najlaqamberdesigns.com

e-ISBN: 978-1-63142-238-6
ISBN: 978-1-63142-239-3

PART 1

CHAPTER 1
PETER

"They're gaining on us," Ilya says as the whine of sirens and the roar of helicopter blades grow louder. Light from the cars on the other side of the highway bounces off his shaved head, creating the illusion that his skull tattoos are dancing as he glances in the rearview mirror with a worried frown.

"Right." Ignoring the adrenaline pumping in my veins, I tighten my arm around Sara, preventing her head from sliding off my shoulder as Ilya zooms around a slower-moving car. I expected the pursuit, of course—one doesn't steal a woman guarded by the FBI without consequences—but now that it's happening, I find myself worried.

My three teammates and I can handle a high-speed chase just fine, but I can't endanger Sara that way.

Reaching a decision, I tell Ilya, "Slow down. Let them catch up to us."

Anton twists around in the front passenger seat, his bearded face incredulous as he grips his M16. "Are you insane?"

"We can't lead them to the airport," Yan, Ilya's twin, points out. He's sitting on the other side of Sara, and he must've caught on to my plan, because he's already rummaging in the large duffel bag we stored under the backseat of our SUV.

"Do you think the Feds know we have her?" Anton glances at the unconscious woman pressed to my side, and I feel an irrational flicker of jealousy as his black gaze roves over Sara's face, lingering for a moment longer than necessary on her plush pink lips.

"They must. Those guys tailing her were stupid but not completely inept," Yan says, straightening with a grenade launcher in his hands. Unlike his twin, he favors a conservative hairstyle and neatly pressed business clothes—his banker disguise, as Ilya calls it. In general, Yan looks like someone who wouldn't know how to handle a wrench, much less a gun, but he's one of the most lethal individuals I know—as are the rest of my team.

Our clients pay us millions for a reason, and it has nothing to do with our fashion choices.

"I hope you're right," Ilya says, tightening his grip on the wheel as he glances in the rearview mirror again. Two black government SUVs and three police cruisers are now four cars behind us, blue and red lights flashing as they pass slower-moving vehicles. "American police are soft. They won't risk shooting if they know we have her."

"Nor will they open fire in the middle of a highway," Yan says, pressing a button to roll down the window. "Too many civilians around."

"Hold off for a moment," I tell him as he moves closer to the window, the grenade launcher in hand. "We want the chopper as low as possible above us. Ilya, slow down some more and get into the right lane. We're taking the next exit."

Ilya does as I say, and we switch into the slower lane, our speed dropping below the posted limit. A gray Toyota Camry zooms past us on the left, and I press Sara closer to me, telling Yan to get ready. The noise from the helicopter is deafening—it's hovering almost directly overhead now—but I wait.

A few moments later, I see it.

The sign for the exit, coming up in a quarter mile.

"Now," I yell, and Yan springs into action, propelling his head and torso out the window, the grenade launcher in his hands.

Boom! It sounds like the mother of all fireworks just went off above us. Brakes screech all around us, but we're already at the exit, and Ilya swerves off the highway just as all hell breaks loose, cars colliding in both lanes with a clang of crumpling metal as the chopper above explodes in a fiery metal ball.

"Fuuuck," Anton breathes, staring at the mess we left behind. With the flaming chopper pieces raining down, a giant Walmart truck is in the process of flipping over, and no less than a dozen cars have already crashed, with more ramming into the pile with each second. The government

SUVs are among the victims, and the police cruisers are trapped behind them. There's no way our pursuers will be able to follow us now, and though I'm not happy about the injured civilians, I know this is how we'll make our escape.

By the time they regroup and send more cops after us, we'll be long gone.

Nobody is taking Sara away from me.

She chose me, and she's staying mine.

———————

We get to the underpass where we left our other vehicle without pursuit, and once we switch cars, we all breathe a little easier. I have no doubt the Feds will locate us, but by the time they do, we should be safely in the air.

We're almost at the airport when Sara lets out a small moan, her eyelids fluttering open as she stirs at my side.

The drug I gave her has worn off.

"Shhh," I soothe, kissing her forehead as she tries to wriggle out of the blanket cocooning her from neck down. "You're okay, ptichka. I'm here, and all is well. Here, drink this." With my free hand, I open a sports bottle filled with water and press it to her lips, letting her suck down some liquid.

"What... where am I?" she croaks hoarsely when I take the bottle away, and I tighten my arm around her shoulders, preventing her from unrolling the blanket and exposing her nakedness. "What happened?"

"Nothing bad," I assure her, setting the bottle down to brush a strand of hair off her face. "We're just going on a little trip."

On the other side of Sara, Yan snorts and mutters in Russian something about major understatements.

Sara's gaze darts toward Yan, then bounces all over the car, and I see the exact moment she realizes what's happening.

"Please tell me you didn't…" Her voice rises in pitch. "Peter, tell me you didn't just—"

"Shhh." Turning her fully toward me, I press two fingers against her soft lips. "I couldn't stay, and I couldn't leave you behind, ptichka. You know that. It's going to be fine. Nothing bad is going to happen to you. I'm going to keep you safe."

She stares at me, her hazel eyes filled with shock and horror, and despite my certainty that I did the right thing, my chest tightens unpleasantly.

Sara warned me about the FBI, knowing I would most likely take her with me, but she probably didn't expect me to do it like this. And maybe there was some other way, something I could've done that wouldn't have involved drugging her and stealing her in the middle of the night.

No. Shaking off the uncharacteristic self-doubt, I focus on what matters: reassuring Sara and getting her to accept the situation.

"Listen to me, ptichka." I curve my palm around her delicate jaw. "I know you're worried about your parents, but as soon as we're airborne, you can call them and—"

"Airborne? So we're still in—? Oh thank God." She closes her eyes, and I feel a tremor run through her before she opens her eyes to meet my gaze. "Peter…" Her voice turns soft, cajoling. "Peter, please. You don't have to do this.

You can just leave me here. It'll be so much safer for you… so much easier to get away if they're not searching for me. You could just disappear, and they'll never catch you, and then—"

"They'll never catch me regardless." My tone is clipped, but I can't help the flare of anger as I lower my hand. Sara had her chance to be rid of me, and she didn't take it. By warning me, she sealed her fate, and it's too late to back out now. Yes, I drugged and took her without asking, but she had to know I wouldn't leave her behind. I told her how much I loved her, and though she didn't say the words back to me, I know she's not indifferent. Maybe this is not precisely what she wanted, but she chose me, and for her to beg me to leave her behind now, to try to manipulate me with her big eyes and sweet voice… It hurts, this rejection of hers, though it shouldn't.

I *did* kill her husband and force my way into her life.

"We're here," Anton says in Russian as the car slows, and I turn my head to see our plane some twenty meters ahead.

"Peter, please." Sara begins to struggle inside the blanket, her voice rising in volume as the car comes to a complete stop and my men jump out. "Please don't do this. This is wrong. You know this is wrong. My whole life is here. I have my family and my patients and my friends…" She's crying now, her struggles intensifying as I bend to grab her blanket-wrapped legs and haul her out of the car. "Please, you said you wouldn't do this if I cooperated, and I did. I did everything you wanted. Please, Peter, stop! Leave me here! Please!"

She's hysterical now, twisting and bucking in the confines of the blanket as I back out of the car, holding her against my chest, and Anton shoots me an uncomfortable look as he helps the twins get the weapons from under the backseat. Though my friend had suggested on more than one occasion that I should just take Sara if I want her, the reality of it must be crueler than he imagined.

Other people might deem us monsters, but we *can* feel—and it would take a heart of steel not to feel something as Sara continues to beg and plead, struggling inside the blanket cocoon as I carry her to the plane.

"I'm sorry," I tell her when I bring her into the passenger cabin and carefully deposit her into one of the wide leather seats at the front. Her distress is like a poison-tipped blade in my side, but the thought of leaving her behind is even more agonizing. I can't picture my life without Sara, and I'm ruthless enough—and selfish enough—to ensure I won't need to.

She might be having second thoughts about her decision, but she'll come around and accept the situation, just like she was beginning to accept our relationship. And then she'll be happy again—happier, even. We're going to build a life together, and it's going to be one she'll enjoy as well.

I have to believe that, because this is the only way I can have her.

This is the only way I can know love again.

CHAPTER 2
SARA

*T*ears of panic and bitter frustration roll down my face as the wheels of the jet lift off the runway, and the lights of the small airport fade into inky darkness. In the distance, I see the light clusters of Chicago and its suburbs, but before long, they disappear too, leaving me with the crushing knowledge that my old life is gone.

I've lost my family, my friends, my career, and my freedom.

My stomach roils with nausea as shards of glass pierce my temples, my headache aggravated by whatever Peter injected to knock me out. Worst of all, though, is the suffocating sensation in my chest, the awful feeling that I can't get enough air. I take deep breaths to combat it, but it only worsens. The blanket is like a straightjacket, keeping my arms pinned to my sides, and I can't get enough oxygen into my lungs.

My tormentor carried out his threat.

He kidnapped me, and I may never see home again.

He's not next to me now—as soon as we took off, he got up and disappeared into the back of the passenger cabin, where two of his men are sitting—and I'm glad. I can't bear to look at him, to know that I was stupid enough to warn him when he already knew everything.

When he had that needle ready and was toying with me.

How did he know? Were there cameras and listening devices inside the hospital locker room where Karen confronted me? Or did the men Peter assigned to follow me spot my FBI tail and tell him? Or maybe he has some connections in the FBI, just like that one contact of his had in the CIA? Is that possible, or am I reaching? Either way, it doesn't matter now; the point is, he knew.

He knew, yet he pretended not to, playing with my emotions while he waited for me to crack.

God, how could I have been such an idiot? How could I have warned him, knowing that something like this could happen? How could I have come home when I suspected— no, when I *knew*—what my stalker was likely to do if he learned about the impending danger? I should've told Karen everything when I had the chance, let her send the agents to my house while the FBI took me into protective custody. Yes, Peter might've still escaped, but he wouldn't have taken me with him—not at that point, at least. I would've had more time to plan, to figure out the best way for me and my parents to stay safe. He would've most likely returned for me, but there was at least a chance the FBI could've protected us.

Instead, I walked right into Peter's trap. I went home, and I let him lie to me. Let him fool me into believing that there was something human—something good—within him. "I love you," he said, and I fell for it, buying into the illusion that we had something genuine, that his tenderness meant he truly cared for me.

I let my irrational attachment to my husband's killer blind me to the reality of what he is, and I lost everything.

The tightness in my chest grows, my lungs constricting until every breath is a struggle. Rage and despair mix together, making me want to scream, but all I can manage is a pained wheeze, the blanket around my body as smothering as a noose around my neck. I'm too hot, too restrained; my head is pounding, and my heart is beating too fast. I feel like I'm suffocating, dying, and I want to claw at my throat, to tear it open so I can suck in air.

"Here, it's okay." Peter is crouched in front of me, though I didn't see him return. His strong hands are loosening the blanket, smoothing my hair back from my sweat-dampened face. I'm shaking and wheezing, in the throes of a full-blown panic attack, and his touch is bizarrely soothing, taking away the worst of the suffocating sensation.

"Breathe, ptichka," he urges, and I do, my lungs obeying him the way they refuse to obey me. My chest expands with one full breath, then another, and then I'm breathing semi-normally, my throat opening to let in precious oxygen. I'm still sweating, still shaking, but my pulse is slowing, the fear of suffocating disappearing as Peter liberates my arms from the blanket and hands me a man's black T-shirt.

"I'm sorry. I didn't have a chance to grab any of your clothes," he says, helping me pull the enormous T-shirt over my head. "Luckily, Anton stashed a change of clothes in the back. Here, you can put on these pants, too." He guides my trembling feet into a pair of men's black jeans, helps me put on a pair of black socks, and removes the blanket altogether, throwing it on the table next to us.

Like the T-shirt, the jeans are huge on me, but there is a belt inside the loops, and Peter tightens it around my hips, knotting it at the front like a tie before rolling up the pant legs.

"There," he says, eyeing his handiwork with satisfaction. "That should suffice for the flight, and then I'll get you a brand-new wardrobe."

I close my eyes, shutting him out. I can't bear to look at his exotically handsome features, can't tolerate the warmth in those steel-gray eyes. It's all a lie, an illusion. He doesn't care for me, not really. Obsession is not love, and that's what he feels for me: a dark, terrible obsession that ruins and destroys.

That has already destroyed my life in so many ways.

I hear him sigh before his big hands wrap around my cold palms.

"Sara…" His deep, softly accented voice feels like a caress over my skin. "We'll make it work, ptichka, I promise. It won't be as bad as you're imagining. Now tell me… do you want to call your parents, explain everything to them?"

My parents? Startled, I open my eyes to gape at him. Then I realize he mentioned this before, only I didn't register it. "You're letting me call my parents?"

My captor nods, a small smile curving his sculpted lips as he remains crouched in front of me, his hands gently clasping mine. "Of course. I know you don't want them to worry, with your dad's heart and all."

Oh God. *My dad's heart.* My headache intensifies at the reminder. At eighty-seven, my dad is remarkably healthy for his age, but he had a triple bypass surgery a few years back and has to avoid stress. And I can't imagine anything more stressful than— "Do you think the FBI spoke to them already?" I gasp in sudden horror. "Did they tell my parents I was kidnapped?"

"I doubt they would've had the time." Peter squeezes my hands reassuringly, then releases them and rises to his feet. Reaching into his pocket, he pulls out a smartphone and hands it to me. "Call them, so you can give them your version of the story first."

"My version of the story? And what version is that?" The phone feels like a brick in my hand, its weight magnified by the knowledge that if I say the wrong thing, I could literally kill my dad. "What can I tell them that will make this in any way okay?"

My tone is caustic, but my question is genuine. I can't imagine what I can say to lessen my parents' panic over my disappearance, how I can explain what the FBI is about to tell them—especially since I don't know how much the agents will reveal.

The plane chooses that moment to hit a pocket of turbulence, and Peter sits down next to me. "Tell them you met a man… a man you fell in love with." He covers my knee with his warm palm, his metallic gaze mesmerizing in its intensity. "Tell them that for the first time in your life, you decided to do something crazy and irresponsible. That you're fine, but for the next few weeks, you'll be traveling around the world with your lover."

"The next few weeks?" A wild hope blooms inside me. "Are you saying that—"

"No. You won't be back in a few weeks. But they don't need to know that yet."

The hope withers and dies, the crushing despair returning. "I'll never see them again, will I?"

"You will." His hand squeezes my knee. "At some point, when it's safe."

"And when will that be?"

"I don't know, but we'll figure it out."

"*We*?" A bitter laugh escapes my throat. "Are you under the impression that this is some kind of partnership? That *we* kidnapped me together?"

Peter's gaze hardens. "It *can* be a partnership, Sara. If you want it to be."

"Oh, really?" I push his hand off my knee. "Then turn this fucking plane around, *partner*. I want to go home."

"That's impossible, and you know that." His bristle-darkened jaw flexes.

"Is it? Why? Because you love to fuck me? Or because you fucking love me?" My voice rises as I jump to my feet, hands balled at my sides. I can see his men in the seats behind us, their faces stony as they stare out the window, pretending not to listen, but I don't care. I'm past embarrassment, past shame; all I feel is rage.

I've never wanted to hurt a living person as much as I want to hurt Peter at this moment.

My tormentor's gaze is dark, his expression hard as he stands up. "Sit down, Sara," he says harshly, reaching for me as the plane hits another bump and I grab at the window wall to steady myself. "It's not safe." He takes my arm to force me back into the seat, and my other hand acts of its own accord.

With the phone still clutched in my fist, I take a swing at him—and don't miss, because at that moment, the plane dips again, throwing us both off-balance. With an audible thud, the phone crashes into Peter's face, the impact of the hit jarring my bones and snapping his head to the side.

I don't know who's more shocked that I managed to land a blow, me or Peter's men.

I can see their incredulous stares as Peter slowly, and very deliberately, releases my arm and wipes at the blood trickling down his cheekbone. The metal shell of the phone must've cut his skin; that, or the unexpected turbulence lent momentum to my blow, intensifying the force behind it.

His eyes meet mine, and my heart jumps into my throat at the icy rage shimmering in the silvery depths. Warily, I back away, the phone slipping out of my numb fingers to hit the floor with a metallic *thunk*.

I haven't forgotten what Peter is capable of, what he did to me when we first met.

I can only take two steps before my back presses against the wall of the pilot's cabin, ending my retreat. I have nowhere to run on this plane, no place to hide, and fear tightens my stomach as he steps closer, his furious gaze holding mine captive as he braces his palms on the wall on both sides of me, caging me between his muscular arms.

"I…" I should say that I'm sorry, that I didn't mean it, but I can't bring myself to voice the lie, so I clamp my lips shut before I can make it worse by telling him how much I hate him.

"You what?" His voice is low and hard. Leaning in, he bends his head until his lips graze the top of my ear. "You what, Sara?"

I shiver at the damp heat of his breath, my knees going weak and my pulse accelerating further. Only this time, it's not entirely from fear. Despite everything, his nearness wreaks havoc on my senses, my body quivering in anticipation of his touch. Only hours ago, he was inside me, and I still feel the aftermath of his possession, the inner soreness from the hard rhythm of his thrusts. At the same time, I'm painfully aware of my hardened nipples poking through the borrowed T-shirt and the warm slickness gathering between my legs.

Even clothed, I feel naked in his arms.

He lifts his head, staring down at me, and I know he feels it too, the magnetic heat, the dark connection that vibrates the air around us, intensifying each moment until milliseconds feel like hours. Peter's men are less than a dozen feet away, watching us, but it feels like we're all alone, wrapped in a bubble of sensual need and volatile tension.

My mouth is dry, my body pulsing with awareness, and it's all I can do not to sway toward him, to remain still instead of pressing against him and giving in to the desire burning me up inside.

"Ptichka…" Peter's voice softens, taking on an intimate edge as the ice in his gaze melts. His hand leaves the wall to cup my cheek, the rough pad of his thumb stroking over my lips and making my breath catch in my throat. At the same time, his other hand clasps my elbow, his grip gentle but inescapable. "Come, let's sit down," he urges, pulling me away from the wall. "It's not safe to be up and about like this."

Dazed, I let him shepherd me back to the seat. I know I should continue fighting, or at least put up some resistance, but the anger that filled me is gone, leaving numbness and despair in its wake.

Even after what he did, I crave him. I want him just as much as I hate him.

My sock-clad feet are chilled from walking on the cold floor, and I'm grateful when Peter grabs the blanket from the table and tucks it around my legs before sitting down next to me. He pulls the seatbelt over me, buckling me in, and I close my eyes, not wanting to see the warmth that now fills his gaze. As frightening as the darker side of Peter is, the man who's doing this—the tender, caring lover—is the one who terrifies me most.

I can resist the monster, but the man is a different story.

Warm fingers brush across my hand, and cold metal presses into my palm. Startled, I open my eyes and look at the phone Peter just handed to me.

He must've picked it up from where I dropped it.

"If you want to call your parents, you might want to do so now," he says softly. "Before they hear anything on their own."

I swallow, staring at the phone in my hand. Peter is right; there's no time to waste. I don't know what I'm going to tell my parents, but anything is better than what the FBI agents are likely to say.

"How do I call?" I glance at Peter. "Is there some special code or anything I need to use?"

"No. All my calls are automatically encoded. Just put in their number as usual."

I take a deep breath and punch in my mom's cell. She's more likely to panic at getting a call in the middle of the night, but she's nine years younger than my dad and has no known heart problems. Holding the phone up to my ear, I turn away from Peter and watch the night sky through the window as I wait for the call to connect.

It rings a dozen times before going to voicemail.

Mom must be sleeping too deeply to hear it, or else she has the phone turned off for the night.

Frustrated, I try again.

"Hello?" Mom's voice is sleepy and disgruntled. "Who is this?"

I exhale in relief. It doesn't sound like the FBI got to them yet; if they had, Mom wouldn't be sleeping so soundly.

"Hi, Mom. It's me, Sara."

"Sara?" Mom instantly sounds more alert. "What's wrong? Where are you calling from? Did something happen?"

"No, no. Everything is fine. I'm perfectly fine." I take a breath, my mind racing as I try to come up with the least worrisome story. At some point soon, the FBI *will* contact my parents, and my story will be exposed for a lie. However, the very fact that I called and told such a story should reassure my parents that, at the time of the call at least, I was alive and well, lessening the impact of whatever the agents will tell them.

Steadying my voice, I say, "Sorry to call so late, Mom, but I'm going on a last-minute trip, and I wanted to let you know, so you wouldn't worry."

"A trip?" Mom sounds confused. "Where? Why?"

"Well..." I hesitate and then decide to go with Peter's suggestion. This way, when my parents learn of the kidnapping, they might think I went with Peter of my own free will. What the FBI will think is another matter, but I'll save that worry for a different day. "I met someone. A man."

"A man?"

"Yes, I've been seeing him for a few weeks. I didn't want to say anything because I didn't know that much about him, and I wasn't sure how serious it was." I can sense Mom is about to launch into an interrogation, so I quickly say, "In any case, he had to go out of the country unexpectedly, and he invited me to come along. I know it's completely crazy, but I needed to get away—you know, from everything—and this seemed as good of an opportunity as any. We're going to be traveling the world together for a few weeks, so—"

"What?" Mom's voice rises in pitch. "Sara, that's—"

"Insane? I know." I grimace, grateful she can't see my pained expression. Between lying to her and the continued headache, I feel like absolute shit. "I'm sorry, Mom. I didn't want you to worry, but it's something I had to do. I hope you and Dad understand."

"Wait a minute. Who is this man? What is his name? What does he do? Where did you meet?" She fires off each question like a bullet.

I turn to look at Peter, and he gives me a small nod, his face impassive. I don't know if he can hear my conversation, but I interpret that nod to mean I can tell my parents a few more details.

"His name is Peter," I say, deciding to stay as close to the truth as possible. "He's a contractor of sorts, works mostly abroad. We met when he was in the Chicago area, and we've been seeing each other ever since. I wanted to tell you about him at our sushi lunch, but it didn't seem like the right time."

"Okay, but... but what about your work? And the clinic?"

I pinch the bridge of my nose. "I'll get it all settled, don't worry." I won't, of course—this kind of bullshit won't fly with my hospital-based practice even if Peter lets me call them—but I can't tell Mom that without making her worry prematurely. She'll have a panic attack soon enough, when the agents show up on her doorstep. Until then, she and Dad might as well think I've gone crazy.

A daughter belatedly acting out is infinitely better than a daughter kidnapped by her husband's killer.

"Sara, darling…" Mom sounds worried regardless. "Are you sure about this? I mean, you said yourself you don't know much about this man, and now you're leaving the country with him? This is not like you at all. You didn't even tell me where you're going. Are you flying or driving? And what is this number you're calling from? It's showing up as blocked, and the reception is all weird, like you're—"

"Mom." I rub my forehead, my headache worsening. I can't answer any more of her questions, so I say, "Listen, I have to go. Our plane is about to take off. I just wanted to give you a quick update so you wouldn't worry, okay? I'll call you again as soon as I can."

"But, Sara—"

"Bye, Mom. Talk to you soon!"

I hang up before she can say anything else, and Peter takes the phone from me, his mouth curved in an approving smile.

"Good job. You have a real talent for this."

"For lying to my parents about getting kidnapped? Yes, a real talent, for sure." Bitterness drips from my words, and I don't bother toning it down. I'm done being nice and agreeable.

We're no longer playing that game.

Peter doesn't appear fazed. "You told them something that will allay the worst of their worry. I don't know how much the Feds will disclose, but this should reassure your parents that you're alive and well as of today. Hopefully, it will be enough until you contact them again."

That was my thought process as well, and it bothers me that we're on the same wavelength. It's a small thing, reasoning alike in this one instance, but it feels like a slip-pery slope, like a step toward that partnership Peter men-tioned. Toward the illusion that there is a "we," that our relationship is in any way genuine.

I can't—I won't—fall for that lie again. I'm not Peter's partner, his girlfriend, or his lover.

I'm his captive, the widow of a man he killed to avenge his family, and I can't ever forget that fact.

Fighting to keep my voice even, I ask, "So I will have a chance to contact them again?" At Peter's affirmative nod, I press, "When?"

His gray eyes gleam. "Once they hear from the FBI and have a chance to digest everything. So in other words, soon."

"How will you know whether they hear from—? Oh, never mind. You're watching my parents too, aren't you?"

"I'm monitoring their house, yes." He doesn't look the least bit ashamed. "So we'll know what the agents tell them and when. Then we'll figure out what you should say and how to contact them again."

I press my lips together. There's that insidious "we" again. As if this is a joint project, like interior decorating or choosing a bottle of wine for a family gathering. Does he expect me to be grateful for this? To thank him for being so nice and thoughtful with the logistics of my kidnapping?

Does he think that if he lets me alleviate my parents' worry, I'll forget that he stole my life?

Gritting my teeth, I turn away to stare out the win-dow, then realize I still don't know the answer to one of my mom's questions.

Turning back to face my kidnapper, I meet his coolly amused gaze. "Where are we going?" I ask, forcing myself to speak calmly. "Where exactly are *we* going to be figuring all this out from?"

Peter grins, revealing white teeth that are slightly crooked on the bottom. Between that and the small scar on his lower lip, his smile should've been off-putting, but the imperfections only highlight its dangerously sensual appeal.

"*We* are going to be figuring it out from Japan, ptichka," he says and reaches across the table to gather my hand in his big palm. "The Land of the Rising Sun is our new home."

CHAPTER 3
SARA

I don't speak to Peter for the rest of the flight. Instead, I pass out, my brain turning off as though to escape reality. I'm grateful for that. The headache is relentless, the drummers beating inside my skull every time I try to open my eyes, and it's only when we start our descent that I wake up enough to drag myself to the restroom.

When I return, I find Peter in the seat next to mine, working on a laptop. I think he might've been there throughout the flight, but I'm not sure. I do remember falling asleep while he held my hand, his strong fingers massaging my palm, and I recall him tucking the blanket around me at some point when the cabin got extra chilly.

"How are you feeling?" he asks, looking up from the laptop as I step around him and sit down in my plush leather seat. Now that the initial shock of the abduction has passed, I realize the jet is quite luxurious, though not very big. Toward the back of the plane, there are two more rows of seats besides ours, each seat big and fully reclining, and in the middle is a beige leather couch with two end tables attached to it.

"Sara," Peter prompts when I don't answer, and I shrug in response, not inclined to soothe his conscience by admitting that I feel better after my long nap. The effects of the drug must've fully worn off, because the nausea and the headache that tormented me are gone.

I *am* hungry and thirsty, though, so I reach for the bottle of water and the bowl of peanuts sitting on the small table between our seats.

"We'll have a real meal soon," Peter says, pushing the bowl toward me. "We weren't expecting to leave the country so suddenly, and this is all we had on board."

"Uh-huh." Not meeting his eyes, I gulp down half of the water bottle, eat a handful of nuts, and wash them down with the rest of the water. I'm not surprised to hear about the lack of food on the plane; the wonder is that he had a plane on standby, period. I know he and his team get paid ridiculous sums of money to assassinate crime lords and such, but the cost of this mid-sized jet must be well into eight figures.

Unable to contain my curiosity, I glance at my captor. "Is this yours?" I wave a hand to indicate our surroundings. "Did you buy it?"

"No." He closes the laptop and smiles. "I got it as payment from one of our clients."

"I see." I look away, focusing on the dark sky outside the window instead of that magnetic smile. Now that I'm feeling better, I'm even more bitterly aware of what Peter has done—and how hopeless my situation is.

If I was at my tormentor's mercy at home, where I was afraid of what might happen if I went to the authorities, I'm now doubly so. Peter Sokolov can do anything to me, keep me captive until I die if he's so inclined. His men won't help me, and I'm about to enter a country where I don't speak the language and don't know anything or anyone.

I love sushi, but that's as far as my familiarity with Japan extends.

"Sara?" Peter's deep voice cuts into my thoughts, and I instinctively turn to look at him.

"Buckle up." He nods toward the seatbelt lying unfastened at my side. "We'll be landing shortly."

I pull the seatbelt over my lap before turning my attention back to the window. I can't see much in the darkness—we must've flown long enough for it to be night in Japan despite the time difference—but I keep my eyes on the sky outside, both in the hopes of seeing something and out of the desire to avoid conversing with Peter.

I'm not going to act like we really *are* lovers going on a trip, to pretend that I'm okay with this in any shape or form. The leverage he had over me—his threat to steal me away if I didn't play along with his domestic bliss fantasy—is gone, and I have no intention of being his compliant victim again. I was beginning to give in, to fall under his twisted spell, but that's all over now. Peter Sokolov tortured me and killed my husband, and now he's kidnapped me. There's nothing between us except a fucked-up past and an even more fucked-up future.

He might have me, but he won't enjoy it.
I'll make sure of that.

CHAPTER 4
PETER

*M*y cheekbone still smarts from Sara's blow as we land at a private airport near Matsumoto and transfer to the helicopter waiting for us there. I'll have a black eye tomorrow—an idea I find amusing now that the initial shock of anger is past. The pain Sara inflicted is minor—I've suffered worse in routine training—but the unexpectedness of my pretty little doctor physically lashing out is what got to me.

It was like being scratched bloody by a kitten, one you just want to cuddle and protect.

She's still angry with me. It's obvious in her rigid posture, in the way she doesn't speak to me or even glance my way as the helicopter takes off. Though it's still dark, I see her staring at the sights below, and I know she's trying to memorize where we're going.

She'll attempt to escape at the earliest opportunity, I can tell.

Anton pilots the chopper, and Ilya sits in the back with me and Sara while Yan is up front. We're not expecting any trouble, but we're armed, so I keep a careful eye on Sara to make sure she doesn't do anything foolish, like trying to grab a gun from me or Ilya.

Given the mood she's in, I wouldn't put anything past her.

Our Japanese safe house is located in the sparsely populated, mountainous Nagano Prefecture, at the very peak of a steep, heavily forested mountain overlooking a small lake. On a clear day, the view is breathtaking, but the main reason I acquired the property is that this particular mountaintop is only accessible by air. There used to be a dirt road on the west slope—that's how a wealthy Tokyo businessman built his summer home up there back in the nineties—but an earthquake-triggered landslide made the slope into a cliff, cutting off all ground access to the property and destroying its value.

The businessman's children were beyond grateful when one of my shell companies purchased the house last year, sparing them from the burden of paying taxes on a place they neither wanted nor had the means to visit regularly.

"So why Japan?"

Sara's tone is flat and disinterested as she gazes out the chopper window, but I know she must be dying of curiosity to break the hour-long silence and actually speak to me.

It's either that, or she's fishing for information that could help her escape.

"Because this is the last place anyone would think to look for us," I answer, figuring there's no harm in telling her the truth. "Nothing connects me to the country. Russia, Europe, the Middle East, Africa, the Americas, Thailand, Hong Kong, the Philippines—at one point or another, I've blipped on the authorities' radar in all those places, but never here."

"Also, it makes for a pleasant hideout," Ilya says in English, speaking to Sara for the first time. "Much better than holing up in some cave in Dagestan or sweating our balls off in India."

Sara gives him an indecipherable look, then turns her attention back to the view outside. I don't blame her. The sky is lightening with the first hints of dawn, and it's possible to make out the mountain slopes and forests below. By the time we reach our mountaintop retreat, she'll get the full impact of the view—and realize she can give up all hope of escape. Because that's another reason for my choice of Japan: the remote location of this specific house.

My little bird's new cage will be both pretty and impossible to flee from.

———

We land forty minutes later on a small helipad next to the house, and I watch Sara's face as she takes in the sight of our new home—a starkly modern wood-and-glass construction that blends seamlessly with the untouched nature surrounding it.

"Do you like it?" I ask, catching her gaze as I help her out of the chopper, and she looks away, pulling her hand out of my grasp as soon as her sock-clad feet are planted on the ground.

"Does it matter? If I said no, would you take me back?" She turns and starts walking toward the edge of the helipad, where the mountainside forms a cliff drop to the lake below.

"No, but if you hate it here, we can consider some of our other safe houses." Following her, I catch her wrist before she gets to the edge of the pad. I don't think she's upset enough to jump off a cliff, but I'm not about to risk it.

"Where? In Dagestan or India?" She finally looks up at me, eyes narrowed. Though it's late spring, it's winter cold at this altitude, the chilly morning wind whipping her chestnut waves around her face and molding the loose black T-shirt against her slender torso. I can feel her shivering, her wrist thin and fragile in my grasp, but her delicate jaw is set in a stubborn line as she holds my gaze.

She's so vulnerable, my Sara, but so strong too. A survivor, like me, though she probably wouldn't appreciate the comparison.

"Dagestan and India are two of the possibilities, yes," I say, letting her hear the amusement in my voice. She's trying to antagonize me, make me regret taking her with me, but no amount of sarcasm or silent treatment will do that.

I need Sara like I need air and water, and I'll never regret keeping her.

Her soft mouth compresses and she twists her arm, trying to break my grip on her wrist. "Let me go," she hisses when I don't immediately release her. "Take your fucking hand off me."

Despite my resolve to remain unaffected, a twinge of anger bites at me. Sara chose me, if not precisely *this*, and I'm not about to put up with her treating me like a leper.

Instead of releasing her wrist, I tighten my grip and pull her toward me, away from the edge of the helipad. When she's sufficiently far from the drop, I bend down and pick her up, ignoring her startled squeak of protest.

"No," I say grimly, pressing her against my chest. "I'm not letting you go."

And ignoring her attempts to twist out of my hold, I carry the woman I love to our new home.

CHAPTER 5
SARA

*P*eter doesn't release me until we're inside the house, and even then, when he sets me on my feet, he keeps his steely fingers wrapped around my wrist, chaining me to his side as I take in my gorgeous new prison.

And it *is* gorgeous. Even with the anger and frustration choking me up inside, I can appreciate the clean, modern lines of the open floor plan and the postcard-pretty views of the mountains and the lake visible through the enormous floor-to-ceiling windows. In the middle of the space, next to an ultra-modern kitchen, a set of plank-style hardwood stairs spirals to the second floor—and that's where Peter leads me, his hand still possessively holding my wrist.

"A Japanese businessman built this twenty years ago, but I renovated it when I bought it last year," Peter says as we go up the steps. "I didn't know we'd be coming here so soon, but I figured it's best to be ready."

I don't respond, because if I try to talk, I might break down and cry. At this very moment, the FBI could be telling my parents about my disappearance, and I undoubtedly have dozens of missed calls and messages from my work, as well as the clinic where I volunteer. One of my patients is supposed to go into labor this week, and I have a C-section scheduled for tomorrow. Or is it today? It's early morning in Japan; does that mean it's evening back home? I don't know what the time difference is, but I can't imagine it's less than ten hours. If so, I must've already missed a full day, and people are looking for me. Maybe even checking with my parents to find out where I am and why I'm not responding to any of their calls or messages.

My poor parents must be sick with worry.

"Can I call them?" I ask thickly as Peter leads me into a spacious bedroom. One of the walls is made entirely of glass, revealing a breathtaking view of snow-capped mountains in the distance and the lake spread out below. Or at least the view would be breathtaking if I could concentrate on it, instead of the suffocating lump in my throat.

Please let my dad be all right.

"Not yet," Peter says, his expression softening as he releases my wrist. If I didn't know better, I'd think he shares my concern about my parents. "We need to review the camera feeds to see what's been happening, and then find a way to reach out to your family without alerting anyone of our whereabouts."

I swallow and turn away before he can see the tears filling my eyes. This is all my fault. If I hadn't come home, if I'd confided in Karen in that locker room, everything would've been different. Yes, my parents and I would've had to go into protective custody, and most likely relocate, but that would've still been preferable to this nightmare. I don't know what I was thinking when I drove home from the hospital last night. Did I imagine that if I showed up at home as normal, Peter wouldn't know that the FBI had spoken to me? That the Feds might not realize that the man they're hunting had been all but living with me, and we'd go on as before?

That if I warned my tormentor about the impending danger, he'd thank me and quietly go on his merry way?

"Don't, Sara." He steps in front of me, forcing me to look up to meet his gaze. His jaw is tight, his eyes gleaming darkly as he says in a low, hard voice, "Don't pretend like you didn't want this. I know you're scared and you're having second thoughts, but you chose me; you chose *us*. That's why you told me they were coming for me, why you came home at all instead of letting them whisk you far away. I waited for you. I knew they were close, and I still waited, because I needed to see if you truly hated me… if you wanted me gone from your life. But you didn't, did you?" He cups my jaw, his thumb brushing over my cheek. "Did you, ptichka?"

"I did." My voice shakes, and to my shame, hot tears trickle down my face. I don't want to show weakness, but I can't help the toxic cauldron bubbling in my chest. "I was exhausted, and I had a headache. I wasn't thinking straight. On any other day—"

"Oh, really?" His mouth twists with cruel amusement as he drops his hand. "Is that the lie you're telling yourself?

That I took you against your will… that you didn't want any of this?"

"I didn't!" I step back, staring at him incredulously. He can't seriously believe what he's saying. "I would never agree to this. My parents, my patients, my friends, my whole life—it's all back there. You *abducted* me, Peter. There's no ambiguity here. You stuck a needle in my neck and you carried me away while I was drugged unconscious. How can you possibly think I came along voluntarily? Did you miss the part where I screamed and pleaded for you to leave me behind when I woke up? Were you deaf when I cried and begged you not to do this?" I'm beyond furious, but the tears won't stop flowing, and I swipe at my cheeks with the back of my hand, trembling with rage from head to toe.

Peter's lips flatten into a hard, dangerous line, and I again glimpse the terrifying stranger who broke into my house and tortured me. Only this time, I'm too angry to feel any fear. If he wants to punish me for this, let him.

I'll only hate him more.

He makes no move toward me, but his voice is harsh as he says, "So why did you do it? Why warn me, Sara? You knew I wouldn't leave you behind. And don't give me that bullshit about not thinking straight. You knew full well what kind of risk you were taking. Why do it if you didn't want to be with me?"

I drag in a shuddering breath and turn away, determined to control the tears that keep streaming down my face. The rage that filled me is dissipating, leaving me weary to the bone and hollow with despair. I want to stand my ground, deny what he's saying, but I can't. Maybe my thinking wasn't as clear as it should've been, but I did know what I was doing.

I wasn't surprised when the needle pricked my neck.

I feel Peter behind me, though I didn't hear him move. "Tell me, ptichka." His voice is soft again, his touch gentle as he clasps my shoulders, drawing me against his hard body. "Tell me why." His stubble rasps across my cheek as he bends his head to kiss my temple, and I tense, fighting the urge to lean back against him and let him cuddle and caress me until I forget that I lost everything.

Until I no longer care that he took away my life.

Lifting his head, Peter turns me around to face him, his gray eyes peering at me intently, and I know he won't let the matter drop. He won't rest until I admit my weakness, that irrational, insane impulse that made me sabotage my chance at freedom.

I lick my lips, tasting the salt of my tears. "I…" I swallow thickly. "I didn't want to see you dead." Even now, the horrifying images won't leave me, my brain visualizing how everything might've gone down in grisly detail. I can almost smell the coppery tang of blood as the SWAT team's bullets rip through Peter's muscled body, can almost see the armor-clad agents bursting through the bedroom door and dragging him off my bed.

Can almost feel the stark, crushing loneliness that would've been my life without my tormentor.

No. No, no, no. I shake off the thought, push it away like the lunacy that it is. I did *not* want this. Just because I missed Peter when he was on one of his assassination missions doesn't mean I wouldn't have moved on eventually. And it wasn't even him I missed. It was the deceptive comfort he provided, the illusion of love and caring. What I felt for him wasn't real, and neither is what he thinks he feels for me. A sick lie is all it's ever been between us, a pathological obsession on his end and an equally perverse neediness on mine.

Peter's eyes narrow, his hands tightening on my shoulders as he processes what I said. "So you warned me out of the goodness of your heart? You were being a Good Samaritan?"

I nod, blinking rapidly to hold back a fresh wave of tears. That wasn't the only reason for my lapse of judgment, but it's the only one I'm willing to admit to.

My captor's face hardens, and he drops his hands, stepping back. "I see."

If I didn't know better, I would've thought I hurt him.

In the next instant, however, he continues as if nothing happened. "This is our bedroom." His voice is cold and flat, utterly emotionless. "The bathroom is through there." He gestures at a door in the back of the room. "You can wash up and relax while we unpack some supplies and prepare breakfast. I'll have clothes brought here for you tomorrow, but in the meantime, there should be a robe in the bathroom and some of my clothes in the closet." He nods toward a set of doors on the opposite side of the room. "If you need anything, I'll be downstairs. Breakfast will be ready in a half hour."

I bite my lip. "Okay, thanks."

He exits the room, and I walk over to the window, my chest aching with grief for everything I lost—and for what I just glimpsed in Peter's eyes.

Pain.

I *did* hurt him, and for some reason, that hurts me.

CHAPTER 6
PETER

"She's not happy, huh?" Anton says quietly in Russian as I take out an oversized carton of eggs he just loaded into the fridge, set it on the counter next to the stovetop, and begin hunting for a frying pan.

"No." I barely restrain myself from slamming the cupboard door when I don't find the frying pan there. "But she'll get used to it."

"And if she doesn't?"

I finally locate the pan in one of the pull-out drawers by the stove. "Then she'll stay fucking miserable." Grabbing the pan, I shove the drawer shut, then curse myself when I see a hairline crack appear in the glossy white wood. Renovating the house one helicopter load at a time was a bitch, and I can't afford to vent my anger on the kitchen counters. Anton's face at training later today will be a much better target.

"You know this had to happen, right?" my friend continues, as though oblivious to the rage simmering in my gut. "That suburban bullshit couldn't continue forever. It's a miracle they didn't bust us sooner. If you want this girl long term—and you do, right?—this is the only way."

I clench my jaw so hard my molars ache. "Drop it, Anton. This is none of your fucking business."

"All right. Just reminding you of the facts. I know it sucks that she's upset and all, but—" He stops, apparently realizing I'm half a second away from kicking his teeth in. Taking out his Swiss army knife, he slices through a netted bag of oranges and puts the fruit into a big wooden bowl on the counter. Then, eyeing the carton of eggs with interest, he asks, "What's for breakfast?"

"For you? Not a thing." I crack five eggs into a mixing bowl, pour in a little milk, and add seasoning before stirring. "You and the twins can fend for yourself."

"That's harsh, man," Yan says, entering the kitchen. He's carrying a huge box filled with more fruits and veggies, as well as bread and frozen meat—food supplies that our local contact loaded onto the chopper before sending it our way.

"Ilya and I are starving, and you like to cook," Yan continues when I don't respond. "How hard is it to make some extra? I promise, *I* will keep my mouth shut about your pretty doctor."

Fighting the urge to snap at him, I crack a dozen more eggs into the bowl. I don't usually feed the guys, but Yan is right: it would be petty to deprive my team of a good breakfast after such a long trip.

I just need them to shut up about Sara, because if I hear one more word on the topic, I'll rip their fucking heads off.

Wisely, both Yan and Anton remain silent, unpacking the rest of the food as I cook the omelet, and by the time, Ilya walks in, I'm almost calm—if one doesn't count the sporadic urge to put my fist through the white quartz countertop.

Ilya sits down on one of the stainless-steel barstools and opens his laptop, reminding me that we have issues besides Sara to worry about.

"What did the hackers say?" I ask when I see him frowning at the screen. "Any leads on that *ublyudok*?"

"Nope." Ilya's face is grim as he looks up. "No credit card transactions, no attempts to contact any friends or relatives, nothing. The fucker is good."

My hand tightens on the handle of the frying pan, my fury returning. The last name on my list—one Walton Henderson III, aka Wally, of Asheville, North Carolina—is the general who was in charge of the NATO operation that went sideways and resulted in the deaths of my wife and son. It was he who gave the order to act without verifying the validity of the supposed lead on the terrorist group, and it was he who authorized the soldiers to use whatever force was necessary to contain "the terrorists."

I already killed all the soldiers and intelligence operatives involved in the Daryevo massacre, but Henderson—the one who has the most to answer for—is still at large, having disappeared with his wife and children as soon as rumors of my target list reached the intelligence community.

"Tell the hackers to do a deep dive on all his friends and relatives, no matter how distant the connection," I say as Yan walks over to sit down on the barstool next to his brother. "They should look for anything out of the norm, like large cash withdrawals, purchases of extra phones, out-of-town trips, property acquisitions or vacation rentals, anything and everything that could indicate they're in league with that bastard. Someone has to know where Henderson went, and my bet is on some random cousin. If in a few months, there's still nothing, we might need to start making in-person visits to Henderson's connections, flush him out that way if need be."

"You got it," Ilya says, his thick fingers flying over the keyboard with surprising agility and grace. "It'll cost us, but I think you're right. People have trouble breaking ties completely."

"Yan, do we have those camera recordings?" I ask when the other twin opens his own laptop. "The ones from Sara's parents' house? We need to see if the Feds spoke to them yet."

"Downloading them now," he responds without looking up from the screen. "This satellite connection is slow as fuck. Says it's going to take forty minutes to get the files off the cloud."

"All right, then let's eat first," I say, turning off the stove. "Anton, can you set the table for the five of us? I'm going to go get Sara."

My men keep their silence as I head toward the stairs, but when I'm halfway up the steps, I see Yan lean toward Ilya, whispering something in his ear.

Sara is just emerging from the bathroom when I enter the room, her slim torso wrapped in a big white towel and her wet hair confined in a crooked bun on top of her head. Her pale skin is flushed, likely from the heat of the water, and her thick-lashed hazel eyes are red and swollen from crying.

She should've looked pathetic, but she looks heart-breakingly beautiful instead, like a Disney princess down on her luck. Maybe the one from *Beauty and the Beast*, though I'm not sure I qualify as the Beast in that tale.

Belle didn't hate her captor nearly as much as Sara seems to hate me.

"Breakfast is ready," I say coldly, trying not to think about her earlier revelation. Knowing that Sara warned me to save my life shouldn't bother me—after all, that's confirmation that she doesn't wish me dead—yet her words felt like a red-hot poker tearing through my chest. I suppose it's because I convinced myself that she wanted to come along, that when she begged me to let her go, it was just cold feet.

It hurt because I deluded myself into believing that one day, she'll love me too.

"Thanks. I'll be right down." She doesn't look at me as she says this, just goes into the closet and emerges a minute later holding one of my long-sleeved flannel shirts and a pair of sweatpants.

"Do you mind?" she says, setting the clothes on the bed, and I fold my arms across my chest, realizing she wants me to turn away while she's changing.

"No, not at all. Go right ahead."

She glances up at me. "I meant that—"

"I know what you meant." I keep my face impassive, even as anger continues to roil my insides. If she thinks I'm going to let her treat me like a stranger, she's sorely mistaken. She might not love me, but she's mine, and I'm not about to pretend I've never felt her orgasm on my cock. If there's one thing we've always had, it's this connection of the flesh, a mutual craving so intense it supersedes simple lust. I want Sara as I've never wanted another woman, and I know she's not indifferent to me.

She wants me, and I won't let her deny it.

The flush on Sara's face deepens, her knuckles whitening as she picks up the pants. "Fine." Glaring at me, she plops down on the bed and pulls the pants on with jerky movements, keeping the towel knotted around her chest until she's got the pants pulled up to her waist and the pant legs rolled up. Then she stands and drops the towel. I catch a glimpse of gorgeous pink-tipped breasts as she pulls on the shirt with angry movements, and my cock stiffens in response, my body reacting to the sight of her nakedness with predictable swiftness.

"Happy now?" She yanks at the drawstring in the waistband of the pants, tying it tightly to keep them from falling down to her ankles, and despite my dark mood, I can't help thinking how adorable she looks in my clothes.

If Anton's jeans and T-shirt were big on her, my sweatpants and flannel shirt are huge. I'm a few centimeters taller and broader than my friend, and these clothes are meant to be loose on me. My young doctor looks like a kid trying on adult clothes—an impression further enhanced by her small bare feet and messy hair.

Unable to help myself, I take a swift step forward, clasp her wrist, and draw her against me, ignoring the angry stiffness in her body as I mold her hips against mine. With my free hand, I gather her damp topknot in my fist, tilting her head back, and then I lower my head and kiss her.

Her mouth is sweet and faintly minty, like she just brushed her teeth. Her lips part on a startled gasp, and I inhale her warm breath, possessing her air like I want to possess everything about her. I want her body and her mind, her fury and her joy. And most of all, I want her love, the one thing she may never give me.

My tongue invades her mouth, stroking the wet, silky depths, and her fingers dig into my sides under the jacket, her nails sharp through the cotton layer of my shirt. The tiny bite of pain jolts my nerve endings, sending more blood surging to my cock, and my balls tighten, the urge to fuck her so intense I almost tumble her to the bed and pull down those ridiculously baggy sweatpants. Only the knowledge that my men are waiting downstairs stops me from doing so.

I want her too much for a two-minute quickie.

With superhuman effort, I release her and step back, breathing harshly. Sara looks the same way I feel, her eyes heavy-lidded and her face flushed as she dazedly gulps in air.

"Go down before the eggs get cold," I say in a strained voice, unzipping my jeans to adjust the painful pressure in my pants. "I'll be there in a minute."

She turns and flees before I finish speaking, and I close my eyes, taking deep breaths and thinking of Siberian winters to make my hard-on subside.

CHAPTER 7
SARA

When I get downstairs, Peter's teammates are already sitting at the rectangular wooden table, their eyes fixed longingly on the large frying pan sitting in the middle. One of them—the one dressed all in black, with shoulder-length hair and a thick dark beard—looks up as I approach.

"Where is Peter?" he asks, frowning. His Russian accent is only slightly more pronounced than Peter's. "Food is getting cold."

"He's coming," I say, the heat in my cheeks intensifying as the bearded man's eyebrows crawl up. He can probably tell what happened upstairs by my swollen lips, if not my shaky inner state. My knees were literally trembling as I walked down the steps, and I'm grateful that Peter's shirt is loose and thick, concealing the hard points of my nipples.

If my kidnapper had chosen to fuck me, I wouldn't have been able to say no, and the knowledge fills me with burning shame.

"Anton, you're being rude," a tall, brown-haired man says with a smooth smile. Unlike his bearded colleague, who could've stepped straight out of an action flick about assassins, this guy wouldn't look out of place in a law firm. His short brown hair is fashionably cut, his face is clean-shaven, and I'd bet a hundred bucks that his subtly striped button-up shirt and gray dress slacks are custom made. Only his cool green eyes bely the neat corporate image; they're hard and emotionless, untouched by the smile that curves his lips.

"You forgot to introduce yourself," the well-dressed man continues, speaking to Anton with a similarly slight accent. Turning toward me, he gestures at his bearded friend and says, "Sara, meet Anton Rezov. He used to fly anything with a motor at our old job, and he's still occasionally useful now. And I'm Yan Ivanov. Oh, and this is my brother, Ilya."

I turn my attention to the third guy, Yan's brother, and realize he's the one who spoke to me earlier, explaining why this place makes a good hideout. He looks the scariest of them all, with a thick bodybuilder-like torso, a shaved skull covered by tattoos, and an oversize jaw that makes me think of a gorilla. But when he smiles at me, the corners of his green eyes crinkle, softening the harshness of his features.

"Pleased to meet you, Dr. Cobakis," he says with a slightly thicker accent and gets up to pull out a chair for me.

"Thank you. It's nice to meet you too," I say, sitting down in the chair. I should hate each of these men—after all, they're accessories to my kidnapping and the murder of my husband—but something about the Russian's genuine smile and the respectful way he addressed me makes it impossible to turn my anger on him.

I'll reserve it all for the man who's coming down the stairs at this very moment, his handsome face dark and closed off.

"Finally," Anton says with relish when Peter reaches the table and takes a seat next to me. Reaching for the pan in the center of the table, Anton cuts out a chunk of the omelet and puts it onto his plate. "I'm so ready to eat."

"Help yourself." Peter's voice is filled with sarcasm that seems to go over Anton's head. The Ivanov brothers display better table manners, waiting until Peter puts a portion onto my plate and then his own before splitting up the remainder.

We eat in silence, demolishing the omelet in a matter of minutes, and then Peter gets up and slices up a few oranges. "Dessert?" he asks tersely, and the guys eagerly jump on the offer. I don't say anything, but Peter brings me a bowl with a sliced-up orange anyway.

"Thanks," I say quietly. Even in this fucked-up situation, the rules of politeness drummed into me since childhood are hard to break. Reaching into the bowl, I fish out a slice of orange and bite into it, relishing the sweet, refreshing juiciness. I must've had low blood sugar on top of everything else, because now that I've eaten, I'm feeling a tiny bit better, the hollow feeling of despair dissipating enough to let me think.

Yes, at first glance, my situation is not the best. As we were flying in, I didn't see anything resembling civilization in the immediate vicinity of this mountain, just cliffs and thick forests, with snow still covering some of the mountaintops nearby. Even if I manage to escape from the four assassins, hiking out of here won't be easy. I've gone camping exactly once in my life, and I'm far from a wilderness expert. Not to mention, if I do reach some farm or village nearby, I'll still face the challenge of communicating my situation to people who might not speak a word of English.

However, it's not as hopeless as it could be. It sounds like Peter intends to let me contact my parents soon, and there's a chance I might be able to communicate my location to them—and thus to the FBI. Also, I'm not tied up or otherwise restrained. From what I can tell, I have the freedom to roam around the house, which increases my odds of escape. If I'm smart and careful, I might even be able to steal some water and supplies, in case my mountain hike takes a couple of days.

All is not lost. One way or another, I *will* fix my mistake and return home.

In the meantime, I have to make sure I don't make things worse by doing something stupid... like falling in love with my captor.

After breakfast, I go up to the bedroom and promptly fall asleep, the time change combined with a food coma making me drowsy despite my long nap on the plane. I wake up when I hear the chopper start, and through the giant window, I see it take off from the helipad next to the house.

A supply run? A work mission? I have no idea, but if Peter is gone with the chopper, that can only be a good thing.

Unfortunately, I see him downstairs when I come down a few minutes later, having splashed some water on my face in order to fully wake up. He's sitting on a barstool behind the kitchen counter, frowning at something on a laptop screen. As I approach, I see headphones in his ears.

He's listening to something on the computer.

Noticing me, he takes out the earbuds and presses a button on the keyboard—probably to pause whatever he was listening to.

"Is that the camera feed from my parents' house?" I ask, and my heartbeat kicks up as Peter nods.

"Yes. The FBI visited them." His expression is carefully neutral.

"And?" I sit down on a barstool next to him, my shoulders tensing. "What did they tell them?"

"It's… interesting." Peter's eyes gleam as he turns to face me. "Looks like the story we gave your parents is consistent with the Feds' suspicions."

I stare at him, my pulse accelerating further. "They think I voluntarily went with you?"

He closes the laptop. "That seems to be the assumption they're operating under, especially now that your parents told them about your phone call. But I think Ryson suspected your involvement with me before that, probably because you didn't tell Karen about me in the locker room."

My hands knot together on my lap. This is both good and bad. I don't want the FBI to think I'm in cahoots with one of their most wanted, but at the same time, I'm relieved. This is infinitely better than my family believing I've been abducted. "So how did my parents react? Were they worried? Upset? Was my dad—"

"They took it well." The hard line of Peter's jaw softens a little. "They're obviously shocked and disturbed that you're involved with someone unsavory, but Ryson was very close-mouthed about who I am and why they're after me. I think he's worried about the story leaking out to the media."

That makes sense. The FBI, or the CIA, or whoever had concocted the lie about the mafia being after my husband—they wouldn't want to expose what really happened in Daryevo. If Peter is right about the mistake that led to his family's massacre, the parties involved would fight tooth and nail to keep the truth from getting out.

The public tends to frown on the slaughter of innocent civilians.

"So my dad is okay?" I press, pushing aside the memory of the horrifying pictures on Peter's phone. "He didn't look sick or anything?"

"Both of your parents looked fine, perfectly healthy." Peter's expression warms further as his palms cover my tightly clenched hands. "They'll be okay, ptichka. They're strong, like you. And you'll be able to contact them soon.

Anton and Yan just left on a supply run, and when they return, we'll have what we need to set up a secure connection. You'll talk to your parents, reassure them, and they'll be okay." He squeezes my hands gently. "Everything will be okay."

I pull my hands away, my eyes prickling with a sudden onslaught of emotion. This, right here, is what makes things so confusing. A man who abducts you isn't supposed to care about your family, much less give a damn about your feelings. What Peter did to me—*everything* he did to me—are the actions of a cruel, selfish monster, yet when he's with me, looking at me like this, it's easy to believe that he loves me, that in his own strange, overpowering way, he wants to make me happy.

Pushing the dangerous thought away, I rein in my unruly emotions and focus on the topic at hand. "But what exactly did the FBI say? And how did my parents respond to what they told them? They must've had a ton of questions—"

"They did, but all Ryson told them is that they're looking for the man who's with you, and they can't disclose why. For the most part, he and the other agents questioned your parents, drilling them about the specifics of your phone call, whether you did or said anything unusual in the past few months, why you stopped the house sale, and so on."

"Right." Because they now suspect me. They think I'm having an affair with my husband's murderer—which, in a way, I am. An unwilling affair, sure, but that doesn't change the facts. I could've gone to the FBI at any time, explained the situation and asked for their protection, but instead, I convinced myself that it would be safer for my parents if I handled my lethal stalker on my own. And who knows? Maybe I was right. Given the authorities' inability to protect the others on Peter's list, he might've found me *and* my parents if we'd tried to disappear. And then more people could've gotten hurt—if not my family, then the agents assigned to protect us.

The three guards who watched over George did end up with bullets in their heads.

"Can I watch the video myself?" I ask, pushing away the awful recollection, and Peter nods.

"If you want. I'll set it up for you on the TV later today." He waves toward the large flatscreen hanging in the living room. "In the meantime, I have to catch up on some work, so feel free to walk around and explore."

I blink, unable to believe it could be so easy. "Okay, I will," I say, trying to conceal my excitement.

If I'm allowed to explore on my own, I can escape as soon as today.

Recalling my bare feet, I glance down and wiggle my toes. "Do you think I can borrow some shoes?" I ask as casually as I can.

"Yan is buying you everything today, but you can try wearing my sneakers for now. If you lace them tightly enough, they shouldn't fall off."

"All right, I'll try that, thanks." I slide off the barstool and hurry toward the stairs, anxious to get on with my exploration.

"Oh, and Sara?" Peter calls out when I'm almost by the staircase. When I turn to look at him, he says, "If you go outside, take Ilya with you. You don't know the area, and there are cliffs everywhere. You don't want to fall."

And oblivious to my deflating excitement, he opens the laptop, his attention on the screen once more.

CHAPTER 8
SARA

Bundled in Peter's thick sweatshirt that goes down to my knees, and with my feet sliding around inside Peter's giant sneakers, I step carefully through the woods, Ilya at my side. He's talking to me, telling me something about local vegetation, but I only half-listen, focusing on memorizing the way to the trail I spotted to the west. It's wide enough to let a vehicle through and appears to lead down the mountain.

"—but was blocked by the landslide," Ilya rumbles, and I snap to attention, realizing he's telling me something useful.

"A landslide?"

His shaved head bobs. "Yes, from the earthquake. It had a big impact here, completely changed this mountain."

"Changed it how?" I ask, hugging myself to draw the sweatshirt closer to my body. It's less windy here among the trees than by the house, but it's still cold from the high elevation. We've been walking in wide circles around the house for almost an hour, and I'm ready to head back inside, where it's warm.

With the Russian assassin dogging my heels, I won't escape today anyway, and when I do, I'll have to make sure I'm properly dressed.

"Other than blocking the road, you mean?" Ilya asks, and I nod, frowning. I hope he doesn't mean the trail I just saw. So far, it's the only thing I noticed that resembles a road. If it's blocked, I'll have to hike down through the woods—a much iffier proposition.

Ilya stops and points at a cliff on the opposite side of the lake below us. "See that? It was a gradual slope before. And there are many like that on this mountain too. Very dangerous. The forest goes right up to the edge of some of these cliffs, so if you don't look where you're going..."

"Right. Dangerous. Got it." That only reinforces my conviction that I need to be well prepared before attempting my escape. The last thing I want is to fall off a cliff. I'll have to take a couple of days to get to know the area, explore it some more so I can know where I'm going. Maybe find out more about this region and learn which way is the closest settlement or whichever place would let me call the U.S. Embassy.

Either way, I have to be smart about my escape, so I don't lose what little freedom I possess.

***

By the time we return to the house, I'm shivering and the tips of my ears feel like icicles. Peter is nowhere to be seen, so I go upstairs and run a hot bath for myself, figuring that should warm me up.

The tall white tub is unusually shaped: square and narrow but deep, with a built-in step inside. I can't lie down in it like in my oval tub at home, but I can sit on the step and have the water cover me up to my neck. It's actually more comfortable this way, I decide, closing my eyes as the heat of the water seeps into me, chasing away the chill and the tension in my muscles. I wouldn't go so far as to describe my current state as relaxed, but I'm definitely feeling better.

If I weren't here against my will, I'd almost consider this a vacation.

"You like the Japanese tub?" a familiar deep voice murmurs behind me, and my eyes snap open as strong hands descend on my shoulders, massaging my slick skin. Instantly, my pulse jumps, the relaxed feeling giving way to the confusing mix of anger, longing, and fear that I always experience in Peter's presence.

Twisting around, I wrap my arms around my torso as I pull out of his reach. He's seen me naked a hundred times, but I'm still conflicted about this intimacy between us, still acutely aware of the sheer *wrongness* of it all. Because if our relationship was twisted before, it's doubly so now that my stalker—the man who waterboarded me at our first meeting—is my captor.

I'm completely in his power, and we both know it.

He stands by the tall tub, his big, sun-bronzed hands resting on the porcelain edge. The sleeves of his thermal shirt are rolled up, exposing the tattoos decorating his left arm. The ink goes from the wrist all the way up to his shoulder, the intricate designs flexing with each ripple of his well-defined muscles. His thick dark hair is mussed, as if he just ran his fingers through it, and his hard jaw is shadowed by a hint of stubble.

He looks all kinds of dangerous, and so uncompromisingly male that my insides tighten. Sexy is too weak of a word to describe Peter Sokolov; what he possesses is pure animal magnetism, a raw, harshly masculine appeal that speaks to something disturbingly primitive within me.

With effort, I shut the mental door on that thought and scoot back as far as the tub allows. "Please go away. I'm bathing."

"I can see that." His gaze travels over my body before returning to my face, his metallic eyes dark with hunger. "So what?"

"So leave me alone." I do my best to hold his stare without flinching. "Unless privacy isn't something your prisoners are allowed?"

His eyes narrow, his fingers tightening on the edge of the tub. Silkily, he says, "My *prisoners* aren't allowed many things, baths included. My *woman*, however, can do what she wants—as long as she understands one simple fact."

"And what's that?"

"That she's mine." He steps back, and before I can respond, he pulls his shirt over his head and drops it on the floor before taking off his socks. Then he unbuckles his belt and unzips his jeans.

I suck in a breath, my arms tightening around my breasts. "What are you doing?"

"What does it look like?" He pushes down his jeans and steps out of them, then does the same thing with his briefs, revealing a thick, hard cock that curves up to his ridged abdomen. The sight floods me with adrenaline even as unwelcome heat gathers between my legs.

I can't do this with him. Not again.

"I'm not having sex with you." Water sloshes over the rim of the tub as I stand, no longer caring that he's seeing me naked.

I have to get out, get away.

Peter catches my arm before I can swing my leg over the rim, and then he steps into the tub, his big body crowding me in the small square space as he pulls me back down into the water. More water sloshes over the rim, displaced by his weight, and I gasp as I find myself ensconced on Peter's lap, my back pressed against his chest and his erection nestled between my ass cheeks. Panicked, I begin struggling, and he loops an arm around my ribcage, holding me in place.

"Oh, ptichka…" His voice is gently mocking in my ear. "Who said anything about sex?"

His teeth graze over my earlobe, and his free hand cups my breast, his thumb stroking possessively over my hard, aching nipple. I freeze, clutching at the muscled band of his arm as my heart drums against my ribs. I'm not afraid of him as much as I'm terrified of my own reaction, of the way my body melts and softens at his touch. And this is so much more than touch. Peter's cock is like a steel pole between my ass cheeks, his balls are pressing against my sex, and his thumb is torturing my nipple as his tongue invades my ear, making me shiver with helpless pleasure.

We might not be having sex by the strict definition of the word, but the net effect is just as devastating.

"Peter, please…" I resume struggling, desperate to get away before I lose sight of what matters. The water makes our bodies slippery, enhancing the erotic sensation of skin rubbing against skin as I tug futilely at his arm. "Please, stop."

"Stop what?" His breath heats my neck as his hand leaves my breast and travels lower, to where my muscles are coiled tight, my flesh pulsing and aching for his touch. "This"—he licks the outer shell of my ear, sending goosebumps down my side—"or this?" His callus-roughened fingers part my folds and press against my clit as his middle finger dips into me, pushing in to the first knuckle. My nails dig into his forearm, my inner muscles clenching greedily at the shallow intrusion, and he chuckles as a faint moan escapes my lips. I want to tell him to stop *all* of it, but my mind goes blank as his fingers move farther back, past my sex. Oh, God, surely he's not—

His finger finds the tight ring of muscle between my cheeks and presses on the tiny opening. "Ah, yes," he murmurs, his voice dark and sinfully soft as I tense at the stinging pressure. "Maybe it's this you want me to stop. Am I right, ptichka?" The pressure on my anus eases as his finger rubs the tightly clenched flesh, as if soothing the attempted violation. "Are you a virgin here, my love?"

The endearment confuses me nearly as much as the foreign sensations rocketing through my body. Something almost like sympathy warms his deep, crooning voice, yet I can hear the lust in it too, a hunger tinged with dark possessiveness. He likes it, the possibility that he'd be my first in this, and the knowledge intensifies the coiling tension inside me, the treacherous heat that thrums low in my core. I shouldn't find this intriguing, shouldn't want it in any way, but I can't deny a certain perverse curiosity. At one point, when George and I were still dating, I brought up the idea of anal sex, but George seemed disinterested and we never discussed it again.

I *am* a virgin in this regard, but if I admit that to my captor, I probably won't be for long.

Gathering the crumbling pieces of my willpower, I yank at his tormenting hand with all my strength. "Just *stop*."

To my surprise, Peter complies, withdrawing his hand and lifting his other arm. "Go then." His voice is tight. "Get out."

I scramble out of the tub, my legs shaking. My wet feet slide on the cool tile as I rush out of the bathroom, barely pausing to grab a towel on the way, and it's not until I'm standing in the bedroom, fully dressed and with the towel wrapped around my wet hair, that my heart slows its frantic beating.

He let me go. I should be glad for the reprieve, but I feel strangely unsettled, frustrated in more ways than one. Once again, my tormentor is pretending like I have a choice, like this is a normal relationship where I can say no. And maybe I can—for a while, at least. So far, he's never physically forced me. But I don't delude myself. He can do whatever he wants with me, and eventually, I *will* end up in his bed, either through more subtle forms of coercion or my own lack of willpower.

I'd almost rather he forced me—because then I could pretend too.

I could imagine I'm normal and sane, a woman who hates the man who ruined her life instead of craving him.

CHAPTER 9
PETER

Sara avoids me until lunchtime, which is just as well. My self-control is fraying, the darkness clawing to the surface. I want to fuck her, and at the same time, I want to subjugate and punish her, make her understand that she is mine.

I want to take her to the edge and bring her over, no matter what it might do to her.

"Don't do it, man," Ilya says quietly as I finish slapping together Sara's sandwich. He's making his own sandwich next to me. "Whatever you're thinking about, you'll regret it."

I bare my teeth in a humorless smile. "Really? You're a fucking psychic now?"

"No, but I don't think you're thinking straight. She doesn't deserve this." He dips a butter knife into a jar of mayonnaise. "The least you can do is give her a little time."

I picture grabbing the knife and crushing Ilya's trachea with it. It's too dull to slice his throat, but it would do a great job of choking him to death. Luckily for my teammate, he doesn't say anything else, and I stride out of the kitchen with Sara's plate.

I find her upstairs, going through a dresser in one of the empty guest bedrooms. Silently, I stop in the doorway and watch her, fascinated by the sight of her lithe, graceful body bending and twisting as she pulls out and closes the drawers one by one. There's nothing in that dresser, but Sara doesn't stop until she's checked every drawer.

Only then does she turn around—and jump up with a startled gasp.

"Peter." She presses her hand to her chest, as if her heart is in danger of bursting out. "I didn't see you there." Her voice is breathless, even as she makes a visible attempt to compose herself. "What are you—"

"I brought you lunch." I step into the room, holding the plate. "I figured you must be hungry." My tone is cool, unlike the fire raging in my blood. Just seeing her like this, still dressed in my overly large clothes, makes me want to pin her against the wall and fuck her so hard we'd both end up raw and bleeding.

Cautiously, she takes the plate from me and steps back, as if sensing the violence simmering within me. As she does so, she nervously bites her lower lip, and I picture myself doing the same, tearing the tender pink flesh with my teeth as I claim that soft mouth, tasting her, consuming her until I satisfy the lust scorching me alive.

"You're not eating?" she asks warily, putting the plate on the dresser, and I shake my head, my eyes tracking her every move. I'm probably scaring her with the intensity of my stare, but I can't help it. I feel like a predator on edge, the hunger inside me so savage and dark it barely resembles something as basic as a sexual urge. It's more of a compulsive need to possess her, to bend her to my will and make her mine so completely she'd never think of looking for things to aid in her escape.

"I ate already," I answer, and though my voice is slightly rough, it doesn't reflect even a fraction of what I'm feeling. Rationally, I know that Ilya is right, that I have to give Sara time to adjust and accept her new life with me, but everything inside me demands that I grab her and make her admit she needs me... that despite everything, she loves me too.

I push the thought away, but not before it fills me with agonizing longing. Because that's what it comes down to, what I want from her the most. Beyond the frustration of unfulfilled lust, beyond the sting of her rejection, it's that acute, irrational craving that tears me up inside and prods at the monster within me.

I want Sara to love me, and I don't know how to make that happen.

"Okay. Um, thanks." Her gaze flicks from me to the plate and then back to my face. "I'll just bring it down when I finish then, right?"

That's my cue to leave, but fuck that. She's uncomfortable with me after what happened in the bathtub, and all of a sudden, I'm glad about that. Some sadistic part of me wants her to squirm, to wonder if I'm going to finally cross that line and claim her over her feigned objections.

"It's all right." My tone is exaggeratedly pleasant as I walk over to the bed in the middle of the room and sit down on the edge, crossing my legs at the ankles. "I can wait."

Sara blinks, then appears to take herself in hand. "Really? You're just going to sit there? Don't you have something better to do, like torturing some innocents?"

"That's on the schedule for later in the afternoon." I give her a sharp smile. "For now, it's just you."

Her face tightens, but she reaches for the plate and picks up the sandwich. Biting into it, she chews and swallows way too quickly, then tears off another large chunk with her straight white teeth.

"Don't choke," I advise lightly when she further accelerates her pace on the third bite. "We don't have a doctor on hand, you know. Well, except for you, but that wouldn't help much if you're the one turning purple."

Sara's eyes narrow, but she doesn't slow down. She demolishes the rest of the sandwich at the same furious pace, then picks up the empty plate and thrusts it toward me. "Here. I'm done."

"Good. Now bring it here." I pat the bed next to me.

Her jaw clenches; then an unexpectedly sweet smile curves her lips. "Oh, you want this plate over there?"

Her eyes telegraph her intent half a second before her arm swings back, and I duck as the plate hits the wall directly behind me, shattering into a thousand pieces. Shards of ceramic rain onto the bed around me, mixing with crumbs of bread.

As if realizing what she's done, Sara inches to the left, toward the door, her eyes locked on me with the same wary expression she wore after she slapped me. I forgave her then, because I knew she was shocked and overwhelmed, but I'm not going to put up with this any longer.

If Sara wants to make me into a villain, I'm happy to oblige.

"You will clean this up." My voice is ice hard as I rise to my feet, brushing shards of broken plate off my sleeves. "This room is going to be perfectly clean again, do you understand me?"

She stares at me, defiance warring with self-preservation in her gaze. Common sense tells her to back down and do as I say, but she doesn't want to give in too easily. Sure enough, her chin comes up. "Or what? Are you going to waterboard me? Threaten me with a knife? Kidnap me? Oh, wait, you've already done all that."

Despite the bravado of her words, her hands visibly tremble as she stuffs them into the front pocket of her sweatshirt. If I were a better man, I'd back off at this point, let her have this small victory. But she's not the only one angry today; the rage inside me feels like a living beast, dark and potent, fueled by her rejection and the knowledge that I may never get what I truly want from her.

If I can't have her love, I'll settle for her hate.

"Oh, ptichka…" I come toward her, enjoying the glimmer of fear in her eyes as she instinctively moves toward the door. Before she can take more than a step, I stop in front of her, cutting off her retreat. Lifting my hand, I brush her hair back from her face and lean in, inhaling her sweet scent as I dip my head and murmur into her ear, "Haven't you learned not to play these games with me?"

I hear her swallow, and when I raise my head to look down at her, I see that her chest is rising and falling in a rapid rhythm. She's scared, my Sara, and for a good reason.

Even I'm not sure how far I'll go today.

Her lips part, as if to offer a rebuttal, and I bend my head again, possessing that soft, quivering mouth with all the violent hunger she arouses in me. My hands slide into her hair, holding her head still, and I swallow her protesting gasp as her arms come up, her slender fingers curling around my wrists in a futile effort to tug them away.

As usual, she's delicious, the inside of her mouth like warm wet silk. Her slender body arches against me as I back her up against the dresser, grinding my erection against her flat stomach, and her plush breasts press against me, her nipples pinched into hard little peaks. I can hear her breathing quicken, and I know that if I were to slide my hand into her pants, I'd feel her growing slick for me, wanting me.

Her body, at least, is drawn to me.

It takes all my willpower to lift my head and step back, to release her instead of devouring her on the spot. But I do—because we need to settle this once and for all.

"You want to know what else I can do to you, ptichka?" My words come out low and hoarse, coated with the lust and anger incinerating my insides. "You want to know what will happen if you push me too far?"

Sara's eyes are wide, her chest heaving as she attempts to catch her breath, and I step closer again, capturing her delicate face between my palms as I gaze down at her. "You want me to explain to you the reality of your situation?" I continue.

She swallows again, and I feel the tremor in her hands as she grips my forearms. "Y-yes." Her voice is barely a whisper, but there's still a hint of defiance in her hazel gaze. "Yes, I do."

My lips curve, and even I can feel the darkness in that smile. "Oh, ptichka, where should I begin?"

CHAPTER 10
SARA

Caught. Trapped.

Even as I hold Peter's gaze, resisting the urge to look away from the hypnotic silver depths, I can feel my strength fraying, my resolve to fight depleting. I've never felt more his prisoner than I do at this moment, have never been so acutely aware of my vulnerability. He's not hurting me, his big palms cradling my face with exquisite gentleness, but those metallic eyes tell a different story.

I'm at my tormentor's mercy, and he has none to spare.

"Let's start with the basics," he murmurs, and I close my eyes as he lowers his head, brushing his lips across my forehead before raising his head to look at me again. Under normal circumstances, the tender kiss would be disarming, but my nerves vibrate like a finely tuned fork as he lowers his hands to my shoulders and says softly, "Your old life is gone, Sara. I let you live it as long as I could, but it's over now. You're going to have to accept that. And the transition can be easy for you… or hard. It's up to you."

My pulse jumps violently. "What do you mean?"

"Tonight's phone call with your parents, for instance." His hands are gentle on my shoulders, even as his eyes gleam darkly. "It doesn't have to happen, you know. Nor does any further contact with anyone from your old life. You could just disappear, make a clean break. That might be even better in some ways. You'd adapt faster if you didn't have constant reminders of what you lost, and—"

"No." The word bursts out of me as my stomach twists in panic, the sandwich I just ate threatening to come back up as I imploringly grip his shirt. "Please, Peter, don't do this. I have to talk to my parents. I have to reassure them. They're too old to worry like this. My dad's heart can't take it—you know that."

He cocks his head to the side. "Do I? I let you speak to them on the plane, and maybe that was a mistake. You insist I kidnapped you, took you against your will. If that's the case—if you're my captive and nothing more—why should I take the risk of letting you contact anyone? If you're just my prisoner, why would I go to the trouble and expense of reassuring your family?"

I stare up at him, my breathing shallow as my hands fall limply to my sides. I understand what he wants now— what he's always wanted from me—and I know that once more, I have no choice but to comply.

"You said—" My voice breaks as acidic tears burn the back of my eyes. "You said that I'm your woman, that you love me. So I'm not just your prisoner, right?"

Peter's expression doesn't change. "I don't know, Sara. That's up to you." He releases my shoulders and steps back. "I will let you think about it as you clean up. The vacuum and the cleaning supplies are in the pantry downstairs."

And turning, he leaves the room.

———————

The guest room is spotless by the time I'm done with it, the bed perfectly made up and clear of the tiniest bits of crumbs and broken ceramic. Housework is not something I enjoy, partially because it takes me forever due to my perfectionist tendencies, but the end result is usually a good one.

In another life, I would've made a decent housewife.

When I'm satisfied with the cleanliness of the room, I bring the vacuum downstairs and go looking for Peter. It's strange, but I feel a bit calmer after his ultimatum. We're back to where we were when his threat to kidnap me was hanging over my head, except it's even simpler now.

No matter what Peter says, I *am* his prisoner, and I only have one choice.

Play along and give him what he wants until I can escape.

I find my captor outside, sparring with Ilya on a small clearing near the house. Despite the chilly weather, both men are shirtless, their broad, muscular torsos gleaming with sweat as they circle around the clearing, occasionally lashing out at each other with a lightning-fast strike. Their movements remind me of martial arts, though I can't pinpoint any specific style. Whatever it is, though, it's savagely beautiful, and I stop, mesmerized despite myself as Peter ducks under Ilya's swinging fist and launches a furious counterattack, moving so fast I can barely follow with my eyes.

They must've been just warming up before, because what follows is a blur of nonstop action. I'm pretty sure Peter lands a hard kick to Ilya's ribcage, and I catch Peter using his forearm to block a blow from Ilya that could've felled a bear. Other than that, the fight progresses at such a furious pace that I can't discern each individual movement, much less figure out who's winning or losing. All I see are two powerful male animals, their muscles coiling and rippling as violence heats the air around them.

After about a minute, they stop and spring apart, panting as they circle each other, and I see blood trickling down Ilya's cheekbone. I can't spot any blood on Peter, so I guess that makes him the winner of that insane round. I'm not surprised. Even though Ilya is built like a tank, he lacks Peter's lethal grace, that certain something that makes my captor so deadly. I have no doubt the bald-headed Russian can kill as well as anyone—just one well-placed strike from that huge fist would probably do it—but Peter comes across as more dangerous, more ruthless.

In a fight to the death, my money would be on Peter any day of the week.

I debate saying something to alert the men to my presence, but before I can do so, Peter glances in my direction and stops in his tracks. "Sara?"

"Um, yeah." I take a breath to calm my racing heartbeat. "Sorry to interrupt, but I was just wondering if you could put the videos of my parents up on that TV for me. Whenever you're done here, I mean—no rush."

I'm being extra polite to make up for my earlier outburst. The truth is, I'm dying to watch those videos and make sure my parents are okay, but I won't gain anything by making demands. If there's anything I learned in that guest room, it's that Peter Sokolov still holds all the power in this fucked-up relationship of ours. Even when I think I have nothing left to lose, my tormentor finds a weakness, a way to manipulate me without hurting me outright—physically, at least.

Emotionally, he's destroyed me ten times over.

"It's fine," Ilya says and gives a wide grin that exposes blood on his teeth. "I think we're done for today, anyway."

Peter doesn't so much as glance at him; all his focus is on me. "Did you clean the room?" he asks, slicking back his sweat-dampened hair. His muscles flex as he lowers his arm, and I catch myself staring at the droplet of sweat running down his flat, ridged abdomen.

Stop it, Sara. Do not ogle your kidnapper.

With effort, I bring my gaze back to Peter's face. "All done." I keep my voice calm despite the clear provocation in his words. "You can check it if you want."

He stares at me for a second, then nods. "All right then. Let's go."

He comes toward me, and I flush as Ilya grins at the possessive way Peter grips my arm. It's irrational, but what Peter and I share feels private, like some kind of secret between the two of us. Obviously, Peter's men are fully aware of the twisted nature of my relationship with their boss—they helped him stalk and kidnap me, after all—but some part of me still cringes at the knowledge that they're seeing me like this. Maybe it's my aversion to airing dirty laundry in public, but I'd almost rather they thought I was Peter's girlfriend, here of my own free will.

Ignoring his sparring partner, Peter leads me toward the house, keeping his restraining hold on my arm. He's still angry with me, I can feel it, and I'm relieved he's carrying out his promise about the videos.

With any luck, by the time the rest of his men return from their supply run, he'll cool down enough to let me talk to my parents.

When we get to the living room, he releases my arm and goes straight to his laptop. Two minutes later, the videos are on the big TV screen in front of me.

"Enjoy," he says curtly and disappears up the stairs.

By the time he returns, I'm halfway through the recording. It's just as Peter told me: for the most part, the FBI agents questioned my parents and avoided answering their questions in return. I can tell that both my mom and dad were stressed and upset, but neither one looked physically ill, at least on the grainy video feed.

"Tell me again how Sara explained stopping the house sale," Agent Ryson says to my mom as Peter sits down on the couch next to me, wearing a fresh pair of jeans and a long-sleeved shirt. He must've showered after his brutal workout, because I smell a faint hint of soap as he reaches across the couch and picks up my hand, interlacing his fingers with mine.

It takes everything I have not to react to that small intimacy and keep my focus on the video. Partially, it's because I don't even know how to react. Should I be glad that he seems to have forgiven my infraction in the guest room? Or should I be upset that the gesture, as simple as it is, makes my chest ache with the same dangerously warm feeling that landed me in this predicament?

"So she never told you that the sale actually went through?" Ryson presses after my mom recounts our sushi lunch conversation almost word for word. "She never explained how it was that she was able to stay in her home after a shell corporation from South Africa purchased the house from the original buyers for double the market price?"

My parents launch into frantic denials mixed with questions and possible explanations, and I watch with a sick feeling in my stomach as my dad's face turns purple before my mom forces him to sit and calm down.

"He's going to be fine," Peter says, his deep voice reassuring, and I realize I'm squeezing his hand so hard my fingers are going numb. I must be hurting him too, but he's not pulling his hand away. The harsh expression he's been wearing all afternoon is gone, his gray eyes regarding me with a warm light as he adds quietly, "I saw the rest of this video, and I promise you, he's fine."

I nod, pathetically grateful for the reassurance, and turn my attention back to the video feed, where the agents have returned to the topic of my phone call, drilling my mom about the exact words I used to talk about my trip. It's clear they suspect I've been lying to the FBI all along, though I have no idea if they consider me simply brainwashed or Peter's accomplice from the very beginning.

"How bad is it?" I ask, turning to face my captor when the video ends with my dad consoling my crying mom in the kitchen after the FBI agents leave. It feels like burning needles are stuck in my heart, even though like Peter said, my parents are okay, relatively speaking.

He doesn't pretend to misunderstand my question. "It's… not good. Now that they know where to look, they've uncovered more evidence of our relationship, starting with our meeting in the nightclub. And of course, there's the fact that you'd been living in the house I own and didn't say a peep to the FBI when they told you I'd been spotted. Between that and the phone call to your parents, they have a pretty strong case for us collaborating. There's also—" He stops.

"There's also what?" I pull my hand away to ball it tightly on my lap. "Tell me."

Peter sighs. "They went through your filing cabinet and found your divorce papers, signed by you but not your husband, dating back to the day before your husband's accident."

"What?" I blink at him, a trickle of dread snaking down my spine. "What does that have to do with anything?"

Peter lays a comforting hand on my knee. "It's not the main theory they're working off," he says gently, "but they *are* considering the possibility that you might've had some involvement in your husband's death—that our relationship might've predated our initial encounter in your kitchen."

"What? That's ridiculous!" I jump up, my throat tightening with shock. "They can't possibly believe that. They know that you tortured and drugged me, and threatened me with a knife. They know that; they've seen the aftermath. Or do they think I made up the drugs in my system and the knife cut on my neck? And the bruises that covered my back for weeks? How can they—"

"It's just one angle they're considering, ptichka." Peter stands up and captures my icy hands in his big, warm palms. There's something almost like remorse on his harshly handsome face. For what he did to me at our first meeting, perhaps? In the next moment, however, his features smooth out and he says, "Don't stress about this. Once they investigate further, they'll realize the truth. Their job is to consider all possibilities, no matter how unlikely, and the fact that you were on the verge of divorcing your dead husband is something they have to latch on to. Haven't you seen any cop shows? The spouse is always the prime suspect, especially if there's reason to believe there was marital discord."

"Marital discord?" A hysterical laugh escapes my throat. "You're kidding, right? This isn't a fucking murder mystery." I yank my hands out of Peter's grasp and step back, my chest heaving. "*You* killed George. You broke into my house, waterboarded and drugged me to get his location, and then you blew his brains out—what he had left of them after the accident, anyway. Or do they think I caused that accident and then hired you to finish the job?" My voice jumps an octave higher. "I mean, that accident *was* my fault, in a way, and you do kill people for hire, so maybe they're on to something, maybe we were secretly in cahoots all along and—"

"Stop it, Sara." Peter steps up to me and catches my wrist, pulling me toward him. It's not until he encloses me in his powerful arms, drawing me against his chest, that I realize I'm so cold I'm trembling from head to toe. Rage and shock are buffeting me like waves in a hurricane, and I close my eyes against the sting of tears as Peter murmurs into my hair, "It's going to be okay, ptichka. This will all blow over. The agents aren't stupid; they'll figure out the truth soon enough. Just give them time."

"What truth?" I wedge my hands between our bodies and push on his chest, opening my eyes to meet his gaze. I feel like I'm crumbling inside, the rage and shock transforming into bitter despair. "The one where I slept with my husband's killer for weeks and then got myself kidnapped by warning him that the FBI were coming? Or the one where I lied to my parents so they'd think I'm in love with said killer?"

Peter's face darkens. "Yes, that truth, Sara. Where you are my victim. That's what you want to be, isn't it?" Releasing me, he steps back, and my body mourns the loss of his heat and the comfort his deadly embrace provides.

With effort, I pull myself together. We can't slide back into that argument, not when I still have to convince him to let me call my parents. "No," I say, shaking my head. "That's not what I meant. In fact…" I stop, then force myself to say it. "You were right. Earlier, when you said that I was lying to myself, you were right. I *did* know what I was doing when I warned you, and it wasn't just because I didn't want to see you dead."

His jaw flexes and his fingertips twitch, as if he's about to reach for me. "What are you saying, Sara?"

"I'm saying…" I take a breath and wrap my arms around myself, feeling like I'm about to fly apart. Even though I'm doing this to manipulate him, everything I'm saying is the truth, and dredging it up is tearing me open. "I'm saying the agents aren't entirely wrong with where they're casting blame."

Peter's eyes narrow. "What are you talking about? You had nothing to do with that bastard's death."

"No, but I have been sleeping with you—with his killer." My voice shakes as tears sting my eyes anew. "And I didn't tell the FBI about you. I didn't ask for their protection, even when I had the chance. So here we are, in this fucked-up situation, and it's all my fault. So I guess on some level, I must've wanted this, right? To lose my freedom and be with you no matter what the cost? I had a choice, and I made the wrong one. I made *all* the wrong choices, and that's why I'm here instead of in the FBI's protective custody, why I'm with *you* instead of leading a normal life."

As I speak, the hard silver of Peter's gaze darkens, and then he does reach for me, one arm looping around my back as his other hand slides into my hair, arching me against him. "Oh, ptichka," he mutters thickly, and my insides clench at the savage hunger on his face. "You couldn't be more wrong. You think you had a choice? You think there was a chance in hell I would've let you go?"

My throat swells with something indefinable, the tears in my eyes threatening to spill over as my hands come up to clutch his sides. "You wouldn't have?"

"No." His eyes glitter darkly as his fingers tighten in my hair. "I'd have come after you. There's no place on Earth they could've hidden you from me. You're mine, Sara, and you're going to stay mine no matter what it takes. No matter what I have to do to keep you." He bends his head, and I feel the warmth of his breath on my lips as he whispers, "No matter who I have to kill to retrieve you."

I shudder in his grasp, my lids drifting shut as his lips touch mine. What he's saying is horrifying, psychotic, yet my body aches at his nearness, my sex filling with liquid heat as his hard cock presses against my stomach. It's as if some perverse part of me wants this from him, as if it revels in the depths of his obsession.

Just like, on some level, I felt relieved when the needle pricked my neck.

Peter deepens the kiss, his tongue invading my mouth, and I let him. I let him because the fire burning inside me is too strong to fight. I tell myself I'm giving in because I have to, because the phone call with my parents is at stake, but deep inside, I know the truth.

I'm giving in because I want to.

Because in some ways, my sickness is as far gone as his.

CHAPTER 11
SARA

*P*eter carries me upstairs, and I hide my face against his shoulder as Ilya walks into the kitchen below. I don't want to know what Peter's colleague thinks about this madness, don't want to think about anything at all. I bared my soul to my captor because I wanted him to forgive me, but now that I have, I feel raw and broken, a mess of shame and need, rage and desire. I hate myself for what I'm feeling, and at the same time, I can't stop myself from clinging to him, from wanting him as much as he wants me.

When we get to the bedroom, he deposits me on the bed and begins to undress, and I watch him through half-closed eyelids. I feel strangely out of it, as if I'm still drugged, but I know it's just the need he awakens in me, the dark, potent desire he evokes in my body. My yearning for him is all-consuming, stealing away all reason and common sense. I want him to hold me and touch me, to take me and possess me. I want his darkness and his twisted love, and most of all, I want *him*.

I want everything from him, no matter how much it terrifies me.

He's coercing you into this. It's a tiny voice of sanity whispering in my mind, reminding me that I'm doing this so Peter wouldn't cut me off from contact with my parents, that I opened up to him for that same reason. My tormentor is too perceptive; he would've known if I'd lied to him or pretended to have feelings I don't have. The truth, in all its pathological complexity, was my best bet, only now I can't shut the spigot off, can't cover up its ugliness with the opaque veil of denial.

It's true that I don't have a choice, but I'd be lying if I said I didn't like that.

Peter's shirt comes off first, and I watch with bated breath as the muscles in his abdomen flex when he reaches for the zipper of his jeans. He has a warrior's body, lean and hard, with powerful, clearly defined muscles and tattoos covering his left arm from shoulder to wrist. Like the small scar bisecting his left eyebrow, most of the scars on his torso are faded, but the one across his stomach is fresh; it's where he was knifed a few weeks ago on the job in Mexico. Those scars are a reminder of what he does, of what he *is*, and my heart constricts as I reflect again on the fact that I'm sleeping with a killer.

My husband's killer.

He's blackmailing you into this.

It's the truth, and it somehow makes it better when he steps out of his jeans and comes toward me naked, his long, thick cock curving up to his navel. It's fucked up, but I don't want to have a choice in this, not when the desire incinerating me is a betrayal of everything I hold dear. Like this, I can tell myself that I'm doing this for a reason… that I'm not completely lost.

"You are fucking gorgeous," he whispers roughly, bending over me, and I close my eyes, unable to bear the intensity in his metallic gaze as he undresses me. The feel of his hands, so strong yet so gentle, makes my body pulse with need, even as my heart bleeds for everything I lost, for everything those cruel hands have taken from me. The tears I've been holding back leak out, trickling down my temples, and I shudder as he kisses them away, his lips soft and warm on my damp skin.

He kisses my lips next, then the tender spot behind my ear and the sensitive column of my throat. It's not until his mouth travels down to my breasts that I realize I'm already naked, my clothes removed while I battled confusing thoughts. His lips close over my nipple, the hot, wet suction making me arch off the bed, and I find my hands buried in his soft, thick hair as my hips shimmy against him, seeking relief from the tension growing inside.

Stop. Please stop.

The desperate cry reverberates in my mind, but I don't voice it. I can't. Not because he wouldn't listen, but because I couldn't bear it if he did. Maybe if I hadn't given in before, it would be easier. If I didn't know what it feels like to have him in me, I might've found the willpower to resist. But I do know, and my body wrestles with my mind, undermining my efforts to control my response, to hold back even as I give him everything.

"Yes, that's it," he breathes against my nipple as his fingers part my folds and find me slick and swollen, so aroused I can scarcely stand it. "Let me have you, ptichka. Let me give you what you need." His callused thumb circles my clit as his middle finger pushes into me, and I moan as my inner muscles clench around the digit, my body craving more of the invasion.

Peter obliges, pushing in a second finger, and the moan turns into a gasping cry as he resumes sucking on my nipple, the dual stimulation making my spine curve and my heart gallop in my chest. I'm close to an orgasm, I can feel it, and when the tension finally crests, I come so hard I cease to breathe for a few vision-dimming seconds. My whole body shudders from the relief of it, the explosion of pleasure rippling down to my toes as Peter's fingers move in and out of my body, stretching me, preparing me for what's to come.

I'm still in the throes of orgasmic aftershocks when he moves up, his knees parting my thighs as he laces his fingers with mine, pinning my hands next to my shoulders.

"Look at me," he orders hoarsely, and I dazedly obey, opening my eyes to meet his burning gaze. His heavy weight presses me down, his masculine scent filling my nostrils as his cock brushes against my inner thigh, hard and massively thick. With my hands pinned to the bed, I'm helpless, completely at his mercy, and there's something perversely exciting in that, something as dark as the need boiling in my core.

"Tell me you don't want this." His tone is harsh, his expression almost violent. "Lie to me, and I'll stop."

My chest heaves convulsively as I hold his gaze, my lungs working overtime. I don't know why he's saying this, but I do know what I want, and it has nothing to do with being able to call my parents.

"Don't stop. Please, don't stop."

I don't know if I say the words out loud, or if I merely mouth them, but Peter's nostrils flare, his starkly beautiful face twisting with fierce hunger. His fingers tighten between mine, nearly crushing in their strength, and my eyes squeeze shut as he bends his head, claiming my lips in a possessive kiss. At the same time, the broad head of his cock pushes into the nook between my legs, sliding between my folds until it finds the wet, aching entrance to my core.

He penetrates me with one deep thrust, his thick length stretching me to the edge of pain, and my gasp is swallowed by his lips as his tongue pushes into my mouth, filling me, devouring me, surrounding me with his scent and taste and feel. His possession is rough, his hunger barely controlled, and as he sets a hard, driving pace, the tension inside me spikes again, climbing toward a new peak. It's too much, too overwhelming, and I wrap my legs around his hips, needing to regain a measure of control, but there's none to be had.

There's only Peter and the violent need consuming us.

I don't know who comes first, or if we get there together. All I know is that by the time the swell washes over me, he's groaning my name, his pelvis grinding against mine as his cock jerks inside me. The pleasure seems to go on forever, sizzling through my nerve endings, and when it's over, he rolls off me, gathering me in his arms as I break down and cry, trembling from the intensity of it all… and the guilt that tears at me.

Once again, I gave in to the man who destroyed my life.

It's only later, when my tears have stopped and Peter is leisurely stroking my back, that something occurs to me, making my blood freeze in my veins.

For the second time, we didn't use a condom.

CHAPTER 12
PETER

I know the exact moment Sara realizes the lack of a condom. Her entire body stiffens, and she lifts her head from its resting place on my shoulder, her eyes wide with horror as she meets my gaze.

"We didn't—"

"I know."

It's the second time—the first was the night I stole her—and though I didn't omit protection on purpose either time, I can't say I'm sorry. The thought of Sara growing round with my child doesn't frighten or repel me; in fact, it fills my chest with a soft, warm glow, one I've only known once before.

With Pasha, my son.

A familiar ache pierces my chest, the pain of loss as sharp as ever. The image of Pasha's body, his little fist clutching the toy car, is carved into my mind with the brutal precision of an assassin's blade. For years, it was the first thing I thought about each morning and the last each evening. It was the nightmare that woke me up at night and the ghost that tormented me during the day. Avenging him and Tamila, my wife who was killed in the same massacre, was my reason for living, and it wasn't until I met Sara that I found a new purpose in life.

Her.

My little songbird, who's now my everything.

At my admission about the condom, Sara looks even more horrified. Grabbing a tissue, she scoots back on the bed and wipes frantically between her legs before clutching the blanket to her chest. Her hazel eyes are huge in her pale face as she says in a choked voice, "Are you *trying* to get me pregnant?"

"No." I get up before I'm tempted to fuck her again. Even with my body humming with post-orgasm relaxation, the idea of Sara pregnant is making me harden again, and I have some urgent emails to answer before dinner. "It just happened. There wasn't a lot of thought involved. But as I told you before, I wouldn't mind—not that it's likely at this time of the month for you. Right?"

Sara nods, but her death grip on the blanket doesn't let up. "It's not likely, but not impossible either," she says in a slightly calmer tone. "A lot of things can throw off a woman's cycle, so you can't assume it's safe based solely on the calendar. Besides, my cycle is on the shorter side, and my period ended a couple of days ago." She takes a breath, then says bluntly, "I need the morning-after pill. Can you get it for me?"

I stare at her, struck by the notion. "Maybe," I say slowly. "What kind of pill is this, and where would I get it?"

I know what she's talking about, of course, but I pretend ignorance to give myself a moment to think. Though I didn't consciously intend for this to happen, now that it has, everything inside me rebels at the idea of reducing the odds of Sara's pregnancy.

It's a new level of fucked up, but in this moment, I realize I *do* want a child with her. I want to tie her to me in every way possible, make her mine so completely she'd never be able to leave.

"There are several brands sold in the US," Sara says. "*Plan B*, *Next Choice*, *My Way*, *ella*… I don't know what's available in Japan, but I'm sure there must be something. These pills work by stopping the release of the egg, preventing fertilization, or stopping the implantation in the uterus. So it's not an abortion pill; it's just emergency contraception. I'm sure if you go into any pharmacy in Japan and explain what you need, they'll give it to you."

She's looking at me with such desperate hope that I can't bring myself to say no.

"All right," I say, doing my best to hide my reluctance. "Let me see if I can reach Anton before they start heading back. Maybe they'll be able to pick it up on the way."

Sara's entire countenance brightens. "Yes, please. The sooner it's taken, the more effective it is. Within the first twenty-four hours is best, and if I take it tonight, we'll still be within the seventy-two-hour window for the last time."

"Got it," I say and head into the bathroom to wash up. "I will call them as soon as I get downstairs."

———————

I keep my promise to call Anton, procrastinating only by the amount of time it takes me to answer an urgent email from our hackers. They located a Henderson family friend who recently booked tickets to Croatia and are asking for a payment to pursue the lead further. I transfer another five hundred grand into an agreed-upon account in the Cayman Islands, and then I contact Anton through our secure satellite phone.

To my relief, they're only minutes away from our mountain retreat. "What do you need?" Anton asks, his words barely discernible over the roar of the helicopter in the background. "The jet lag is kicking my ass, but if it's something urgent, we can turn around and go get it."

"No, it's okay," I say, suppressing an unwelcome spurt of guilt. "By the time you fly back there, all the pharmacies will be closed anyway." Or at least that's what I'm going to tell Sara and hope it doesn't occur to her that something as simple as a locked door is no obstacle for my team.

We can obtain anything at any time, locks and legalities be damned.

"All right." Anton must indeed be tired, because he doesn't react to my strange statement. "We'll see you in ten."

He hangs up, and I go upstairs to tell Sara the bad news.

I will get her that pill, but not today.

Tomorrow will be soon enough.

CHAPTER 13
PETER

Sara takes the news well, probably because I inform her at the same time that we have what we need to make the secure call to her parents. While Ilya and Yan set it up, I instruct Sara on what to say.

"Not a word about our location or how many of us there are," I tell her as I lead her downstairs. "Nothing about how long it took us to get here or how we got here. And if you try to hint about sushi or mountains or helicopters or to plant any other clue, I'll know, and this will be the last time you contact your family. Understand?"

Sara's face is pale, but she nods. "What *can* I say, then?"

"You can tell your parents you're with me—the Feds know that much. You can say you're happy and in love, and that they shouldn't worry about you. Keep it brief; the idea is not to answer their questions but to reassure them that you're alive and well. The less you say, the better for all concerned."

"Okay." Stopping at the foot of the stairs, she takes a breath and squares her shoulders. "I'm ready."

The call goes through two dozen relays, bouncing off satellites and cell towers all over the world before showing up as a blocked number on Sara's mother's cell. I know for a fact that all phones connected to Sara's parents are tapped by the FBI, but it doesn't matter. There's no way they'll be able to trace the call. The main danger is Sara saying something she shouldn't, but hopefully, she's smart enough to avoid that.

I don't bluff when I make threats.

Lorna Weisman, Sara's mother, is quick to pick up the phone. "Hello?" Her voice is tense as it comes through the speaker.

"Hi, Mom," Sara says. She's sitting on the couch next to me, the phone on loudspeaker on her lap so I can hear the conversation. "It's me, Sara."

"Sara! Oh, thank God! Where are you? Are you okay? What's going on? The FBI came and—"

"I'm fine, Mom." Sara's tone is calm and soothing, despite the overly bright glitter in her eyes. "Please don't worry. I'm with Peter, and all is well. I know things are probably confusing, but I'm well and everything with us is great. I'll tell you more when I get home, but for now, I just wanted to call because I figured you must be worried."

"Sara, darling, listen to me." Lorna sounds on the verge of crying. "The FBI said he's a criminal, one of their most wanted. You have to get away from him. Where are you? Please, darling, tell me, and we'll send someone for you. He's not a good man, Sara. He's dangerous; he can hurt you. You have to—"

"Mom, don't be ridiculous." Sara's voice sharpens. "I'm perfectly fine, and Peter is wonderful to me. Look, I can't talk long, but whatever it is they're telling you, don't believe them. He *is* a good man, and we're very happy together. He loves me, and I... Well, I think I might be in love with him too."

She glances at me, and I give her an approving nod, ignoring the irrational pang of pain in my chest. She's just acting as I told her, and it's pointless for me to wish that this were real, that she were truly in love with me.

"But, Sara—"

"Mom, I have to run. I'll call again soon. In the meantime, please don't worry about me and tell Dad not to worry either." Her voice thickens, as if she's about to cry too. "I love you both, and I'll talk to you soon, okay?"

"Wait, Sara—"

But she hangs up, her slim shoulders shaking with sobs as she jumps to her feet and runs upstairs, leaving me behind with the phone.

CHAPTER 14
SARA

I don't know how long I cry before the bed next to me dips and Peter gathers me into his arms, placing me on his lap as though I'm a distraught child. His big hand strokes my back as I wrap my arms around his neck, hiding my wet face against his shoulder, and it feels good, his touch, his warmth. It feels necessary, even though I hate him right now... even though the pain in my mom's voice is unbearably fresh in my mind.

"They'll be all right, ptichka," he says softly when my sobs quiet down. "We're keeping an eye on them, and they're handling everything well. And now that you called, they know you're fine too."

"Fine? They think I've gone crazy, disappearing with a wanted criminal like that." My voice shakes, my vision blurry with tears as I push at his shoulders, lifting my head to meet his gaze. "And with the FBI looking for us..."

"I know." His gray eyes are warm as he gently wipes the moisture off my cheeks. "It's not optimal, but it's the best we can do for now."

"Right." I finally find the strength to push myself off his lap and stand up. My eyes feel gritty after all the crying, and I have a splitting headache, but I'm determined to regain control. I can't keep seeking comfort from the man who took everything from me, can't keep crying and clinging to my kidnapper.

I'm stronger than that.

I have to be.

"Are you hungry?" Peter asks, getting up as well. "I'm about to make dinner for us."

I wipe the remnants of tears with the back of my hand and nod. "I could eat."

"Good." His smile is so bright it's almost blinding. "I'll see you downstairs in an hour."

I expected Peter's men to join us for dinner, as they did for breakfast, but they're conspicuously absent. When I ask Peter about it, he explains that they're training outside and will eat their meal later.

"Why didn't you join them?" I ask, reaching for a piece of salmon. We're having Japanese-inspired food today—fish and white rice, with pickled veggies on the side. "Don't you guys train together?"

Peter smiles. "We normally do, but I wanted to spend time with you tonight."

"Because I've been such great company today?"

His smile widens. "We've had our moments."

I fight a flush, knowing he's referring to the sex earlier. I've been doing my best not to think about it, though my body still feels tender from his rough possession. It's stupid to feel embarrassed when we've been sleeping together for the past several weeks, but I can't help it. This thing between us is too confusing, too fucked up. And then the no-condom thing—

No, I can't think about that. Peter promised me a pill tomorrow, and I have to believe he'll keep that promise. Even if, for some bizarre reason, he wouldn't mind getting me pregnant, he has to realize that a baby under the circumstances would be a disaster for all involved. He's a wanted man, an assassin on the run. What kind of life would that be for a child? Peter is too smart not to understand that.

He's also obsessed with you.

I suppress that scary little whisper and dig into my food. There's no point in worrying about that tonight; tomorrow, if Peter doesn't come through with the pill, will be soon enough. In any case, I'm so tired I can barely lift my fork, much less stress about a potential pregnancy. It must already be morning back home, and despite my morning nap, I'm feeling the effects of jet lag, combined with the aftermath of extreme stress. Once I finish eating, I'm going to pass out and hope my head will be clearer tomorrow.

I need it to be, so I can plan my escape.

"I forgot to tell you," Peter says as I'm finishing up my salmon. "Yan got you a bunch of clothes. They're over there." He nods toward the entryway, where, for the first time, I notice several shopping bags.

"Oh, thanks." Suppressing a yawn, I push my empty plate away and get up. I have no intention of being here long enough to need that many clothes, but I do need shoes and warm basics for escape. "I'll check them out right now."

Peter gets up and starts clearing the table while I sort through Yan's purchases. All the tags show bigger sizes than I'm used to, but the clothes look like they'll fit me, so I must be a Medium or a Large among the petite women of Japan. The shoes are the right size too. I try them on right away, excited to find a pair of comfortable sneakers and warm boots, along with less practical sandals and high-heeled pumps.

"Does your colleague think I'm going to be going out clubbing?" I ask Peter when I go through the rest of the bags and find some equally impractical dresses in addition to common-sense basics like yoga pants, jeans, sweaters, and T-shirts. There's underwear too, most of it lacy and pretty, and a couple of slinky silk nighties—a man's idea of what a woman would wear to bed.

"Yan is good with clothes, so I told him to get whatever he thought was best," Peter says, grinning as I hold up a low-cut tank top that wouldn't look out of place at a summer beach bash. "I guess he went a little overboard with some items."

"Uh-huh." I stuff everything back into the bags and grab a couple, about to lug them to the closet upstairs, when Peter comes up to me and snatches them out of my hands.

"I've got it," he says, picking up the rest, and I watch, bemused, as he carries all the bags upstairs.

This is yet another example of his extreme solicitousness, I realize as I follow him up the steps. Back home, not only would Peter free me from all chores when I was tired, but he also wouldn't let me carry anything heavier than a plate of food when he was around. I don't know if he thinks I'm incapable of lifting a shopping bag, or if someone taught him to always carry things for women, but it definitely adds to the sense that he's pampering me.

When he's not drugging, kidnapping, or threatening me, that is.

"Was this a part of your upbringing at the orphanage?" I ask, following him into the bedroom walk-in closet, where he puts the bags down and starts hanging up my clothes next to his. "When you were a boy, did someone instruct you on how to be a gentleman or something along those lines?"

Peter stops and looks at me, eyebrows raised. "You're kidding, right?"

I frown and reach for one of the bags, taking out a sweater to fold. "No, why?"

He laughs darkly. "Ptichka, do you have any idea what orphanages in Russia are like?"

I bite my lip as I put the sweater on the shelf next to me. "No, not really. I'm guessing not so good?"

He resumes hanging up the clothes. "Let's just say that gentlemanly behavior wasn't high on my list of priorities when I was a child."

"I see." I should be helping Peter, but all I can do is stare at him, struck by how little I still know about the man who's taken over my life so completely. I know he was raised in an orphanage—he told me he ended up in a juvenile prison camp after he killed the headmaster of that orphanage—but that's as far as I've gotten, and all of a sudden, it's not enough.

I want to know more about Peter Sokolov.

I want to understand him.

"What happened to your family?" I ask, leaning against the closet doorframe. "Did you ever know your parents?"

"No." He doesn't pause in his methodical unpacking of the bags. "I was left on the doorstep of the orphanage as a newborn. They think I was three or four days old at the time. Their best guess is that my mother came from one of the nearby villages. She might've been a schoolgirl who fooled around and got pregnant or something along those lines. I didn't show any signs of fetal alcohol syndrome, and I tested negative for drugs, so that ruled out prostitutes and such."

"And no one's ever come forward to claim you?" I ask, trying to ignore the painful squeezing in my chest. I don't know why, but picturing this dangerous man as an abandoned newborn makes me want to cry.

Peter lowers the hanger he's holding and gives me a mildly surprised look. "Claim me? No, of course not. No one claims the kids at those places—that's why they're called orphanages. Well, nowadays, rich foreigners like to pop in and adopt a baby or two if they can't have brats of their own, but that wasn't the case when I was growing up."

I swallow, the ache in my chest intensifying. "Did you ever try to find out about your mother? To find her or your father? I mean, you have the resources now…"

Peter's jaw flexes, and he turns to fully face me. "Why would I waste my time looking for someone who abandoned me?" His eyes gleam with a hard, dark light. "There's only one thing I'd want to do if I found her, and even *I* draw the line at matricide."

He turns away, continuing to fold and hang my clothes, and I force myself to join him in the task despite my shaking hands and knotted stomach. His revelations both terrify me and fill me with crushing pity. It's obvious to me now that the rage I glimpsed in Peter goes deeper than the tragedy that befell his wife and son, that he was shaped by forces I can scarcely comprehend.

That his focus on family—and his obsession with me— might have roots going all the way to the darkness of his childhood.

CHAPTER 15
SARA

I fall asleep in Peter's embrace as soon as we lie down, and I wake up sometime later to the feel of him sliding into me from behind, his muscular arm looped around my rib-cage to hold me still. I'm not wet enough, and the first few thrusts burn, but then his hand moves down to my sex, finding my clit, and my body softens, melting for him as the fire ignites in me again.

It takes only a couple of minutes for me to come, and he's right behind me, his thick cock jerking inside me as he reaches his peak with a muffled groan. He holds me then, not bothering to pull out, and I fall back asleep like that, with him still buried in my body. In my dreams, he kisses my temple and tells me how much he loves me, but when I wake up in the morning, I'm alone in bed, with the bright light streaming through the floor-to-ceiling windows.

As I shower, I find traces of dried semen on my thighs—evidence that we didn't use protection once again. I wash it off quickly, trying not to give in to the panic bubbling inside me, and get dressed to go looking for Peter.

He has to get me that pill.

He has to keep his promise.

To my surprise, he's nowhere to be found downstairs. Neither are any of his men.

My pulse jumps, then settles into a rapid rhythm. Could it be? Could they have left me alone and gone to take care of some business? Before I let myself get too excited, I grab my boots and go outside to check if they might be training there.

Nothing.

Everyone's gone, and so is the chopper.

"They'll be back this afternoon," a man's voice says behind me, and I jump up with a startled squeak.

Spinning around, I face Ilya, who's stepping out of the house behind me. He must've been in one of the guest bedrooms upstairs—the only places I didn't check yet.

Taking a breath to settle my racing pulse, I ask, "Did Peter go too?"

The big Russian nods, his tattooed skull gleaming in the sunlight as he leans against the doorway. "He left breakfast on the stove for you."

"Oh, okay. Thanks."

He goes in, and I follow him back into the house, shivering from the cold wind. I'll definitely have to dress warmly when I make my escape, with layers and everything. And I might get the chance sooner than I expected.

With any luck, Ilya won't be watching me too closely today.

Sure enough, he doesn't join me for breakfast. Instead, he disappears into his room upstairs while I scarf down the oatmeal Peter left for me and then clean up. When Ilya still doesn't return a few minutes later, I quietly go upstairs, layer on two sweaters and a parka, grab a hat, and just as quietly go downstairs. I still don't know the area, but I can't pass up this kind of opportunity. Dropping by the kitchen, I hurriedly grab a water bottle, a packet of peanuts, and an apple, and stuff everything into a plastic bag that I zip up in my parka.

My boots are by the front door, so I pull them on, and then I exit the house, careful not to make any noise as I close the door behind me.

I don't take a full breath until the house is out of sight and I find the trail I saw on the west side yesterday. I keep to the side of it, ready to dive deeper into the forest at the first sign of pursuit, but none seems to be forthcoming.

Maybe my luck will hold and Ilya won't realize I'm gone until some time from now.

The air is cold and clear as I half-walk/half-run on the trail. I'm not in good enough cardio shape to keep that pace for long, but my goal is to get as far down the mountain as I can before anyone discovers I'm missing. I don't delude myself that I can evade a team of former Spetsnaz soldiers without a significant head start, but it's worth a shot.

Maybe I can at least get to a phone before they catch me.

I push myself all through the morning, stopping only for a five-minute bathroom/drink break around noon. Then I resume my rushed pace, ignoring the burning in my leg muscles and my lungs. By the time the sun is at an early afternoon angle in the sky, I'm forced to slow to a walk. It's fortunate that I'm hiking *down* the mountain, or I wouldn't have lasted this long. Though the trail is wide enough for a car, it seems to have gone unused in recent years, and it's filled with obstacles I have to navigate around, everything from fallen tree trunks to enormous pot holes and ditches filled with water. It must be because of that landslide Ilya mentioned. I'll have to go around, through the forest, when I get to that point, but for now, the trail is easier, even with all the obstacles.

Just a little longer, I tell myself as I clamber over another fallen tree and skid down a steep part of the trail, nearly tripping over a rock as I fight to remain upright. Soon, I'll stop to drink again and eat a snack, but not yet.

I have to get farther before they start searching for me.

I force myself to keep going for another hour, at which point I sink to the ground, exhausted. For the past twenty minutes, I've had the unsettling sensation that I'm being followed, but I'm pretty sure I'm just being paranoid.

My captors wouldn't bother following me; they'd just grab me and bring me back.

Regardless, I carefully inspect my surroundings, ready to jump up and run at any moment. As I'd suspected, though, everything is quiet, the giant cedar trees swaying slightly in the chilly breeze. Relaxing, I unzip my parka and take out the plastic bag I stuffed there. Opening the water bottle, I gulp down what water I have left and then eat the peanuts and the apple I brought with me.

It's not much, but it will suffice.

Feeling marginally better, I stand up and, for the second time today, jump up with a startled scream.

A gray, pink-faced monkey is staring at me from the trees.

Or more precisely, it's staring at me and the apple core I left on the ground, its gaze darting between me and the potential food.

I burst out laughing, both at the expression on the monkey's face and my own reaction. My skin is tingling from the adrenaline surge and my heart is pounding like I just got attacked by a bear, but I'm so relieved I could kiss that little pink face.

A mountain monkey has been stalking me, not a Russian mercenary.

"You can have it," I tell the monkey, gesturing toward the apple remnants when I'm finally able to stop laughing. "It's all yours."

"How generous of you, ptichka," a familiar voice drawls from behind, and I freeze, my pulse skyrocketing again.

I was wrong not to trust my instincts.

With a sinking feeling, I turn around and face the man I fled from.

Peter Sokolov is leaning against a tree, his sensuous lips curved in a sardonic smile.

CHAPTER 16
PETER

Ilya messaged me as soon as Sara left the house, and I told him to follow her. Not because I was worried we'd lose her—Yan added tracking chips to all the shoes he got for her—but because I didn't want her hiking alone. My little doctor is used to suburban environments, not mountain forests, and I didn't want to risk her getting hurt. I was already on the way back, so as soon as Anton dropped me off, I followed the GPS signal from Sara's boots. It took me only an hour to catch up to Ilya, and then I took over the job of tracking Sara—my favorite pastime in recent months.

"How did you find me?" she asks, recovering from the shock of seeing me. Her voice is strained and a touch breathless, but she holds her chin high, facing me without flinching. "How long were you following me?"

"Since late morning," I say, straightening away from the tree. "You have more endurance than I thought. I would've expected you to take a break long before now."

Her hazel eyes narrow. "Is that why you let me get this far? To show me how weak I am and how fast you can catch me?"

"No, ptichka." I come toward her. "To show you something else."

She takes a step back, then stands her ground, likely figuring it's pointless to run. And it is. I would catch her in a heartbeat. And then I would punish her, as the monster inside me demands.

I would ensure she never ran from me again.

It takes all my willpower to suppress that urge, to keep from giving in to that dark desire. It makes perfect sense for Sara to attempt her escape, to try to return to the life she's always known. She wouldn't be who she is if she didn't try, and I know that. I accept it—rationally, at least.

On a more visceral level, I want to subjugate her and make her love me, to clip her wings so she'll never, ever leave.

"Come," I say, reaching out to take her cold, trembling hand when I stop in front of her. "It's just a little farther this way."

And leashing the simmering rage within me, I lead her down the trail.

CHAPTER 17
SARA

𝒫eter's expression is unreadable as we walk together down the trail, yet I can sense the anger within him, the lethal volatility that's as much a part of him as those steel-gray eyes. Despite that, his grip on my hand is gentle, his big hand shielding my palm from the cold air even as it prevents my escape.

"How did you find me so fast?" I ask, concealing my anxiety. At this point, I'm almost certain Peter wouldn't physically hurt me, but that still leaves a number of ways he can make me pay.

"Ilya followed you," he says, glancing at me. The chilly breeze reddened his high cheekbones and the tip of his nose, and with the sporty parka he's wearing, he looks like one of those hardcore athletes who scale Mount Everest for fun. "Did you think he wouldn't know you left the house?"

Of course. I should've known it was too easy.

"Why didn't he stop me then? Why just follow me?"

"Because I told him to."

I dig in my heels, forcing him to stop. "Why? Are you trying to teach me a lesson? Is that it?"

"No, Sara—though it is a bonus." A glimmer of amusement appears in his eyes.

"What, then?" I demand. "Why let me get this far?"

"So I can show you this," he says, and tightening his grip on my hand, he leads me to a thin patch of trees a little farther down the trail.

I've been walking cautiously this whole time, but I still almost miss the sudden disappearance of ground under our feet. If it hadn't been for Peter yanking me to a stop, I might've tumbled down.

Gasping, I step back, holding on to Peter's hand with all my strength as I gape at the sheer drop below us. By some fluke of nature, the trees go right up to the edge of the cliff, some roots even extending beyond it. It gives the illusion that there's solid ground where there's none, and I remember Ilya talking about this phenomenon yesterday, when he mentioned the landslide.

"Is this from the earthquake?" I ask when I get over my shock.

"Yes." Peter tugs me back, away from the cliff's edge. When we're sufficiently far, he releases my hand and says, "This is what I wanted you to see. I know Ilya told you yesterday that this mountain is all cliffs, but you must not have believed him, so I wanted you to see it with your own eyes. This was the only slope that was gradual enough to walk or drive on before the earthquake, and it's not usable anymore. The only way off this mountain is with the chopper, ptichka." He smiles, his eyes gleaming like polished silver.

I stare up at him, my stomach filled with ice. I must've tuned out when Ilya was talking about this, because I don't remember him mentioning this at all. No wonder my captors have been so unconcerned about my escape; they knew I had nowhere to go.

"This whole mountain is ringed by cliffs? On all sides?"

I must look as crushed as I feel, because Peter's expression inexplicably softens. "Yes, my love. You didn't understand that yesterday?"

I shake my head dejectedly. "I must not have been listening too closely."

He doesn't say anything, just takes my hand again, and we walk together up the trail, back toward the house. My steps are slow, the exhaustion from my morning hike hitting me like a wrecking ball. And it's not just physical weariness. Emotionally, I'm wrung out, so tired I feel numb inside.

I don't know why I placed such hopes on this escape. Even when I was back home, with my family and the FBI just a phone call away, I knew there was nowhere I could run to avoid Peter's reach. I was his prisoner then, just as I am now, and I don't know what made me think that escaping from this mountaintop was going to make things better.

Why I imagined I could be free if I made it down.

Peter would've come after me. Even if, by some miracle, I escaped and made it to the supposed safety of the FBI's protection, I would've never been truly safe. I would've had to look over my shoulder every hour, every day, and eventually, he would've been there, standing with that cruel smile on his handsome face.

There's no way out of this for me, and in my panic, I forgot that.

Despair is a crushing force on my chest, constricting my breath and coloring the world around me gray. I know I need to regroup, to come up with some new plan, but the hopelessness of my situation is too encompassing, too absolute. My legs feel like lead as I take each step, and the ice inside me is spreading, the chill wrapping like chains around my heart.

There's just no way out.

"It doesn't have to be like this, Sara," Peter says quietly, and I look up to find him watching me, his gaze oddly sympathetic. It's as if he understands, as if he empathizes on some level. Except if he did, he wouldn't do this.

He wouldn't destroy my life to satisfy his obsession.

"Not like this?" I ask hollowly, stopping in front of a fallen tree. We need to climb over it, and I lack the energy to do so. "Then how? How do you envision this working?"

His lips twist as he releases my hand and turns to face me. "You can just give in, ptichka. Accept what is between us."

"And what is that?"

"This." He lifts his hand to stroke my cheek, and I find myself leaning into his touch, seeking the magnetic warmth of his fingers.

Feeling the perverse need pulsing in my core.

I should pull away, jerk out of his reach, but I'm too tired to move. Too tired to protest as he bends his head and presses his lips to mine, his kiss soft and gentle, so tender it makes me want to weep.

He kisses me like I'm something precious, something rare and beautiful. Like he wants me more than life itself. My eyes drift shut and my hands come up, clutching at his shoulders as he deepens the kiss, inhaling my air and feeding my need.

What if you do give in?

It doesn't seem so wrong in this moment. Not when I'm so weary and lost, so utterly devoid of hope. He's the cause of my despair, yet everything is warmer and brighter with his touch, more bearable with his affection.

What if you do accept it?

The question circles through my mind, taunting me, teasing me with possibilities. What would it be like if I stopped fighting? If I let go of my old life and embraced my new? Because at this moment, it doesn't seem so crazy that he could love me, that we could share something meaningful and real.

That if I let myself forget the things he's done, I could maybe love him too.

"Sara," he breathes, lifting his head, and in his heated gaze, I see the future we could have. The one where we're not enemies, where the past doesn't paint our present in shades of black.

I see it and I want it—and that's what terrifies me most.

"Let me go." Somewhere, I find the strength to pull away, to reject the dark lure of his affection. "Please, Peter, stop."

His gaze cools and hardens, molten silver turning to cold steel. Without another word, he takes my hand and resumes leading me up the mountain, back to my prison.

Back to our new home.

———————————

We walk up the trail for another hour and a half before I begin stumbling over every root and stone, my legs so heavy with exhaustion I literally can't lift my feet. Going up is ten times more difficult than going down, and after pushing myself to the limits earlier today, I can't keep up any longer.

Gulping in icy air, I sink down on a big rock. "I need… a break," I wheeze out, bending in half. There's a sharp cramp in my side, and my lungs burn like I just ran ten miles. "Just a… few minutes."

"Here, drink." Peter sits down next to me, looking as cool and fresh as if we've been leisurely strolling all this time. Unzipping his jacket, he hands me a new water bottle and says, "I know you're tired, but we can't slow down. A storm is expected tonight, and we need to be home before then."

I gulp down most of the water before giving him back the bottle. "A storm?"

"Rain and sleet, mixed with snow at higher altitudes." He finishes off the water and stuffs the empty bottle back inside his jacket. "We don't want to get caught in that."

"Okay." I still haven't caught my breath, but I force myself to stand. "Let's go."

Peter rises to his feet, studying me with a faint frown. Then he turns around and says, "Climb onto my back."

An incredulous laugh bubbles up my throat. "What?"

"I said, 'Climb onto my back.' I will carry you."

I shake my head. "Don't be ridiculous. You can't carry me that distance. We still have a solid three hours of hiking—maybe four or five, since we're going uphill."

"Stop arguing and get on my back." He gives me a hard look over his shoulder. "You're too tired to walk, and this is the easiest way to carry you."

I hesitate, then decide to do as he says. If he wants to exhaust himself by giving me a piggyback ride, who am I to argue? "Okay." With the last of my strength, I clamber onto the rock and from there onto his broad back, gripping his shoulders as I circle his waist with my legs.

"Hold on tight," he says, and looping his arms under my knees, he starts walking, covering the ground with long, steady strides.

CHAPTER 18
PETER

I set a brisk pace, determined to get back to the house quickly. Already, the sky is darkening on the horizon, the air cooling and thickening. The storm is coming faster than predicted; we have maybe a couple of hours before it hits, and I can't ping the guys to pick us up. After dropping me off, Anton took the helicopter to pick up a few supplies in Tokyo, and he wouldn't be back in time.

I should've chosen some other day for this demonstration.

Oh, well. No point in worrying about it now. As we get to a flatter part of the trail, I pick up the pace further, and Sara shifts her grip on me, looping her arms around my neck as she leans forward.

"Is this okay?" she murmurs in my ear, and I nod.

"Fine. Just don't choke me," I tell her.

"Are you sure you don't want to let me down? Because I've rested now and I can walk—"

"You'll slow us down."

My tone is brusque, but I'm not inclined to waste my breath on speaking. Not because my little bird is heavy—at barely fifty kilos, she weighs less than the packs I jog with when I train—but because I can't afford to go any slower. The wind is gusting up, blasting us with an icy chill, and though we're both warmly dressed, I want to get Sara indoors before the weather worsens.

The first drops of sleeting rain hit when we're less than a half hour from the house. "Let me down," Sara demands, and this time, I listen. I've been carrying her for over three hours, and by now, she *is* sufficiently rested. We'll move faster if she's on her own feet.

Gripping her hand, I begin to jog, towing her behind me as the sky opens up and the wind starts driving icy water into our faces.

"Oh, thank God," Sara gasps out as the house comes into view. The sleet is now mixed with snow, and the wind feels like it's cutting through our bones. My jeans are soaked through, my legs are numb with cold, and I can no longer feel my face. I can only imagine how miserable Sara must be. Unlike me, she's never been trained to divorce herself from pain and discomfort, has never known what it's like to focus solely on survival. If I could shield her from this storm with my body, I would, but the most important thing right now is to get her inside, where it's warm and dry.

Another hour of this, and we'd run the risk of hypothermia.

When we're less than thirty meters from the house, Sara stumbles, tripping over a branch, and I pick her up, carrying her clasped against my chest as I cover the remaining distance. Getting to the door, I knock with my boot, and as soon as Yan opens the door, I carry my half-frozen burden straight to our bathroom upstairs.

Putting her down, I turn on the shower, making sure the water is warm but not too hot, and then I strip us both, removing our wet, icy clothes before ushering her under the spray. Sara's lips are tinted blue, and she's shivering so hard she can barely remain upright. I'm not in much better shape, so I wrap my arms around her in a full-body hug, and for a few minutes, we just stand under the water, shaking as its warmth soaks into our frozen skin.

"We c-could've died." Sara's teeth are still chattering as she pulls back and meets my gaze. Her hazel eyes are almost black in her white face, her dark lashes spiked with wetness. "P-Peter, we could've d-died out there."

"Yes." I tighten my arms around her again, pressing her against me until I can feel every shallow breath she takes. "Yes, ptichka, we could have."

Another hour or two in that storm, and she wouldn't have made it. I didn't let myself think about it before, didn't let my focus waver from the task of getting her home, but now that we're here—now that she's safe—the realization that she could've died hollows out my stomach and wraps my heart with ice. I've only known fear like this once before, when I saw those methheads threatening her with knives.

120

That time, I could eliminate the threat—and I did—but I couldn't protect her from this storm.

If it had come two hours sooner, I could've lost her.

The thought is terrifying, unbearable. When I lost Pasha and Tamila, it felt like my world had ended, like I would never know anything but rage and agony again. The fury that drove me was absolute—because that was the only way I could get through each day, the only way I could eat and breathe and function.

The only way I could live long enough to find those responsible and make them pay.

It wasn't until Sara that I began to feel alive again, to want something more than brutal vengeance. She became my new focus, my new reason for existing.

I can't lose her.

I won't lose her.

"You will never do this again." My voice is low and hard as I grip her shoulders and pull back to meet her startled gaze, the fear inside me swamped by fierce determination. "You will not run from me, Sara. Ever. There's nobody out there who can help you, no place you can hide from me. And if you try this futile stunt again, you'll regret it—I give you my word on that. You think you know what I'm capable of, but you haven't even scratched the surface. You have no idea of the lengths I'll go to, ptichka, no clue what I'm willing to do to have you. You're mine, and you're staying mine—now and for as long as we're both alive."

I can feel her muscles tensing as I speak, and I know I'm scaring her. It's not what I want, but I have to keep her from these escape attempts.

I have to keep her safe.

"Peter, please…" Her soft hazel eyes fill with tears, her palms coming up to press against my chest. "Don't do this. This isn't love. Even you must realize that. I'm sorry for everything you've lost, for what George did to your family. And I know—" She swallows, holding my gaze. "I know there's something between us, something that shouldn't be there… something that doesn't make any sense. You feel it, and I feel it too. But that doesn't make this right. You can't stalk someone into loving you, can't intimidate her into caring. For as long as you're keeping me here, I'm your captive, no matter what you make me say… no matter what you coerce me into. Whether I run or not, I'm not yours—and I never will be. Not like this."

Every word she speaks is like a knife puncturing my liver. "How then?" My words come out harsh and desperate, violent in their intensity. "Tell me, Sara. How can I have you? What other way can we be together when I'm a wanted man?"

Her gaze mirrors my torment. "We can't," she chokes out, her delicate nails scraping over my skin as her hands curl into fists against my chest. "This isn't meant to be, Peter. *We're* not meant to be. Not with the past we share—not with who and what we are."

"No." My rejection is visceral, instinctive. "No, you're wrong."

Realizing I'm gripping her shoulders with biting force, I release her and step back, then turn away to turn off the water, using the small task to regain some control. Now that I'm no longer freezing, my body is starting to respond to her nakedness, my hunger for her sharp and dark, aggravated by the volatile brew of anger and frustrated longing. If I don't calm down, I will take her, and I will hurt her.

I will fuck her until she breaks and admits she belongs to me.

She's crying when I turn back to face her, the tears mixing with the wetness on her cheeks. "Peter, please…" She reaches over to grip my hand, her slender fingers wrapping around my palm imploringly. "Please, just let me go. This isn't what you want, not really. I can't be your family. I can't be their replacement. Can't you see that? It's just not meant to be. What you want is not—"

"*You* are what I want." Tugging my hand out of her hold, I fist it in her hair and wrap my other arm around her waist, molding her against me. She sucks in a sharp breath, her peaked nipples brushing against my chest, and my cock throbs, hard and ready against her stomach as I say thickly, "You, Sara, are everything I want. I don't give a fuck about the past, or what is or isn't meant to be. We make our own fate—we choose our own destiny—and I chose you. I don't care if the whole world thinks it's wrong, if I have to fight an army to hold on to you. I found you, I took you, and I'm keeping you—and I'm never going to set you free."

CHAPTER 19
SARA

I expect Peter to fuck me then, right there in the shower, but he releases me and steps out of the stall, jerking a towel off the rack and wrapping it around me as I follow him out. He dries me with brisk motions, and then he grabs a towel for himself. His movements are rough, uneven, his eyes glittering darkly as he finishes toweling off and throws our towels back on the rack.

He's angry or hurt or a combination of both, none of which bodes well for me.

Clasping my elbow, he leads me to the bedroom, and when we get to the bed, I fall onto it, my legs refusing to support me for a second longer. A wave of dizziness sweeps over me, my stomach growling with emptiness, and I realize I haven't had anything to eat since those peanuts on the trail.

Peter must realize that too, because he stops and eyes me with a dark frown. "Do you want dinner?"

I nod and force myself to sit up, wiping the tears off my face with the back of my hand. "Please."

"All right." He strides to the closet, grabs a robe, and throws it to me before putting one on himself. "Let's go eat."

As we consume the stir-fry Peter quickly made, I fight the disconcerting sensation that I'm waiting for the guillotine to fall. My captor hasn't said a word since offering me dinner, and I have no idea what's going through his mind. Whatever it is, though, he's watching me with a hard, intent stare, and that scares me.

The dinner delayed whatever he was going to do to me, but he still plans to do it.

It's possibly the worst timing ever, but I can't put it off any longer. The clock is ticking in my head, every passing hour increasing my anxiety. "Peter…" I put my fork down, trying not to look as nervous as I feel. "Did you get the pill?"

His jaw tightens, and for a second, I'm convinced he'll say no. But he just gets up and walks over to the counter, where a white paper bag is sitting next to a laptop.

Picking it up, he brings it to me, and I eagerly grab it from him. Inside is a pink pill in glossy white packaging with Japanese writing on it. Only the manufacturer's name is in English, but I'm certain it's the pill I need.

Tearing through the packaging, I pop the pill out and swallow it with half a glass of water. With any luck, we're still in the safety zone, and the pill will do its job. Not that it matters, given what Peter says.

Child or not, he'll never let me return home.

The despair threatens to overwhelm me again, and it's all I can do to tell him in a semi-normal tone, "Thank you. I appreciate it."

No matter how strained things are between us, I have to keep in mind that he didn't have to give me this pill—that he could've forced his will on me in this matter, too.

Peter nods curtly and begins clearing the table. I'm still dead tired, but I make myself get up and help him just as Ilya and Yan come down the stairs, discussing something in Russian. Yan is laughing, but Ilya looks pissed, making me wonder if the two brothers are having an argument.

Peter barks something at them, and Yan glances at me with a grin before replying in rapid-fire Russian.

Ilya looks like he's about to blow, but he just grabs an apple from the bowl on the table and stomps back up the stairs.

"What were you just talking about?" I ask, frowning as the brown-haired Russian sits down behind the counter and opens the laptop lying there. I've been eyeing that computer all through the meal, wondering how to get my hands on it, and I'm disappointed to see a password-protected start page before Yan angles the screen away from me.

"I was just telling my brother that he needs to find himself a nice girl," Yan explains in English, his grin widening as Peter shuts the dishwasher door with unnecessary force. "You know, like Peter did with you."

"Oh, I see." Given Peter's reaction, I suspect the language Yan used with his brother was quite a bit saltier, but I'm not about to pry further.

I'd rather not know what this little band of killers truly thinks of me.

Yan busies himself with the computer, and I wipe down the table and the empty counters, feeling the need to do something even though I'm ready to collapse. I don't know what awaits me upstairs tonight, but I feel peculiarly on edge, my instincts screaming that I'm in danger. Maybe it's the hard, closed-off expression on Peter's face or the barely controlled violence in his movements, but I'm reminded of our meeting in Starbucks all those weeks ago, back when my captor was nothing more than the lethal stranger who tortured me and killed George.

Back when I didn't know how dangerous he could really be.

Outside, the storm is raging, the wind driving icy rain into our windows. I shudder, remembering how it felt to be out in that, and tie the robe tighter around my body.

"Cold?" Yan asks, and I turn to find him looking at me with a half-smile. Unlike me and Peter, he's fully dressed, his dress slacks and button-up shirt stylish but far too formal for lounging around the house. I have a feeling he doesn't care, though—either about the appropriateness of his clothes or much of anything in general. Even when he's smiling or laughing, there is a cold, distant quality about

Yan Ivanov, as though he doesn't feel the emotions he's displaying.

I wouldn't be surprised if Ilya's smooth-mannered brother is a psychopath, in the clinical sense of the word.

"I'm fine," I say and glance over at Peter, who finished putting away the leftovers and is now watching me with narrowed eyes, his powerful arms crossed over his chest.

"Are you done?" he asks in a hard voice, and my heart sinks as I realize I can't put off whatever's about to happen any longer.

I made a mistake, and I'm about to pay the price.

CHAPTER 20

When we get to our room, Peter leads me to the bed. Stopping in front of it, he removes his robe, letting it drop to the floor, and then he unties mine and pushes it off my shoulders, leaving me naked. He seems fully in control, the volatile anger leashed for the moment, and despite my nervousness, my thighs clench on a surge of heat as he brushes his knuckles over the sensitive skin of my upper breasts before cupping each mound and gently rubbing his thumbs over my nipples.

"You look scared," he observes, his silvery gaze hard and opaque. "Are you afraid I'll hurt you?" His fingers close on my nipples, pinching with startling force, and I gasp, my hands flying up to grip his wrists.

"Tell me, Sara." He pinches my nipples harder, the pressure bordering on pain. "Do you think I'll hurt you?"

"I—" I gulp, my heart hammering as I tug futilely at his wrists. "I don't know."

"I *could* hurt you." His sculpted mouth twists as he releases my nipples, leaving them erect and throbbing as his hands slide down my body to grip my hips. "And sometimes I want to. You know that, don't you, ptichka? You've sensed it." His cock presses against my stomach, hard and insistent, and my breath catches in my throat, my core tightening with a heated ache despite the chill spreading through my veins.

"Yes." I can't bring myself to lie, even though that might be smarter, might pacify the monster peering at me through the dark metal of Peter's eyes. "Yes, I have."

"Oh, ptichka…" Mock sympathy fills his voice as he gives me a hard push. "Of course you have."

Startled, I fall backward onto the bed, but instead of climbing over me, Peter bends down and straightens a moment later with the tie from my robe in his hand. Anxiety shoots through me as I comprehend his intentions, and I react instinctively, rolling away as he climbs onto the bed next to me.

He catches me before I can roll off the bed, and I find myself face down on the mattress, my lower body pinned by his weight and my arms forced behind my back as he knots the tie around my wrists. His movements are quick and sure, ruthless in their efficiency, and only seconds pass before my hands are thoroughly restrained, the terrycloth fabric looping around my wrists in a soft but unbreakable hold.

I yank on the restraints, panting into the mattress, but there's no give in the tie, no way for me to get free. "What are you doing?" My panic intensifies as I feel him climb off me. "Peter, please… what are you doing?"

"Shhh." Gripping my elbow, he tugs me to my knees and turns me around to face him. His face is taut with lust, his eyes gleaming darkly as he says, "I'm giving you a taste of what it means to be my captive. Because that's what you want, isn't it? To run and have me catch you? To have me do this, so you can be free of blame?"

I open my mouth to deny it, but before I can utter a word, Peter stands up on the bed. Fisting his hand in my hair, he arches my head back, pulling my face toward his groin, and I gasp, yanking at my wrist restraints as his thick cock slaps against my cheek. His musky male scent fills my nostrils, his ball sac rubbing against my jaw, and my breathing quickens as I realize what he's about to do.

"Peter, please—" I begin, then clamp my lips shut as the head of his cock presses against my mouth. With his hand in my hair and my arms tied behind my back, I can't turn my face away, can't move so much as an inch. In the weeks since Peter has invaded my life, he's taken me more times than I can count, pleasuring me with his mouth and hands and cock, but he's never made me pleasure *him* before. And for the first time, I realize it was a mercy… a small choice he'd left up to me.

A choice he's now taking away.

"Open your mouth." His voice throbs with dark lust as he slaps his cock against my cheek again. "Open your fucking mouth, Sara."

I keep my lips tightly sealed even as my heart rate jumps into the anaerobic zone. It's stupid to fight a blowjob when we've fucked dozens of times, but I can't help feeling that by doing this, I'd be giving in even more… losing the last bit of me that still belongs to George. Not the alcoholic or the spy who lied to me, but the man I fell in love with back in college, the one who was my first everything.

Peter's face tightens, his eyes narrowing as he growls, "You want to do it the hard way? Fine." With his free hand, he pinches my nostrils closed, cutting off my air, and when I open my mouth to drag in a breath, he shoves his cock in, all the way to the back of my throat.

I choke, my eyes watering as my gag reflex kicks in, but he's merciless as he starts thrusting, fucking my mouth with a hard, relentless rhythm. I don't even have a chance to bite; with his fingers pinching my nostrils, all I'm focused on is getting enough air and trying not to gag. Panicking, I instinctively yank at my bonds, my eyes scrunching shut as saliva drips down my chin, but his thick length pistons in and out, and there's nothing I can do, no place I can escape to.

I don't know how long he ruthlessly uses my mouth, but I can feel myself getting dizzy, the lack of air combining with my exhaustion, and a dream-like lethargy sweeps over me. I've never felt so helpless, so utterly in my tormentor's power, and as Peter continues fucking my mouth, I do the only thing I can.

I stop fighting and give in to him.

The punishing thrusts don't stop and he doesn't release my nose, but my panic eases as my body goes soft and pliant in his grasp. I'm a rag doll, a toy to be taken and played with, and there's peace in that, a twisted kind of acceptance. My throat relaxes, letting him in, and the gag reflex subsides as I embrace his rhythm. Each time he withdraws, I gulp in a breath, and the air sustains me as he pushes in deep, filling my throat, controlling me so completely my very life is in his hands.

"Yes, that's it. That's so good… Just like that, my love…" His lust-soaked groan vibrates through me, and I open my lids a sliver, squinting up at him with watering eyes. Savage ecstasy is contorting his features, the tendons standing out in his muscled neck, and as his gaze meets mine, I feel something inside me shifting, changing in some fundamental way.

I'm yours, my body tells him, accepting all he has to give. It's a complete surrender of myself, yet it feels right, feels comforting and peaceful. In this moment, I want to belong to him, to stay cocooned in his enormous strength.

To give up and let him keep me.

All fear fades, all thoughts about the future disappearing. I feel like I'm floating, like I'm above and beyond myself. If there's still discomfort, I don't feel it, yet my senses are heightened, my sex wet and thrumming with arousal. It's oxygen deprivation, my medical training tells me, but the reason doesn't matter.

Nothing matters but Peter and his pleasure.

I hold his gaze as the climax takes him, maintaining the connection as his seed spurts into my throat. Eyes streaming, I swallow every salty drop, and it's only when his fingers release my hair that the strange high fades and reality kicks back in.

Shaking, I collapse onto my side, feeling like I'm crumbling into pieces as he frees my hands from the tie. My eyes are wet, but I'm no longer crying. I can't. The plunge into despair is too sudden, too frightening and deep. And underneath it all is sick arousal, a hunger that burns in my core.

"It's okay, my love," he murmurs, gathering me into his embrace, and my shaking intensifies as his hand slips between my thighs, two rough fingers thrusting into me as his thumb presses on my clit. "You're going to be fine. This is normal. Let me take care of you, ptichka, and you'll be okay."

But I won't be. I know it, and he knows it too.

It takes mere seconds for me to come, to convulse in his arms with shattering pleasure. And as he holds me, stroking my hair, I know that this is it.

The cage he promised me is here.

PART II

CHAPTER 21
SARA

The first two weeks are the toughest. I cry almost every day, my anger and despair so intense I want to yell and throw things. But I don't. Instead, I walk around Peter on eggshells, determined to avoid further punishment—and to make sure my captor lets me keep in contact with my parents.

I still don't understand what happened that night, how that blowjob broke me so completely. Sex with Peter has always had an element of darkness, but I thought that I could handle it, that I was used to the rollercoaster of fear, shame, and need. But that night was something different, something more perverse... something that cracked me open and twisted me up inside.

That night, I danced with Peter's inner monster, and in the process, discovered one in me.

He hasn't touched me like that since, though each time we have sex, I sense the desire in him, the need to dominate and torment. It's there no matter what he does, no matter how tenderly he treats me. It's part of him, this darkness, this urge to punish and avenge. He might fight it, but it's there—because regardless of what Peter says, the past does influence our present.

He'll never forget my husband's role in the massacre of his family, and I'll never get past what he did to George.

The good news is that we're back to using condoms. I don't know if Peter saw the wisdom in avoiding extra complications at this stage of our fucked-up relationship, or if he's actually respecting my wishes, but despite the copious amount of sex we're having daily, there haven't been any further slip-ups. Still, I anxiously count the days until my period, and when it arrives, two and a half weeks into my captivity, I sob with relief, for once grateful for the cramps and the discomfort. Peter doesn't seem nearly as pleased, but when we resume having sex after the worst of my symptoms are over, he continues to use protection.

Another positive is that my failed escape attempt hasn't lost me any outside contact privileges. Every afternoon, Peter lets me watch the recordings from my parents' house, and every couple of days, he lets me call them. The calls are always brief, both as an extra precaution against the FBI tracing them and because there's not much I can say. As far as my parents are concerned, I'm jetting around the world with my lover, happily oblivious to the danger he presents and to my responsibilities back home. Pretty much all I can do on those calls is assure my parents that I'm fine and inquire after their well-being before swiftly hanging up to avoid their endless questions and entreaties.

"You know, you can elaborate on our love affair a little," Peter says after listening to the calls for about a week. "Give them some color to make it seem more authentic."

"Really? Should I tell them how often you fuck me, or describe how big your cock is?"

Peter grins at my sarcasm—the one bit of defiance he doesn't mind on occasion. "If you want," he says, leaning back on the couch. "Or you can say that I make breakfast for you every day. I'm no expert on parents, but that seems like something they'd appreciate more."

I bite back another sarcastic remark and do as he suggests on the next few calls, telling my parents about some of the little things Peter does for me. It can't be anything that would point to our location, so I stick to more personal stuff, like the fact that he's a great cook and his back rubs are amazing. Neither is a lie; now that we're settled in the new place, Peter is back to making gourmet meals for me, and I'm beyond pampered with daily massages. I think it's because he can't keep his hands off me, and since we can't have sex twenty-four-seven, he settles for touching me in other ways, using every opportunity to stroke and rub me from head to toe. Especially toe. I'm beginning to suspect my captor might have a little foot fetish, given how often he gives me the best foot rubs of my life.

I don't tell my parents about the foot rubs—despite my sarcastic query, I'm not comfortable discussing anything remotely sexual with them—and I also keep quiet about the more intimate ways he takes care of me, like brushing my hair and washing me in the shower. It's like I'm his human doll, something between a child and a sex toy. He did that back home as well, but I worked so much it was more of an occasional thing. Now, however, it's a daily occurrence, and though I should probably find that kind of attention disturbing, I enjoy it too much to object.

I've been self-sufficient and independent for so long it feels good to let Peter baby me.

Of course, no amount of pampering can make up for losing my life and the job that defined me. I went from working upward of eighty hours a week to total leisure, and I have no idea how to fill that extra time. Peter takes up some of it—now that I'm always within his reach, he fucks me two or three times daily—and with the fresh mountain air, I sleep more, at least nine or ten hours a night. I also share leisurely meals with Peter and his men, and weather permitting, I go on long walks with him or whoever he assigns to guard me.

It's not a bad routine, and we do have books and movies, but three weeks in, I'm ready to climb walls.

"Don't *you* feel cooped up?" I ask Peter during one of our morning walks. The air is chilly, but fortunately, it's neither rainy nor windy, as was the case for the last few days—another reason for my aggravation. "I mean, I know you work on your laptop, but still…"

Peter shrugs his broad shoulders. "I'm enjoying this downtime. It's rare, so my guys and I take advantage while we can. We have a big job coming up, so we won't be resting for long."

"What kind of job?" I ask, driven by a dark curiosity. "Another assassination?"

He stops and gives me an even look. "Do you really want to know?"

I hesitate, then nod. "Yes. I do." It's not as if I'm ignorant of what Peter is or what he does. I experienced his lethal skills firsthand the night we met. If some drug lord paid him and his team an obscene amount to take out another dangerous criminal, I might as well hear all about it.

If nothing else, it might be entertaining, in a horror flick/James Bond thriller kind of way.

"There's a banker in Nigeria who's stepped on some toes," Peter says, reaching over to take my hand as he resumes walking. "One of those toes hired us to take care of the problem."

"A banker? That doesn't sound like someone who'd require your particular skillset." Or like the ruthless crime lord I pictured. Not that I delude myself that Peter's job is something noble. Still, some naïve part of me must've been hoping that most of his targets are at least somewhat deserving of what comes their way.

"This particular banker has a small army and pretty much owns the little town he lives in, as well as most of the local law enforcement," Peter explains as we head toward a narrow trail I never noticed before. "By all indications, he's one of the richest men in Nigeria, and he didn't get there by making car loans."

"Oh." I readjust my mental image of the man. "So he's not a nice guy?"

A humorless grin flashes across Peter's face. "You could say that. At last count, he's murdered over a dozen of his opponents and tortured or maimed at least fifty more, not counting their families. The man who hired us is a cousin of one of the victims; his daughter was gang-raped to teach his family a lesson."

Horror constricts my throat, and I'm suddenly savagely glad Peter is going after this monster.

Glad and irrationally worried, because this is far more dangerous than I thought.

"How will you…?" I stop, not knowing how to phrase it.

"Get to him?"

I nod, glancing up at his coolly amused face. "Yes."

"The usual way. We'll find out everything we can about his security, learn his routines, and when the time is right, we'll strike."

I push down the irrational bubble of fear in my chest. Peter and his guys are highly trained, and in any case, it's stupid to worry about the safety of the assassin who abducted me. Instead, I focus on what's most relevant to my situation. "So you're going to be gone for a while?"

"No, not unless something goes wrong. Anton and Yan will fly over there next week for reconnaissance, but Ilya and I will only get involved in the final stages of the operation. I'm guessing that will be in a week or two, and I shouldn't be gone for more than a couple of days."

I chew on the inside of my cheek. "What about me? Are you going to leave me here while you go to Nigeria?"

"Yan will stay behind with you," Peter says, turning off the trail toward a clearing as I try to hide my disappointment. Despite what he told me the day of the storm, I haven't completely given up on the idea of escape. Yes, he showed me that one cliff, and during our walks, I've seen a few more, but that doesn't mean the entire mountain is impassable. There might be a way down that Peter doesn't want me to know about, and given enough time and freedom, I might find it. What I would do afterward—how I would stay out of Peter's clutches even if I made it back home—is a different matter, but I need to focus on one problem at a time.

I have to have some hope, or the despair will swallow me whole.

"Don't you need your entire team?" I ask, doing my best to sound only mildly interested. "I thought you guys operated as a unit."

"We do, but we'll adjust." Peter shoots me a sardonic look as we enter the clearing. "Don't worry, ptichka. We won't leave you stranded here alone."

I don't respond, because there's no point—and because we've reached our destination: a cliff with a magnificent view of the lake below.

"Wow." I exhale, taking in the stunning scenery as we stop a few feet from the cliff's edge. "How gorgeous."

After the rain of the past few days, the air is crystal clear, and the sky is a perfect pale blue, without a cloud in sight. In the absence of wind, the lake below us is so still it looks like a giant mirror, reflecting the majestic mountains surrounding it.

If I weren't here against my will, I'd think it's the prettiest place on Earth.

"Yes, gorgeous," Peter agrees, his voice unusually husky as his hand tightens on mine, and I turn to see his metallic gaze burning with hunger. My heart skips a beat as answering heat ripples through my body, chasing away the high-altitude chill.

It's always like this now. One look, one touch, and I'm a goner. Even when we're just holding hands, my heart beats a little faster, and when he looks at me like this, my bones turn soft and liquid, my body quickening with arousal.

Flushing, I pull my hand out of his grasp and step back to avoid swaying toward him. We had sex less than two hours ago, and I'm still sore. It's disturbing how much I want him and how little control I have over my response. The chemistry between us has always been explosive, but ever since that blowjob, there's something different about my desire, something that seems rooted in the very wrongness of it all.

No. I force the thought away, refusing to give in to it. Peter was wrong. I don't want to be his captive. This isn't a sexual game we're playing; it's my life, my future. Everything I've worked for is gone, stolen by the man looking at me with those burning silver eyes. Whatever twisted cravings he's awakened in me, I'll never be okay with this forced relationship.

I can't be.

Yet as he reaches for me, drawing me back toward him, I don't resist. I don't fight as he bends his head and crushes his lips against mine. The fire sweeping through my veins burns away all reason, all morality and common sense. My fingers tangle in his hair, my body molding against his, and as he backs me up against a tree, I give in and embrace the darkness, letting my own inner monster roam free.

CHAPTER 22
PETER

As the preparations for the Nigeria job ramp up, I find myself reaching for Sara with increasing desperation, my need for her blazing out of control. When I'm not training with my men or working on the logistics for the mission, I'm either with her or thinking about her. It's like an addiction, this craving that never goes away, and the worst part is that no matter what I do, I can't get Sara on board.

I can't get her to accept her life with me.

It's not that she fights me physically. On the contrary, she responds whenever I touch her, and in her eyes, I see the same hunger, the need that's burning me alive. She might deny it, but she likes it when I'm rough in bed, even more than when I'm gentle. When I take control, it sets her free, easing the torment of her guilt and shutting off her overactive brain. Our desires complement each other, our connection sizzling with dark heat, yet even as her body embraces mine, I feel the chill of her mental distance, the attempts to keep herself from me.

On some level, I understand it. I took her from her life, from her family and the job she loved. It bothers me, that last part, because I know how much of Sara's identity was tied up in being a successful doctor. Music might've been her passion and medicine the pragmatic, parent-approved choice, but she still enjoyed her occupation. I saw it every time she came home, tired yet exhilarated by the challenge of bringing life into this world and healing her patients' ills. Now she seems lost, broken in some indefinable way, and I hate it.

My ptichka loves helping people, and I took that away from her.

To cheer her up, I decide to get a couple of musical instruments and recording equipment on the next trip out, so Sara can record herself singing along to some of her favorite pop songs. I also enlist Ilya to help me convert a portion of the open living room area downstairs into a dance studio, in case Sara wants to take up salsa or ballet again.

"What are you doing?" Sara asks when she sees us putting up the wall, and I explain my idea to her. She doesn't seem overly excited, but then again, she rarely does these days.

It's as if some of her inner spark has gone out, and I don't know how to bring it back.

"This is fucked up, man," Ilya mutters as Sara goes upstairs after yet another call with her parents, her shoulders stiff and her hazel eyes filled with tears. "Seriously, that girl doesn't deserve this."

I shoot him a dark look, and he shuts up, but I know he's right.

I'm destroying the woman I love, and I can't stop.

No matter what, I can't let her go.

By the time Anton and Yan return from their reconnaissance mission, the dance studio needs only mirrors, and I resolve to get those on the return flight from Nigeria, along with the musical instruments and the recording equipment. I also download thousands of popular music videos onto an internet-disabled iPad and give it to Sara—something she thanks me for, though again, with muted enthusiasm.

It's getting to the point where I'd almost rather she actively fought me, like in the first couple of days after I took her.

Not for the first time, I think about the morning-after pill I gave her and the condoms we're continuing to use. Maybe it was a mistake to listen to the remnants of my conscience and give in to Sara's pleas in this regard. When her period came two weeks ago, I felt like I lost something, and no matter how hard I try to force the idea of Sara with child out of my mind, I can't stop dwelling on it.

I can't stop wanting it.

My little bird, pregnant. I can picture it so clearly when I look at her—the swollen belly and the full, ripe breasts, the glow of life developing inside her… Her pretty nipples would get extra sensitive, her slim body lush and soft, and when the child would be born, she'd love it.

She'd care for our baby, the way my birth mother never cared for me.

It's tempting, and the desire gnaws at me more each day. Up here, Sara is completely in my power. If I left the condoms off, there'd be nothing she could do, no morning-after pill she could get from somewhere on her own. She'd have my child and she'd love it, and then someday, she'd grow to love me too.

We'd be a family, and I'd finally truly have her.

She'd be mine, and she'd never want to leave.

———

The night before Ilya and I depart for Nigeria, I make a special dinner for Sara and the team, whipping up each person's favorite dishes, along with a couple of Japanese recipes I've been itching to try out.

"Why don't we eat like this every day?" Anton complains, scooping up a second serving of *vinegret*—a traditional beet-based Russian salad. "Seriously, man, you've got to step it up. All we had yesterday was rice and fish."

I give him the finger, and the Ivanov twins laugh before tucking into their favorite dish—lamb kebobs done the Georgian way, complete with a spicy dipping sauce. Even Sara smiles as she loads her plate with a little bit of everything, including my attempt at tempura vegetables.

As we eat, the guys and I discuss some of the job's logistics, and Sara quietly listens, as is her habit during mealtimes. The distance she keeps from me extends to my men; she rarely talks to them, at least when I'm around. The only one she seems to like is Ilya, and even with him, she's reserved, her manner polite but far from warm. I think she feels uncomfortable around my teammates; either that, or she hates them for being my accomplices.

I don't mind her attitude toward them. In fact, I prefer it. Over the past six weeks, I've caught all three eyeing Sara with varying degrees of interest, and I've barely stopped myself from slitting their throats. I know they don't mean anything by looking—any red-blooded male would appreciate Sara's trim, graceful beauty—but I'm still tempted to kill them.

She's mine, and I don't share. Ever.

In any case, I'm glad it's Yan who's staying behind. Of the four of us, he has the coolest head, and though I trust all three of my teammates, I have the greatest confidence in Yan's self-control. He wouldn't touch Sara, no matter the temptation, and that's precisely what I need.

I have to know she's safely guarded, so I can focus on the job.

"So what about the townspeople?" Yan asks as Ilya outlines our escape route after the hit. We're all speaking English out of deference to Sara, and to my surprise, I see her face whiten as I explain about the bombs we're planning to set off as a distraction.

If I didn't know better, I'd think she's worried for us.

We go through more of the bombing logistics and are in the middle of discussing contingency plans when Sara abruptly stands up, her chair scraping across the floor.

"Please excuse me," she says in a shaky voice, and before I can stop her, she runs to the staircase and disappears upstairs.

CHAPTER 23
SARA

I feel sick, literally ill with anxiety. My stomach is cramping, and it feels like a truck drove over my chest. Ever since Peter told me about the Nigerian banker, I've been trying not to think about the danger, but tonight, listening to the men talk about the insane security at the banker's compound and what they'll do in case one of them gets injured or killed, I couldn't ignore it any longer.

Tomorrow, Peter and his teammates will go up against a monster in his heavily guarded lair, and there's no guarantee they'll come out alive.

Locking myself in the bathroom, I hurry to the sink and splash cold water on my face, trying to breathe through the suffocating tightness in my throat. It feels like a panic attack, only the fear I'm feeling has nothing to do with my own situation—a situation that could, in fact, be resolved by Peter's death.

A bullet to the brain or the heart—that's what he once told me it would take for him to leave me be. And I know it's true. For as long as my tormentor is alive, I'll never be free of him. Even if I somehow managed to escape, he'd come after me. So I should hope he gets killed—shot or blown apart by one of those bombs. Then his teammates might return me home, and my old life could resume.

I could have it all back if he were dead.

It's what I should want, but instead, dread and anxiety consume me. The thought of Peter hurt in any way is unbearable, even more so today than the night he stole me. Over the past six weeks, I've done everything I can to rein in my emotions, to respond to him in physical ways only, but I've clearly failed.

Whatever messed-up feelings I developed for my husband's killer are still there; if anything, they've grown during my captivity.

Feeling increasingly ill, I grab a towel and rub it over my wet face. My stomach is a giant knot, and I can feel the blood pulsing in my temples as I drag shallow breaths into my tightening ribcage. The face reflected in the bathroom mirror is chalk white, with red splotches where I rubbed too harshly with the towel.

Tomorrow, Peter could be killed.

"Sara?" A knock on the door startles me, and I drop the towel, pivoting to face the doorway.

"Ptichka, are you okay?" Peter's deep voice holds a note of worry.

My lungs are still not functioning properly, but I manage to gulp in a breath and choke out, "I'm fine. Just one sec."

Grabbing the towel from the floor with shaking hands, I throw it into the laundry hamper in the corner and smooth my palms over my hair, trying to calm down. My panic attacks have all but subsided in recent weeks, and I don't want Peter to know that I unraveled just from hearing about the dangers he'll face.

Taking several deep breaths, I walk over to the door and unlock it. Peter immediately steps in, a worried frown creasing his forehead as his gaze rakes me over in search of injuries.

"What happened? Are you okay?"

"Yes, sorry. Just got a stomachache," I say in an almost steady voice. "I'm fine, though."

Peter's frown deepens. "Is it that time of the month?"

"No, just—" I stop and do some mental calculations. To my surprise, he's right. My last period was nearly four weeks ago—which does explain some of what I'm feeling.

"Actually, yes," I say, relieved to grab on to the excuse. "I didn't realize that, but yes, that must be it."

Some of the tension leaves Peter's face. "My poor ptichka. Come here." Reaching over, he pulls me into his embrace, and I wrap my arms around his waist, breathing in his warm scent as he strokes my hair. The worst of my panic is easing, the solid, muscular feel of him lessening my anxiety, but the dread about tomorrow refuses to go away.

What if he gets killed?

"Do you want to lie down?" Peter murmurs after a moment, pulling back to gaze down at me, and I shake my head. My chest is still too tight, and my stomach is cramping for real, but being alone with my worry would only exacerbate the situation.

Stepping out of his hold, I manage a small smile. "I'm okay. Sorry if I ruined dinner. Everything was delicious."

There are still traces of worry in his gaze, but he nods, accepting my words at face value. "Do you want some dessert?" he asks. "It's apple pie. I can bring it up here for you, if you're not feeling up to—"

"No, I'll come down. I have to take an Advil anyway."

And taking a deep breath, I walk out of the bathroom, determined to do whatever it takes to distract myself from thoughts about tomorrow.

CHAPTER 24
PETER

When we get to the kitchen, Sara's demeanor changes so suddenly it's as if someone flipped a switch, turning on a different personality. A kind of frenetic energy seems to take hold of her, and after she gulps down two Advils, she starts rushing around the kitchen, putting away the leftovers and getting fresh plates for dessert with the speed of someone racing to catch a train.

"I got this, ptichka. Just relax," I tell her, guiding her to her chair when she tries to grab the pie out of the oven without mitts. "You're not feeling well, so just take it easy."

"I'm fine," she protests, but I ignore her, carefully taking the pie out of the oven myself and carrying it to the table while the guys watch the whole thing in bemusement.

Sara sits still for a few moments, letting me cut the pie into five pieces, and then she jumps up again. "Here, let me serve it," she says, grabbing Ilya's plate. Then, apparently realizing she doesn't have the right utensils, she runs over to the kitchenware drawer and returns with a spatula.

This time, I let her do her thing, though I have no idea what's come over her. Her eyes are too bright, feverish with some repressed excitement, and her face is still too pale. Maybe she's coming down with something? But then she should be tired, not running around in a frenzy.

"Here," she says, shoving the pie in front of Ilya. "Do you want anything else? Like whipped cream?"

"Um, no, thank you." My teammate blinks at Sara. "I'm good."

She gives him an uncharacteristically bright smile and grabs Anton's plate next. Plopping down a slice of pie on it, she hands the plate to him, and then does the same thing for Yan and me before snagging a piece of pie for herself.

Sitting down, she stabs a fork into her slice and looks up, surveying our puzzled faces.

"So," she says in a voice so cheerful I hardly recognize it, "do you guys have apple pie in Russia too, or is this more of an American thing? You know, as American as apple pie and all that?"

Yan recovers first. "We have apple pie," he says with an amused grin. "It doesn't look exactly like this, but we make pies and little pies—*pirozhki*—filled with apples and berries, as well as meat, potatoes, mushrooms, cabbage, green onions, and eggs."

"Cabbage, green onions, and eggs?" Sara wrinkles her nose. "Really?"

"Well, not together," Yan clarifies. "It's eggs and green onions, or cabbage. Oh, and mushrooms can also be with onions and cheese."

Sara cocks her head, regarding him with interest. "Oh yeah? What other kinds of baked goods do Russians like?"

"Oh, there are lots," Anton says, jumping into the conversation. Unwittingly, Sara has touched on my friend's biggest weakness—sweets and baked goods—and Ilya and I exchange exasperated looks as he launches into a long list of his favorite cakes and pastries, describing each one in drool-inducing detail.

"Wow," Sara says when he pauses to catch his breath. "Peter, do you know how to make all of these?"

"Some," I say, putting down my fork. "If you want, I can try my hand at the Napoleon when we return—that's the Russian version of *mille-feuille*, the multi-layered custard Anton was telling you about."

"Yes, please," Anton replies, though I wasn't addressing him. "How do Americans say it? Pretty please with a cherry on top?"

Ilya and Anton laugh, but Sara's face tightens for a fraction of a second. In the next moment, however, she joins them in laughter, and I have to wonder if I imagined it. Not that it matters—her behavior is strange enough as is.

As we eat dessert and drink tea—a Russian tradition the guys tell Sara all about—I watch her, trying to figure out the reason for her sudden animation. It's as if a different person took over Sara's body. She's joking and laughing with my men, as though she has not a care in the world. Yet under the table, she's shifting in her chair and holding her arm curled around her stomach—a clear sign of the cramps that plague her.

It bothers me, this puzzle, and when all of the apple pie is gone, I tell the guys to take care of the cleanup. Sara jumps up to help them, but I catch her wrist before she can start running around again.

"Come," I say. "It's time for bed."

She doesn't offer any objections, even though it's barely nine o'clock, and when we get to the bedroom, she starts to undress without prompting, her eyes still gleaming with that feverish light.

My physical response is instant. As soon as she takes off her shirt and unclasps her bra, my cock goes rock hard and prickles of heat run over my skin. And when she lets the bra fall to the floor before shimmying out of her jeans, my heart starts slamming against my ribcage. What turns me on the most, though, is that she holds my gaze throughout, the feverish gleam in the hazel depths transforming into the seductive glow of desire.

Her thong is last, and then she comes toward me, her slim hips swaying with unconscious grace.

Impossibly, I harden even more, and it takes everything I have not to seize her as she stops in front of me, her slender hands reaching for the top button of my shirt.

"I thought you weren't feeling well." My voice is hoarse, filled with the lust pounding through me in savage waves. "Ptichka, you don't have to—"

"Shhh." Reaching up, she presses a delicate finger to my lips. "I don't want to talk."

My heartbeat roars in my ears as she lowers her hand and starts working on the buttons of my shirt. It's the first time Sara's initiated sex with me like this, and as her fingers brush against my skin, the heat inside me turns volcanic, the urge to fuck her so strong my hands curl into fists. She's working with exquisite concentration, her sexy lower lip tucked between her teeth as her hair tumbles in thick, shiny waves around her face, and I literally shake with the need to reach for her, to grab her and take her, over and over again.

Yet I don't move. I can't. Her willing touch is a gift I didn't expect tonight, didn't even dare to hope for. I don't know what's going through her head or why she's doing this, but I'm not about to protest.

Finishing with the buttons, Sara pushes the shirt off my shoulders and, glancing up at me through the dark fringe of her lashes, reaches for the zipper of my jeans.

Her touch is more hesitant now, almost wary, but it doesn't matter. The blood rushing through my veins feels like lava. Her naked body is so close I can smell her, feel her… all but taste her sweetness on my tongue. Her nipples are tight and hard, the pale globes of her breasts swaying gently as she wrestles with the buckle of my belt, and a groan escapes my throat as she frees my throbbing cock and sinks onto her knees before me.

"Sara…" I can barely speak as she cradles my balls in her soft palm and wraps her other hand around my shaft. Leaning in, she licks it delicately from root to tip, sending heat rocketing up and down my spine. My balls draw up high and tight, and I know I'm seconds away from coming. Dragging in a breath, I try to think of something else, something to delay the explosive rise of tension, but she wraps her lips around me, taking me into her soft, wet mouth, and I lose all semblance of control.

Groaning, I clutch her head, tangling my fingers in her hair as I thrust all the way in, making her gag and choke as I hit her throat. It's not what I wanted, not what I meant to do tonight, but the lust riding me is too violent, too potent to resist. On her knees, with her chestnut waves streaming over her slender back and her eyes watering as I fuck her face, Sara is the sexiest thing I've ever seen. And knowing she's there of her own accord...

"Fuck!" The expletive bursts out of me as her hand tightens on my balls, and the orgasm boils up, the pleasure spiking out of control. My muscles clench, my spine curving as ecstasy pounds through my veins, and with a hoarse shout, I come, my seed jetting straight into her throat.

She swallows every drop, sucking on my cock until it softens, and all the while, her hazel eyes stare into mine. It's like she's drinking in my pleasure, feeding on my need for her. It reminds me of the time I punished her, only tonight I don't see the same dazed submission in her gaze. She's doing this because she wants to, not because I broke her, and when the last of the rippling pleasure fades, I pull her to her feet and lead her to our bed, determined to make it right.

"Lie down," I tell her, guiding her onto the bed, and she obeys, stretching out on her back. Her gaze is shadowed, her lids half-lowered as she watches me climb over her, and

I know she's still in the grip of whatever's been driving her tonight.

The puzzle of it gnaws at me, but now is not the time to pursue it. I'm still breathing heavily with the aftershocks of pleasure, but I want more. I want to taste her as she comes, feel her slender arms wrap around me. More than a sexual need, it's a compulsion.

With Sara, I can never get enough.

So I indulge myself. With my most urgent hunger sated, I take my time playing with her body, kissing and caressing every centimeter of her warm, sweet-scented flesh. She's delicious, my Sara, her pale skin smooth and sleek, her delicate curves soft yet firm to the touch. Her moans, her breathy little gasps, her whimpers as I lick her—I'd give the world to stay like this forever, to keep hearing her cries as she unravels on my tongue.

Two orgasms, three, then four... I lose count after a while, consumed by her, addicted to her pleasure. I bring her to completion with my fingers and my mouth, and then take her gently, cognizant of her pre-period discomfort. She doesn't object, clinging to me as I rock carefully back and forth, and after I come, I go down on her once more, tasting our combined wetness as I suck her clit. Her fingers clenching in my hair, her panting breaths and pleading groans—it's like a drug I overdose on, binging on her scent and taste and feel. And when she's lying there spent, glowing and exhausted, I take her in my arms, feeling her heart beat against mine as we fall asleep.

CHAPTER 25
SARA

I wake up to a peculiar mixture of wellbeing and malaise, and it takes a solid minute to recall why.

Peter.

He left for Nigeria this morning after making love to me all night.

It feels surreal now, like a dream I'm waking up from. I can't believe I came on to him like that, and then what followed... Groaning, I roll over onto my side and swing my legs off the bed. My stomach is cramping in full force, and when I get to the bathroom, I'm not surprised to discover that my period is starting. What does shock me is that we again forgot condoms last night, and no alarm bells rang in my mind.

It's like I subconsciously want to get pregnant.

No. I shove away the horrifying thought. I definitely do *not* want a child like this. I just wasn't thinking clearly last night. After listening to the men talk about the dangers they'll face, I was so sick with worry, and so desperate to distract myself, I all but attacked Peter, seducing him despite how shitty I was feeling. I'm pretty sure he would've left me alone last night—he's always considerate when I feel ill—but I needed a distraction, and that's precisely what I got. By my second orgasm, I forgot all about Nigeria *and* not feeling well, and by the fourth, I could barely recall my own name.

I'm in desperate need of a shower, so I ignore the twisting discomfort in my stomach and step into the stall to wash from head to toe. Then I towel off, brush my teeth, and trudge back into the bedroom to get dressed. To my surprise, I discover a glass of water and Advil on the dresser—Peter must've left them there for me this morning.

Feeling pathetically grateful, I swallow the medicine and lie down, waiting for the worst of the discomfort to pass. It's stupid, but I already miss my captor... miss his attentiveness and care. I know it's just because I'm feeling low, but I want him here to rub my belly, to hold me and make me feel like I'm the center of his world.

I want him here and not halfway around the world, where bullets fly and bombs explode.

No. No, no, no. I squeeze my eyes shut, but it's too late. The anxiety I thought I banished returns with a toxic blast, the panic tightening my chest and throat. It's stupid, utterly irrational, but I don't want to see my tormentor dead. I can't even imagine it. His impact on my life is so absolute, so all-encompassing, I can't picture it without him.

I don't want to picture it.

My chest squeezes even tighter, and I focus on my breathing, trying to relax my tense muscles and slow my wildly beating pulse. I tell myself that Peter will be fine, that he can handle whatever comes his way. Danger is his comfort zone, assassinations his chosen profession. There's no reason to think that something will go wrong, no reason to imagine he will not return.

Except he got hurt on that Mexico job.

No. Breathing deeply, I force away the insidious reminder. It's stupid to worry just because of a one-time slip. Over the years, Peter has done plenty of dangerous jobs without getting hurt.

In fact, he killed my husband and his three guards without getting so much as a scratch.

My stomach roils, worsening my cramps, and my throat fills with bile at the recollection. How could I have let myself forget, even for an instant, what kind of man Peter is and what he's done? Up here on this mountain, my old life may seem less real, but that doesn't mean it didn't happen.

It doesn't mean the husband I loved did not exist.

Closing my eyes, I focus on George and the happy memories we had together. There were so many: our first dates, the trip to Disney World, the barbecues at my parents' house... My parents loved him, thought the world of him, and for years, so did I. We laughed and cried together, went out and stayed in. He was there for my college graduation, and I was there for his. Then things got tough: my med school and my residency, his never-ending trips abroad. And still, we were together, our love bolstered by the knowledge that our lives were just beginning, that we were young and could withstand it all.

Of course, that was before the drinking and the moods... before his secrets destroyed our marriage and brought Peter to our door.

Opening my eyes, I stare at the ceiling, feeling the now-familiar pain of betrayal. I wish I could forget that part, to pretend that everything Peter told me is a lie, but I can't deny the facts.

The boy I met in college wasn't the man I married, and for years, I had no idea why.

Spy, not journalist. It still seems so impossible to believe. Would George have ever told me? If the tragedy at Daryevo and all the things that followed hadn't happened, would I have ever learned about his real job? Or would he have kept me in the dark our entire lives, lying to me with a smile?

Realizing my thoughts are veering toward bitterness, I try to focus on the happy times, but it's useless. What George and I had might've been good once, but it wasn't toward the end, and I can't forget that. I can't wipe away the pain and the guilt, the shame and the despair I battled as our marriage slowly fell apart, crushed by the weight of his addiction. I lost my husband long before the accident that broke his skull, before Peter showed up with his deadly plans of vengeance.

I lost him when Peter lost his family; I just didn't know it at the time.

My stomach is still cramping, but the pills are starting to kick in, so I get up and start getting dressed. I can't bear to think about George any longer, because even the happy memories are now tainted by the knowledge that it was all a lie, that I never truly knew the man I married.

The man whose killer I'm worrying about now.

Desperate to suppress a fresh swell of anxiety, I grab the iPad Peter gave me and turn on a music video, singing along with Ariana Grande as I put on my clothes and brush my hair. The music lifts my mood slightly, and by the time I go downstairs, I'm able to greet Yan, who's sitting behind the counter with a laptop, with a normal-sounding, "Good morning."

"Good morning," he replies, looking up from the screen as I start making myself coffee. As always, Ilya's brother is dressed as though for work at an investment firm, his brown hair neatly styled and his face smoothly shaven. He's smiling at me, but his green gaze remains cool as he says, "Peter left oatmeal for you on the stove."

"Oh, thanks." My chest squeezes with unsettling warmth as I walk over to the stove and ladle the oatmeal into a bowl. I should be used to it by now, but it still amazes me how Peter never seems to tire of taking care of me. This morning, of all days, he must've had so many more important things on his mind, yet he thought of me, leaving me Advil and now this breakfast.

"Any news?" I ask Yan as I sit down at the table. "Have you heard anything from them?"

The Russian shakes his head. "It's eight more hours before they land." His tone is light, but I catch a note of tension underneath.

In his own possibly psychopathic way, he's worried.

My anxiety ratchets up again, my appetite disappearing, but I force myself to eat as Yan turns his attention back to the computer screen. Peter might be gone for a couple of days or more, and I can't starve myself just because I'm worried sick. Nor does it make sense for me to worry about a man I should hate, but I'm giving up on that battle.

Foolish or not, I don't want to see Peter hurt or dead.

Finishing my meal, I go upstairs and distract myself by reading and watching the music videos Peter downloaded onto the iPad for me. Between that and some light household chores, I keep busy until lunchtime, at which point I go downstairs again.

Yan is nowhere to be seen, so he must be either in his room or training somewhere outside. For a second, I'm tempted to repeat my escape attempt—the weather is much warmer now, and as far as I know, no storm is coming—but I decide against it. I'm still not familiar enough with the topography of this mountain, and blindly stumbling around cliffs doesn't seem like a great idea, especially when I'm feeling shitty from my period.

At least that's what I tell myself to explain why I push all thoughts of escape out of my mind and pop another Advil before making myself a sandwich.

When I come down again for dinner, Yan is there, finishing a bowl of leftover oatmeal and setting up what looks like audio recording equipment—a pair of bulky, over-the-ears headphones with an attached microphone that plugs into the computer.

"Anything?" I ask, walking over to the fridge after I take another Advil, and Yan shakes his head.

"Should be soon, though," he says before gulping down the rest of his tea. "I'll let you know when they land."

"Thank you," I say and get busy making myself a veggie stir-fry. I can feel the tension gathering between my shoulder blades, the anxiety I battled all day returning as I chop and dice vegetables before seasoning them liberally with soy sauce.

"Do you want some?" I ask Yan when he glances up to see what I'm doing, and he politely declines, putting on the headphones for what appear to be some audio reception tests. He still looks unusually tense, his expression grimly focused as his fingers fly over the keyboard of the laptop.

When the stir-fry is done, I sit down to eat and covertly observe Yan, my unease growing with each bite. By my calculations, it's already been eight hours since breakfast, and the tension radiating off the usually suave Russian doesn't help.

"Do you normally keep in touch with them throughout the mission?" I ask when I can't bear the silence any longer. "Or do you wait for them to contact you?"

Yan looks up from the screen and removes the headphones. "I'm usually with them," he says, swiveling the bar-stool to face me, and I realize why he seems so on edge.

He's used to being there, in the thick of things, not watching from the sidelines.

"I'm sorry you had to babysit me," I say, pushing my half-eaten plate away. I might as well try to get to know my remaining jailer instead of obsessing about Peter's fate. "I'm sure you must be worried about your brother."

Yan shrugs, an expression of cool amusement veiling the tension on his face. "Ilya can take care of himself."

"Yes, I'm sure." Picking up my own cup of tea, I ask, "Is he your younger or older sibling?"

His amusement appears to deepen. "Older by three minutes."

"Oh." I blink. "He's your twin?"

He nods. "An identical one, if you can believe that."

"Wow. You guys don't look anything alike." Sipping the tea, I study his clean, vaguely aristocratic features. Now that I look closer, I see the similarities to Ilya's bone structure, but there are quite a few differences too. Yan's nose is straighter, and his square jaw is more proportional—not quite as chiseled as Peter's, but still strong and nicely defined. The biggest difference, though, is the hair.

Yan has a full head of it, with not a hint of skull tattoos in sight.

"My brother's been unlucky in some fights," he explains, noticing my scrutiny. "Had his nose broken and his face bashed in quite a bit. Also, he did some steroids when we were young and stupid—wanted to bulk up."

"I see." Steroids would account for some of the differences, including that of size. Not that the man sitting before me is small by any means. He's roughly Peter's height, and just as muscular. His twin brother, however, is massive, as big as any bodybuilder I've seen.

"Is he your only sibling?" I ask, and Yan nods.

"Yeah, it's just the two of us."

I put down my cup. "Do you have any other family?"

"No." His expression doesn't change; there's nothing to indicate either grief or regret. He might as well have been answering whether he has an extra pair of socks.

I want to dig deeper into that, but there's another topic that interests me more. "When did you meet Peter?" I ask, leaning forward on my elbows. "You worked together before, right?"

"We did." Yan closes the laptop, swiveling the barstool to face me fully. "Ilya and I were part of his team for three years prior to Daryevo."

The mention of the village reminds me of the horrific images on Peter's phone, and the stir-fry sours in my stomach. "Did you know them?" I ask, trying to keep my voice steady. "His wife and son, I mean?"

"No." The Russian's green eyes are as bright as gems, and just as cold. "Anton is the only one who's met them. The rest of us didn't know Peter had a family until they were killed."

"Oh." I don't know what to say to that. Clearly, Peter didn't trust the man sitting in front of me—at least not enough to risk exposing his most precious secret. Yet here they are, working together again.

"If I were him, I would've kept it on the down low too," Yan says, a hard-edged smile spreading across his face, and

I realize he caught on to my discomfort. "We don't do families and babies in our world."

"Really?" So it wasn't a trust issue so much as a deviation from the accepted lifestyle on Peter's part. "Then I take it none of you have ever been married?"

"Only Peter," Yan confirms. "And you know how that turned out."

I swallow the lump in my throat and reach for my tea again. "Yes. I do."

Yan watches me drink the rest of the tea before saying quietly, "This won't last either, you know."

I lower the cup. "What do you mean?"

"This." He waves his hand, indicating me and our surroundings. "Whatever this is, it won't last."

I stare at him, confused. "You mean… he'll let me go?"

"No." The Russian's gaze is cold again, utterly unreadable. "That he won't do. He's an obsessive man, and you are his obsession. He'll never let you go, Sara. Not unless one or both of you are dead."

I suck in a sharp breath, but before I can respond, something pings and Yan turns away, facing the laptop.

"They landed," he says, putting on the headphones. "Now the fun can begin."

CHAPTER 26
PETER

The first part of the operation proceeds smoothly. So smoothly, in fact, that I get nervous. It's never a good sign when everything goes according to plan. There's always a snag to be dealt with, some kind of kink to be worked out. Unforeseen obstacles are to be expected, because nothing is ever a hundred-percent predictable, and thinking that it is—believing that the plan, no matter how flexible, accounts for all variables—is the fastest way to get killed.

So when we get into the banker's compound and quietly eliminate the exact number of guards we planned for, I begin to feel uneasy. And when we hijack all the cameras, giving Yan remote access, and make our way to the banker's bedroom suite without encountering a single staff member deviating from his or her routine, my danger meter goes on high alert—and I'm not the only one.

"You smell it, right?" Anton mutters as we stop in front of the bedroom door.

"Smell what?" Ilya whispers, sniffing the air with a frown.

"The shit about to hit the fan," I say in a low voice. "It's too easy. Too much like what we planned."

Comprehension lights Ilya's gaze. "Fuck."

None of us are superstitious, but we have a healthy respect for luck, and we all know that too much good luck can be just as deadly as an unlucky streak. A steady stream of small obstacles keeps one's mind and reflexes sharp, while smooth sailing lures one into complacency. Not that we're ever relaxed on a job—the adrenaline rush ensures we stay alert—but there's a difference between regular battle alertness and the hyperawareness that comes along with fighting for our lives.

This job has been smooth sailing so far, and when we hit a rough patch—which we will, because luck is a fickle bitch—it's going to suck extra hard.

There's nothing we can do about it, though, short of aborting the mission, so I gesture to Anton to get ready, and Ilya steps in front of the door.

One hard kick from his massive foot, and the door flies off its hinges, crashing to the floor. Inside, there is a panicked squeal, and as the three of us rush into the room, we see our target on the floor, his fat folds jiggling while his naked mistress cowers behind the bed.

The banker's tiny, pig-like eyes are white with terror, his round frame shaking as he scrambles to cover his deflating cock with a pillow. "Stop! Please, I can pay you. I swear, I can pay you. I'll top whatever they're paying you. What do you want? A hundred thousand euros? Half a million dollars? I have it. I have the money, I swear!" Seeing that we're not stopping, he switches from English to an accented mixture of French and German, and then a Hausa dialect, frantically repeating the offer until Anton stabs him in the throat to shut him up.

"Omuya's cousin sends his regards," I say in English, watching the man flail about as he chokes on the blood spurting out of his neck. It takes mere moments for him to die—an easy death, all things considered.

The asshole's mistress breaks into violent sobs behind the bed. Ignoring the noise, I snap a picture of the body as proof for the client, and then tell Ilya in Russian, "Tie her up and let's go." Normally, we'd eliminate the woman too, but I want a witness this time.

I want the authorities searching for us in Africa, far away from Sara and Japan.

Slinging the strap of his M16 over his shoulder, Ilya rounds the bed and reaches for the crying woman. Figuring he can handle it, I head for the door, my shit storm instincts still on high alert.

Suddenly, a shot rings out.

I spin around, my ears ringing from the blast, but it's too late.

Ilya is on the floor, a dark red stain spreading out from his head.

CHAPTER 27
SARA

I pace around the second floor, going from room to room as I battle my anxiety. The moment the team landed, Yan told me to leave him alone so he could focus on doing his part: monitoring the banker's compound remotely in case of unexpected problems. And he wasn't just trying to get rid of me. As I left the kitchen, I caught a glimpse of several security camera feeds on his computer screen, and what appeared to be a view from an aerial drone.

To distract myself, I tried to read again, then watched some music videos, singing along with some of my favorite artists. I even went to the unfinished dance studio and attempted a couple of ballet routines I learned as a child, along with some stretching at the barre to ease the period-induced tightness in my lower back. None of it held my attention for longer than fifteen minutes, so now I'm mindlessly going from window to window, as if by staring at the darkness outside, I can make the helicopter appear.

After about two hours, my cramps worsen and I'm a raw mess of nerves, so I go down to the kitchen to take more Advil. Yan is still sitting behind the counter with his computer, the headphones covering his ears, but there's nothing cool about his expression now. He's starkly pale, and lines of tension bracket his tight-lipped mouth as he speaks urgently into the microphone in Russian.

My heart stops, then launches into a panicked gallop.

Something went wrong.

Icy fear prickles through my body, my stomach twisting with an awful premonition, and I barely manage to stop myself from demanding to know what happened. That wouldn't help, and I don't want to distract Yan from what he's doing. Instead, I rush across the kitchen and stop behind him, frantically peering at the screen over his shoulder.

He pays me no attention, all his focus on the computer as he barks out what sounds like instructions. At first, I can't tell what's going on, but then, on one of the camera feeds, I see it.

Two bodies sprawled next to a bed.

One is an obese dark-skinned man, his naked bulk swimming in a pool of red, and on the other side of the bed is a naked woman. Looking closer, I notice blood splattered around her as well.

They're both dead.

Nausea rises in my throat, and I clap my hand over my mouth, trying to remain silent. Yan is still speaking in that urgent tone, and on another camera feed, two men in SWAT-like gear appear in a hallway. They're walking fast and carrying a large man by his arms and legs.

It's Peter and Anton carrying Ilya, I recognize with a mixture of horror and relief. Ilya's head is bandaged with what appears to be a pillowcase, but I can see the blood seeping through.

Yan's twin is severely injured, maybe even dead.

Scarcely daring to breathe, I bite my palm as I watch them round a corner. On yet another camera feed, a dozen armed men are rushing down another hallway, and I see the furious alarm on their faces as they stumble across more bodies. The other guards, perhaps? Either way, they regroup quickly, continuing down the hallway as Yan speaks even more urgently into the microphone.

Peter and Anton disappear from the camera view, then appear a moment later on another feed, and I see that they're approaching a parlor with a door leading to a large garage. They're all but running at this point, Ilya's body swinging hammock-like between them, and with a sinking feeling, I realize the reason for their urgency.

The hallway with the armed guards leads to the same parlor.

It's a race with the deadliest of stakes—and the guards appear to be winning.

I must've made a sound, because Yan glances over his shoulder, his jaw tightly clenched as his eyes lock with mine. He doesn't say anything, though, just turns back to the computer, and I continue watching, unable to take my eyes off the horror unfolding half a world away.

On the drone feed, two explosions tear through a small structure next to the main house, and the guards halt before separating into two groups. One group continues toward the parlor while a few guards rush back—toward the bombs the team must've set as a distraction.

Still, the delay is not enough. The guards get to the parlor a couple of seconds before Peter and his team.

The Russians appear to be ready. Still running, they swing Ilya higher, and Peter crouches mid-stride, letting Ilya's stomach land on his shoulder as Anton lets go of the unconscious man and grips his assault rifle. Grimacing with effort, Peter straightens, holding Ilya's massive bulk draped over his shoulder, and I watch, stunned, as he resumes running, steadying Ilya's body with one hand as he pulls a grenade out of his pocket with another.

With all the sound going through Yan's headphones, I can't hear the blast of automatic gunfire, but I see the bullets tearing through the walls as the Russians burst into the parlor with the guards. Two guards are mowed down by Anton's fire, but the rest take shelter behind a column, and I bite back a scream as Peter stumbles, Ilya nearly flying off his shoulder. In the next instant, however, he recovers, hanging on to his human burden, and I see the savage resolve on his face as he brings the grenade up and tears the pin off with his teeth.

Boom! A bright flash, and two camera feeds go dark. I'm not touching Yan, but I feel him jerk, as though he got shot. A stream of frantic Russian pours from his mouth as he pounds at the keyboard, bringing up more camera feeds, and it's not until I spot movement on the bird's-eye

drone view that I take a breath and realize I'm crying, the
tears leaving a burning trail on my ice-cold skin.

Yan must've spotted the same hint of movement, because he zooms in on the drone feed just as a huge SUV
bursts through a slowly opening garage door, taking out a
chunk of the door panel as it barrels toward the compound
gate.

A sobbing breath hisses through my teeth, and I bite
my palm again.

At least one of them is alive, and well enough to drive.

Shaking, I watch the SUV tear through the iron gate
amidst a hail of bullets, then rocket down a narrow road
with two guard SUVs in hot pursuit. The drone follows
long enough to show one pursuing SUV careening off the
road, as though they shot its tires, but after a few more seconds, the cars disappear in the distance, leaving the drone
behind.

Yan mutters what sounds like a Russian curse and
again pounds furiously at the keyboard. A new window
pops up, this one with an audio feed graph, and I realize
he must be tuning in to some radio signal. Sure enough, a
minute later, he resumes speaking in frantic Russian, and I
exhale a shaking breath.

Someone in that SUV must be alive.

*Is it Peter? Are they hurt? How far to the plane? Is Ilya
still alive? Is Peter hurt?*

The questions threaten to burst out, but I dig my nails
into my palms and remain silent, not daring to distract Yan
as he pulls up a map and rattles off instructions in rapid-fire Russian. His posture is as tense as ever, his attention

laser-focused on the screen, and I know they're still in danger.

If they're all alive, that is.

Taking a breath, I try to calm myself, to stop the tears from streaking down my frozen face, but the fear is too strong. I'm sick with it, poisoned by the surfeit of adrenaline. I've never known this kind of debilitating worry for another. My heart pounds violently in my ribcage, each beat marking another second of wretched waiting.

Peter has to be all right. He has to be.

One minute, two, three, ten… I stare at the tiny clock in the corner of the screen as Yan falls silent, joining me in waiting.

Twelve minutes.

Fifteen.

Eighteen.

I don't move. I barely even breathe.

Twenty.

Twenty-two.

Yan's posture changes, taking on a new alertness. Gripping the microphone, he speaks a few terse sentences in Russian, then removes the headphones and swivels to face me.

Ravages of stress still mark his features, but the tension I saw earlier is gone. "It's over," he says. "They're in the air, on their way to Egypt. A bullet grazed Ilya's skull, but they stopped the bleeding, and he's already briefly woken up. With any luck, he'll be okay."

I grip the counter, bracing myself. "And Peter?"

"Bruised and a little bloodied, but not injured. Same goes for Anton."

I exhale, dizzy with relief, and swipe at the wetness on my cheeks with the back of my trembling hand.

Peter is alive.

Bruised and bloodied, but alive.

I want to sink to the floor, the post-adrenaline slump hitting me like a bullet, but I steady myself against the counter, forcing my overloaded brain to function. "So why—" I clear my throat, chasing the hoarseness from my voice. "Why are they going to Egypt?"

"Ilya still needs medical attention, and there's a clinic," Yan explains, then gives me an arrested stare.

"What?" I ask, my heartbeat accelerating.

"You're a doctor," he says, cocking his head. "Aren't you?"

"I… yes." Doesn't he know that? "I'm a licensed OB-GYN."

"Do you know how to stitch a wound?"

I'm beginning to see where this is heading. "Yes, of course. I also did a rotation in ER during my residency, but—"

"Hold on." He pivots to face the laptop and puts on the headphones.

"Wait, Yan. He needs a hospital," I protest, but he's already speaking into the microphone in Russian.

Frustrated, I wait for him to finish, and when he turns to face me again, I tell him firmly, "This is a bad idea. Your brother could have a concussion or internal bleeding. He needs a CT scan, antibiotics, proper medical equipment… He—"

"Has survived worse, believe me," Yan interrupts, his face resolute. "What he needs is rest and recovery time, and we can't give him that in the clinic—not with the authorities about to scour the African continent for us. We have antibiotics and basic medical supplies here—we stock that in all of our safe houses—and now we have a doctor too."

I frown. "No, listen. It's still not—"

"You should get some sleep, Sara," Yan advises, reaching for his headphones. "You look tired, and we'll need you sharp and rested when they land."

CHAPTER 28
PETER

Sara is standing by the helipad as we land, her slender figure small and fragile next to Yan's solid frame. My chest squeezes at the sight, my longing for her painfully sharp, and it's all I can do not to grab her as soon as our helicopter skids touch the ground. Instead, the first thing I do upon jumping out of the chopper is help Ilya out. The wound where the bullet grazed his skull is no longer bleeding, but he's still weak from loss of blood and more than a little concussed.

If the banker's mistress had used something other than a pearl-handled .22 revolver and had better aim, we'd be bringing him home in a body bag.

My overworked shoulder burns and my bruised ribs ache as Ilya leans on me—my bulletproof vest stopped two bullets during our escape—but I don't complain. I'm lucky. Fuck, all three of us are lucky. The shit definitely hit the fan, and it was spectacularly shitty. Between the banker's mistress finding the revolver under the mattress and some vigilant guard hearing the gunshot, our way out of the compound was as rough as the way in was smooth.

On a scale of one to ten, this job ended up as a seven—not as bad as some, but definitely worse than others.

"Here, I got him," Yan says, stepping in to support Ilya, and I step aside, letting him help his brother. Anton is coming out of the chopper behind us, but I pay him no attention. He caught some shrapnel from the grenade in his arm and shoulder, but I know he'll be fine. Instead, I focus on the one person I can't live without.

Sara.

My beautiful little songbird.

The wind is blowing her chestnut hair around her face, the sun highlighting shades of red within the rich brown waves. Her gaze is solemn as she stares at me, her face devoid of all expression. Yet I sense her longing, feel it deep within my bones.

She might not admit it, but she needs me.

She feels our connection, too.

Five long strides, and I scoop her up, lifting her into my arms as I crush my mouth to hers. Behind us, Anton lets out a low wolf whistle, but I tune him out. I don't give a fuck what the guys think, don't care that they see my weakness. Nothing matters but the way her slim arms fold around me, and the sweet, hot burn as I taste her lips. The minty flavor of her breath, the slick glide of her tongue, her warm Sara scent—I absorb it all, filling the emptiness inside me, pushing the darkness of my world away.

I don't deserve her, but I have her.

She's mine to love and cherish, mine to hold.

I don't know how long I kiss her, but by the time I lift my head, the others are already entering the house. Reluctantly, I lower Sara to her feet, but I can't bring myself to let go of her.

"Did you miss me, ptichka?" I ask softly, my hands resting on her supple waist. "Did you worry when I was gone?"

The sun brings out the greenish flecks in her soft hazel eyes, highlighting the turmoil within them. "I…" She licks her kiss-swollen lips. "I didn't want to see you dead."

"So you've said. But did you miss me?"

She gives me a tortured look, then pushes at my chest, stepping out of my hold. "I have to go," she says tightly. "Ilya's head won't stitch itself."

Turning, she runs into the house, and I follow, both disappointed and encouraged.

She's not yet ready to admit it, but sooner or later, I will break her.

I will make her love me, no matter what it takes.

Sara follows the Ivanov twins into Ilya's room, and I go into our bedroom to take a shower before I crash. I washed up on the plane, but I still feel the urge to scrub off all the violence and death.

I don't want the ugliness of my world to taint Sara in any way.

It takes me over twenty minutes to shower and change—with the numbing effects of adrenaline wearing off, my sore muscles and bruised ribs object to every movement—and by the time I get to Ilya's room, Sara is halfway done with his stitches. I stop in the doorway and watch her work, enjoying the tiny frown of concentration on her face. I had cameras installed in her office at the hospital, so I'm intimately familiar with that expression. She'd often wear it when taking notes on her patients or reading some new study that had come out in her field.

"Hand me that gauze," she tells Yan when she's done, and I grin at her authoritative tone. My little bird is in her element, and for the first time in weeks, I see a hint of her former spark. Yan was right to suggest this; not only is having Sara take care of Ilya's wound infinitely safer for us, but it's good for her mood, too.

Her movements are quick and efficient as she bandages Ilya's head, and my teammate closes his eyes, looking blissed out as the painkillers we gave him earlier kick in.

"Any other injuries?" Sara asks, glancing over her shoulder at me and Yan.

"I don't think so, but I'll check," Yan says. "I know Anton caught a little shrapnel, so you might want to take a look at him. I think he's in his room."

She nods and gets up. "What about you, Peter?"

I want her hands on me, so I shrug and promptly wince from the movement. "Just some scrapes and bruises," I say, doing my best to sound stoic but in pain.

Yan, who's seen me walk around with broken bones without a peep, gives me an "are you fucking kidding?"

look, but is smart enough not to say anything as Sara frowns and comes up to me.

"Show me," she orders, reaching for my shirt, but I catch her slender wrists before she can start an examination right then and there.

"How about we go to our room so I can sit down?" I suggest, ignoring Yan's open eye roll. "We'll be more comfortable there."

Sara frowns up at me, apparently divining my agenda. "I still have to examine Anton. Here, sit." Twisting her wrists out of my hold, she grabs my hand and leads me to a chair in the corner as Yan—the cock-blocking bastard—snickers quietly.

"Let me see," Sara says, deftly pulling my shirt up over my head, and I wince for real as the movement pulls at my sore shoulder.

It's all worth it, though, because in the next moment, Sara's cool, gentle hands press against my torso, carefully feeling each rib for breaks. Her touch should hurt, but as her delicate fingers glide over my bruises, all I feel is a surge of warmth, mixed with an aching tightness in my groin.

"Does this hurt?" she murmurs as her hands move up to my shoulder, and I shake my head, mesmerized by the green striations in her soft hazel eyes.

"It's just—" I clear my throat. "Just muscle soreness, I think."

"Hmm." Carefully, she lifts my arm and moves it in a circular motion. "No pain like this?"

"No." I breathe in deeply, inhaling her sweet scent. "Just some soreness."

"Okay." She gently lowers my arm and, to my disappointment, steps back. "Looks like you're right—it's just some bruising."

"I also scraped my back," I say, turning to show her. "Might need to be bandaged."

Sara leans in, her hands grazing my shoulders before moving down to mid-back, where I feel the faint stinging.

"This?" she asks, touching the wounded area lightly, and I nod, though the pain is barely noticeable.

"It looks like it's already healing, so no bandage required," Sara says as I turn back to face her. "I'm guessing someone already cleaned it?"

"Anton did that on the plane," I admit grudgingly. For once, I wish my team and I weren't so well versed in first aid. "Are you sure you don't need to bandage it?"

"No. It will heal better like this. Anything else?"

I lift my hands to show her the scrapes on the bottom of my palms, and Yan bursts out laughing.

"What do you want her to do with that? Kiss it and make it better?" he says in Russian, ignoring my furious glare. "Seriously, man, you want to indulge in doctor-patient play, do it later. Let her finish treating actual wounds first."

Sara frowns at us both before asking Yan, "What did you just say?"

"I told him that Anton needs your attention," Yan replies, still grinning. "And that he shouldn't hold you up with his kinky sex games."

Sara's face pinkens, and she turns away, grabbing the first aid kit to stuff the gauze and other supplies back in.

"I'll go take a look at Anton right now," she says stiffly, and hurries out of the room without looking at either one of us.

I get up and put my shirt on. "I'm going to smash your fucking face into your skull at training tomorrow," I tell Yan grimly. "As soon as I get some sleep, you're going to be eating your own teeth."

The asshole just laughs as I stalk out of the room, following Sara, and even Ilya seems to have a smile on his face as I loudly slam the door behind me.

Anton better not enjoy Sara's ministrations as I just did.

I'll kill that motherfucker if he does.

CHAPTER 29
SARA

Anton has a few gashes and shallow puncture wounds where the shrapnel from the grenade got his arms, but otherwise, he's okay. I change his bandages as Peter glowers from the other side of the room, and then I give Anton some instructions on how to take care of the wounds. Not that Peter's teammate needs them; from what I can tell, these men are pros at treating basic injuries.

"Thank you, Dr. Cobakis," he says when I'm done, and I smile at him.

Even scary-looking bearded assassins seem to respect the medical profession—when they're injured, at least.

Peter says something sharp in Russian and crosses the room to stand next to me. "All done?" he asks irritably, glaring down at me, and I match his frown with one of my own.

"Yes, for now." I have no idea what his problem is, but he's been acting like a bear with a thorn in its paw ever since he entered the room.

If it weren't so ridiculous, I'd think he's jealous of my attention to his injured friend.

"Then let's go." Grabbing my hand, he leads me out, and my pulse jumps as I realize he's bringing me to our room.

"Peter…" I feel myself getting breathless as I try to keep up with his long strides. "What are you doing? You need to rest."

He gives me a sidelong glance but doesn't stop. His jaw is tightly clenched, his grip on me so hard it's almost painful. Towing me along, he enters our room and purposefully shuts the door behind us.

"Peter…" I back up as soon as he lets go of my hand. "You're hurt. I don't know what you're thinking, but you need to—"

My words end on a gasp, because Peter stalks after me, closing the distance between us in a few decisive strides before sweeping me up against his chest. Three seconds later, I find myself on the bed, with two hundred pounds of furious, aroused male sprawled on top of me.

"What are you—"

His mouth slants over mine, hard and hungry, and his hands tear at my clothes, literally ripping my shirt in half. I tense, startled by the violence, but he doesn't stop, working my jeans down my legs with rough, jerky movements as he devours me with his brutal kiss. As he yanks down my underwear, I spare a moment's thought for the sheets and the bloodied pad I'm wearing, but his fingers twine with mine, pinning my hands above my head, and I forget all about it, swept up in the savage storm of his lust.

It's overwhelming, even frightening, yet the desire is still there, lurking underneath the fear. My muscles instinctively lock tight even as warm slickness lubricates my sex, the tension intensifying my arousal. I burn for him, craving the danger and the roughness, and as he plunges into me, I cry out from the shock of it, from the dark pleasure and stinging pain.

He pauses then, lifting his head to meet my gaze, and I remember our first time, the way he took me, losing all control. He hurt me then too, but unlike that time, there's no hate in my heart today, no bitterness or stifling shame. The pain feels good, pushing away the remnants of my worry, reminding me that he's alive.

Reminding us both that we're alive.

"Sara…" My name is a hoarse exhale on his lips, his molten silver gaze holding me captive even as he throbs inside me, his thick cock stretching my inner tissues, filling me to the brim until I ache. "Ptichka, I need you so fucking much…"

"And I need you." The words feel like they come from the very center of my being, torn out of me by the impossible fire burning in my veins. I can't fight it any longer, can't pretend I hate this beautiful, lethal man. It's not love between us, nor anything resembling friendship, but our connection is undeniable, the bone-deep chemistry binding us together in coils of dark need and violent attraction.

I want this from him: the roughness and the tenderness, the fear and the all-consuming heat.

He's everything I never knew I needed, and as his eyes darken at my admission, I realize what this means.

I *am* his, as terrifying as that thought may be.

Closing my eyes, I wrap my legs around his hips, taking him even deeper, and as he begins thrusting, his muscled ass flexing against my calves, I give in to the inevitable.

I give in to him.

PART III

CHAPTER 30
SARA

By the time the second month of my captivity transitions into the third, I find my resentment slowly lessening, the desperate longing for my old life transforming into a kind of bittersweet ache. I continue to look for opportunities to escape, but someone's always in the house, watching me, and as the days bleed into one another, I stop worrying about the impossibility of getting away and begin to enjoy some parts of my leisurely routine. The warm weather helps—we're in the hottest month of summer now, and there's a lot more to do outside—and so does the fact that outside of a few supply runs, Peter has been spending pretty much all his time with me.

"You haven't had a job in a while," I comment as we head down to a mountain stream where we've been swimming on particularly warm days. "Is it because of what happened to Ilya the last time, or you just don't get clients that often?"

"We get contacted all the time, but we're selective in the work we take on," Peter says, raising a low-hanging branch to let me pass underneath. "The risk-reward ratio has to be just right, especially now."

He doesn't say why, but he doesn't have to. From what he's told me, and from what I've gleaned from my brief conversations with my parents, the authorities are intensifying their manhunt, throwing all their resources at the problem that is Peter. Partially, it's because of my disappearance; even with my twice-weekly calls, my parents are convinced I'm in danger and spend their days harassing the FBI for updates. But the main issue is the last target on Peter's list, a former US general who's proving to be as elusive in his own way as Peter and his team.

"Wally Henderson is highly connected," Peter explained to me a couple of weeks ago. "He caught wind of what's going on long before anyone else on my list, and he staged a disappearance worthy of Houdini. So far, every lead our hackers have followed has led exactly nowhere. As far as we can tell, he's not in contact with anyone from his former life—neither friends nor coworkers nor distant relatives—and he hasn't made a single slip. No appearances on social media by his teenagers, no credit card use, nothing. A lot of his background is classified, but rumor has it, he was a CIA operative at some point, possibly a field agent working deep under cover. And while we haven't been able to discover the specifics of how he's doing it, it seems he's been pressuring the authorities to turn up the heat from wherever he's hiding."

"You think he knows he's the last name on your list?" I asked.

"I'm sure he does," Peter replied. "Like I said, he's connected, and not just in Washington D.C. He knows everyone in the international intelligence community, and he's leveraging that to make me as high priority as any ISIS leader."

I've been trying not to think about the implications of that, but it's impossible. I can't put my worry for Peter out of my mind. By all rights, I should cheer for the general and hope the authorities find my captor, liberating me in the process, but rational thinking seems to be beyond me these days.

"Why don't you stop these jobs altogether?" I ask now as we approach the stream. "You must have enough money already."

Peter shoots me an oblique look. "There's no such thing as enough money when you're on the run," he says and pulls off his T-shirt, exposing a powerfully muscled torso. "Private planes and helicopters don't come cheap."

I look away to avoid flushing as he steps out of his shorts—he's commando underneath—and wades into the stream after kicking off his boots. I see him naked all the time, but that doesn't lessen the impact of his tautly muscled body on my senses. Nature has blessed my captor with a perfectly proportioned male frame—broad shoulders, narrow hips, long, strong-boned limbs—and intense military training has given him a physique Olympic athletes would envy. But it's not his looks that fill my veins with liquid heat; it's the knowledge that if I so much as glance at him in a certain way, the dark fire that always simmers between us will blaze out of control, and I'll end up in his arms, screaming his name as he takes me against the slippery rocks.

"You know, you wouldn't need all those planes and helicopters if you didn't venture out as much," I point out when he's safely covered by the water. My voice is huskier than I would've liked, but at least my face is not bright red. "You'd be safer, and you wouldn't have to... you know."

"Kill people?" he suggests dryly.

"Right." I busy myself by stripping down to my swimsuit as Peter turns to float on his back, leisurely moving his arms to offset the current. I don't like thinking about the gruesome reality of Peter's profession, not in any kind of depth, at least. I'm obviously aware that he's a killer, but as long as I don't dwell on it, it's more of an abstract concept than something that's constantly at the forefront of my mind.

Today, though, I can't push it out of my thoughts, and as I wade into the deeper portion of the stream next to Peter, I find myself asking, "Do you like it? Is that why you do what you do?"

I expect him to deny it, to claim necessity or upbringing as the driving force behind his career choice, but he turns upright to face me, a dark smile curving his lips as he answers, "Of course I do, ptichka. Did you ever imagine otherwise?"

I stare at him, my skin pebbling with goosebumps as the current rushes around me, the water covering me up to my chest. The stream that felt refreshing a moment ago now feels like liquid ice, as chilling as that storm we were caught in. "You like killing?"

He nods, his eyes bright silver in the sunlight. "Death, like life, has its own allure," he says softly, stepping closer to draw me against his large, warm body. "It's a dark allure, but it's there, and every soldier knows it. As a doctor, you must've seen it sometimes: the way pain transforms into the bliss of nothingness, agony into the peace of nonexistence. Death ends all struggles, heals all hurts. And dealing death... there's nothing quite like it. You feel it: the vulnerability of yourself and everything surrounding you, but also the power. The control. It's addictive, once you've experienced it... once you've held someone's life in your hands and extinguished it on purpose."

His words wash over me like a dark wave, terrifying and fascinating at the same time. I have seen some of what he's talking about, have even felt the power he's describing. Only for me, it was when I would save a life, not take one. I can't imagine the lack of empathy it takes to use that power to destroy instead of healing, to take away someone's very existence.

I was right to think him a monster. He *is* one, yet that realization doesn't repulse me as it should. His admission, as horrifying as it is, doesn't lessen the heat growing inside me as he molds my lower body against his, one hand gripping my hip and the other reaching up to frame my face. He's already turned on, his erection hard against my stomach, and as he leans in, his lips pressing hungrily against mine, I close my eyes and wind my arms around his muscled neck, letting his touch burn away the chill of knowing what he is.

I'm in bed with the devil, and at this moment, there's nowhere else I'd rather be.

That evening, we have dinner, all five of us, and as has been the case since the Nigeria job, Peter's men converse with me throughout the meal, telling me a bunch of amusing stories about Russia and some of the former Soviet Republics. I'm still not completely comfortable around the mercenaries—I'm keenly aware that they'd kill me or anyone else without hesitation if Peter were to order it—but they've been excessively friendly since I treated Ilya and Anton's wounds. It's during meals like these that I learn about the customs of my captors' country—they do consider it polite to remove shoes when entering someone's home—and even pick up a few words in Russian.

"*Vkusno. V-koos-nah.*" Ilya repeats the word for me slowly, softening the "v" so it sounds like an "f." "That means delicious, or tasty. So if you want to tell Peter you like something, you can point at that dish and say, 'Vkusno.'"

"Vikusno," I try, pointing at the roast chicken Peter prepared. "Fi-koos-nah."

"There's no 'i' in there," Yan says, looking amused. "And don't emphasize the first consonant so much. Just say it quickly, without breaking it up into three syllables. *Vkusno.* Try it."

"Vkusno," I parrot to the best of my ability, and all the guys, including Peter, laugh.

"That's pretty good, ptichka," he says, cutting more of the chicken for me. "They might make a Russian speaker out of you yet."

I grin at him, absurdly pleased, and when he urges me to sing for them after dinner, as he often does with no success, I agree for once and belt out one of my favorite Beyoncé songs, the one I've been practicing in the recording studio he set up for me. Peter's men listen, open-mouthed, and when I'm done, they clap and cheer so hard the dishes rattle on the table.

It's the best evening I've had in months, and when Peter leads me upstairs, I embrace him willingly, even eagerly. We make love, and afterward, I don't think of George and the fact that I'm sleeping with his killer. I don't even think of my parents.

For that night, I belong to Peter and no one else.

CHAPTER 31
SARA

The next morning, I'm back to fighting my feelings for my captor, but as the days go by, I'm aware that I'm losing the battle. He's wearing me down, making me forget why I'm even trying to resist. He hasn't said he loves me since we got here—probably because I threw the words in his face when we first arrived—but I can't deny that in his own twisted way, Peter cares for me.

It's there in the way he looks at me, the way he touches me and holds me. Even when our sex is rough, with the darker edge that still frightens me sometimes, he always soothes me in the aftermath, stroking and cuddling me until I feel safe and warm, cherished and adored. His power over me is absolute, and there's something perversely comforting in that, something that taps into a part of me I never knew was there.

I wasn't dissatisfied with my sex life with George. Over the years, we'd learned each other's bodies and knew exactly what to do to get each other off. Before his drinking began, we had sex regularly, at least once or twice a week, and though we weren't particularly adventurous after the first year, we played some sexy games on occasion, even used some toys. It was enough, I thought; it was as it should be. I never imagined the kind of sexual chemistry I now have with Peter, never thought a physical connection so strong could exist.

He fucks me so much I'm sore on most days, his appetite for me never fading. And I respond, though he often exhausts me with his sexual demands. I've never known someone who has so much energy. Over the past few weeks, Peter and his men have been training hard each day, doing hours of bodyweight exercises, running through the forest with rock-filled backpacks, and practicing hand-to-hand combat that looks as deadly as their weapons, yet he still finds the strength to go on hikes with me, swim when the weather allows, cook for everyone, and of course, have sex with me two or three times a day.

"Don't you ever get tired?" I murmur as I lie draped over his chest one night, my heart still racing from the intensity of the orgasm I just had. Normally, I pass out right after our evening sex, but I napped this afternoon, so for once, I can stay awake a little longer.

"Tired?" He shifts underneath me, positioning my head more comfortably on his shoulder. His fingers tangle lazily in my hair, his heartbeat strong and steady against my ear. "Of what?"

"Just physically tired," I explain. "You seem inexhaustible sometimes, like a cyborg of some kind. Don't you ever want to just laze around and do nothing? Or slack off and not train with the guys one day?"

"I'm lazing around right now," he points out with amusement. "And I have to train; otherwise, we run the risk of getting killed."

I bury my nose against his neck, breathing in his warm, clean scent. Nap or not, I'm getting drowsy, the light tugging of his fingers in my hair inducing a state of near-hypnotic relaxation. Suppressing a yawn, I mumble against his neck, "That's not what I meant. Don't you ever just get *tired*? Like a normal human being? You know, limbs heavy, muscles sore, don't want to move?"

His powerful chest heaves with a laugh. "Of course I do. I just have a higher pain tolerance than most. I wouldn't have survived to adulthood otherwise."

He says it lightly, his tone still amused, but my Peter revelation radar goes on high alert. He rarely talks about his youth—almost never, in fact—so when I do get a chance to learn something new, I jump on it, even though what I learn horrifies me most of the time.

"What was it like?" I ask, my drowsiness gone. Lifting my head off his shoulder, I meet his gaze in the dim light coming from the bedside lamp. "That juvenile prison camp you were sent to, I mean."

Peter's face tightens, all traces of amusement disappearing as he shifts me off his chest, turning to lie on his side facing me. "Like hell," he answers bluntly as I pull a pillow under my head. "A cold, dirty hell, populated by demons in

203

human form. Pretty much exactly as you'd imagine a labor camp in Siberia to be."

I shudder, remembering a book I once read about prison camps during Soviet times, and reach for a blanket to ward off the chill spreading over my skin. "Was it like a *gulag*?"

"Not like." A grim smile cuts across his face. "It *was* a gulag at one point, used to punish, and quietly kill off, dissidents and other undesirables. When the Soviet Union fell apart, the place wasn't utilized for some time, but then someone got the bright idea to repurpose the facilities into a correction camp for juvenile delinquents. And that's how Camp Larko was born."

I fight the urge to look away from the darkness in his eyes. "How long were you there?"

"Until I was seventeen. So almost six years."

Six years starting from when he was just a child—nearly all of his teenage years. My hand squeezes into a fist under the blanket, my nails cutting into my palm. "Why did they send you there? Was there no other alternative?"

His mouth twists bitterly. "Not in Russia. Not for an orphan criminal like me."

"But you were not even twelve." I can't fathom that someone would be so cruel as to send a child to the frozen hell I read about in that book. "What about school? What about—"

"Oh, they taught us." His teeth flash in another mirthless smile. "We had exactly two hours of instruction each day. The other fourteen, though, were reserved for work—that's what we were there for, after all."

Fourteen hours? For someone who was still a child? Swallowing the lump forming in my throat, I force myself to ask, "What kind of work?"

"Mining, mostly. Also road repair and laying pipes. Some construction work too, but that was only around our camp, to fix the Soviet-era shit that was crumbling all around us."

I stare at him, not knowing what to say. I knew he hadn't had an easy life, of course, but somehow I never imagined this, never realized that most of his formative years—a time when other boys his age played video games and challenged their parents on curfew—were spent doing hard labor under hellish conditions.

Trying to ignore the ache banding my ribcage, I reach out from under the blanket and brush my fingers over the tattoos covering his left arm and shoulder. "Is that where you got these?"

Peter glances down, as if just now recalling the ink that's there. "Most of them, yes," he says, folding his other arm under his head. "A couple I got later on, when I joined my unit."

"What do they all mean?" I ask softly, tracing the intricate designs with my fingers. The one on his shoulder resembles a bird's wing and a few more look like demonic skulls, but the rest are just abstract lines and shapes.

Peter's gaze turns opaque. "Nothing. It was something to do, that's all."

"That's a lot of ink to do on a whim."

He's silent for a few seconds. Then he says quietly, "I had a friend at that camp. Andrey. He was into this stuff—a real artist, you know. After we were there for a couple of years, he ran out of space on his own skin, so I let him practice on me. Every time something happened to us, good or bad, he wanted to commemorate it with a tattoo, and because he was so good, I gave him free reign with the designs."

"Oh." Intrigued, I rise onto my elbow. "What happened to that friend?"

"He died." Peter says it casually, as though it doesn't matter, but I hear the dark echo of grief underneath, the rage that passage of time wasn't able to cool. Whatever happened to his friend, it had been bad enough to leave a scar… bad enough that remembering it now still has the power to hurt him.

"I'm sorry," I murmur, but Peter doesn't respond. Instead, he reaches over to turn off the light, then pulls me against him in our usual sleeping position.

I close my eyes and focus on my breathing, trying to calm down enough to fall asleep, but it's impossible. Even the heat of Peter's large body can't chase away the lingering chill from his revelations. My mind buzzes like a ravaged beehive, the questions refusing to leave me alone. There's so much I still don't know about the man who holds me every night, so many things I don't understand about his past. Everything about his life in Russia is foreign to me, as strange and mysterious as if he'd come from another planet.

Finally, I can't take it anymore. Wriggling out of Peter's hold, I turn on the bedside lamp and turn over onto my side to face him. As I suspected, he's not sleeping either, his silver gaze shadowed with memories as his eyes meet mine.

"You said you were recruited from that place straight into your unit," I say, propping myself up on my elbow again. "Why? Do they normally do that in Russia?"

He gazes at me silently, then turns over onto his back, lacing his hands under his head as he stares at the ceiling. "No," he says after a moment. "They usually recruit through the army. But in this case, they needed someone with a specific psychological profile."

I sit up, holding the blanket against my chest. "What kind of profile?"

His eyes cut over to meet my gaze. "No inconvenient family ties or attachments, no scruples, and only minimal conscience. But also young enough to be trained and molded into what they needed."

"Which was what?" I ask, though I suspect I already know.

Peter sits up, his expression carefully neutral as he leans against the headboard. "A weapon," he answers. "Someone who wouldn't balk at anything. You see, the insurgents were getting more ruthless, more fanatical with every year. The bombing of the subway in Moscow was the last straw. The Russian government realized they couldn't limit themselves to civilized, UN-approved methods of combatting terrorism; they had to meet them on their level, fight them using every tool available. So they formed this off-the-books Spetsnaz unit, and when they couldn't find enough trained soldiers to fit the desired profile, they decided to get creative and look elsewhere."

"In Camp Larko," I say, and Peter nods, his eyes like polished steel.

"Those of us who lasted there for any extended period of time tended to be strong, able to handle long hours of physical exertion under extreme conditions. Hunger, thirst, cold—we could endure it all. And as you can imagine, many of us fit the profile they were looking for."

A shiver dances over my skin, making me draw the blanket tighter around myself. "So why did they choose you over the others?" I ask, fighting to keep my tone steady.

His lips quirk in a dark smile. "Because right before they arrived, I killed a guard," he says softly. "I staked him out in the snow and made him admit his crimes before I gutted him like a rabbit in front of the entire camp. My methods were… Well, let's just say it was exactly what they were looking for. So instead of getting punished for the guard's death, I got a new career, one that fit both my inclinations and my skillset."

My palms grow slippery where I'm holding the blanket. "What *were* the guard's crimes?" I ask, though I'm not sure I want to know.

The darkness in Peter's gaze deepens, and for a moment, I'm afraid I went too far, brought up too many bad memories. But then he leans back against the headboard and says evenly, "He liked to boil boys alive."

I stop breathing as bile surges up my throat. "What?" I gasp out when I'm able to speak.

"In the showers, we had either ice-cold or scalding water, nothing in between," Peter says, his face tightening as his gaze grows distant. "The pipes would constantly malfunction, so we'd use buckets to mix the water before washing. Some guards, though, would punish us by making us stand under the water as it was, ice cold for minor infractions, scalding when we really misbehaved. One guard, in particular, liked the hot water remedy. He got off on it, I think. The others would just do it for a few seconds at a time, maybe half a minute tops, giving the boys superficial burns. But this guard, he'd push it. A minute, two, three, five… By the time Andrey landed on his shit list, he'd killed two fifteen-year-olds by boiling the meat off their bones."

I taste vomit in my throat. "Andrey… your friend Andrey?" I whisper through numb lips.

"Yes." Peter's chiseled face takes on an almost demonic look of fury. "Andrey, who should've never been in that shit hole in the first place. My friend, who refused to let that prick fuck him and died in agony instead."

"Oh God, Peter…" I press my trembling fist to my mouth, then reach for his hand, feeling his fingers twitch with barely suppressed rage as he fights to control himself. "I'm so, so sorry."

He grips my hand like a lifeline and closes his eyes, breathing in deeply. When he opens them again, his expression is calm, but I now know the depth of the pain and fury that lurk beneath that controlled mask.

I was wrong to think that his family's deaths made him into a monster. He was one long before Daryevo, the horrors he'd encountered in his lifelong struggle for survival stripping away whatever capacity for goodness he might've once possessed. His early victims were no angels, but once he went down the dark path of vengeance, he became like them, hurting innocent and guilty alike.

Carefully extricating my fingers from his grip, I move back to the middle of the bed. "What about that headmaster?" I ask, holding my captor's gaze. I'm already sick to my stomach, but I have to know how deep the damage goes. "What did he do to make you kill him?"

Peter smiles grimly. "You haven't had enough for tonight? No? All right, if you must know, he liked little boys. The younger, the better. I was lucky, because at eleven, I was already big, almost like a teenager. Way too old for him when he started at the orphanage. But the little ones... I would lie there at night and hear them scream and cry in their rooms when he came to them. Each night, I'd die a little bit inside, because there was nothing I could do, nobody I could tell who'd listen. The teachers, the police— they either didn't care or didn't dare make waves. This motherfucker was connected, you see; he was from some important family. So nobody did anything, and then a new boy was brought in, all of two years old. When I heard him go to the child, I couldn't take it anymore. I took one of the kitchen knives, crept up behind him, and while he was busy assaulting the kid, I slit his throat."

Of course. My dark knight taking vengeance again. I close my eyes against the hot sting of tears, my heart breaking for both Peter and the little boy. I suspected it was something like that, only I was afraid it was Peter himself who'd been the victim. Not that it means he hadn't been. Opening my eyes, I meet his steely gaze. "What about you?" I ask unsteadily. "Were you ever...?"

"No." His mouth flattens. "At least not as far as I know. I was always very good at defending myself, even when I was little. I don't recall much before age three, though, so I suppose it's possible—I *was* a pretty kid, according to old pictures. In any case, by the time I was in kindergarten, I knew how to use my fists, teeth, rocks… any kind of weapon I could get my hands on. The one fucker who tried something with me when I was five got his finger bitten off, and after that, I was generally left alone."

I stare at him, relief battling with agonizing pity. And anger. I feel so much anger at the cruelty of the world that shaped him into the dark, tormented man he is today, into this ruthless, amoral killer who, despite everything, craves love and family. Did he find respite from his demons when he had Tamila and his little boy? Is that why he accepted her pregnancy so easily, becoming a husband and father when he could've simply walked away? Did they give him back pieces of his soul, only to rip it all away with their brutal deaths?

If so, it's no wonder that their loss sent him spinning—and that vengeance was his default response.

At my long silence, Peter's face tightens further; then a mocking smile curls his lips. "Too much for you, ptichka? I suppose I should've come up with some rosy story, one filled with rainbows, puppies, and piñatas."

"No, I just—" I stop, my throat swollen with emotions. Gathering my composure, I try again. "I just wish someone had been there for you, the way you were for that little boy."

He blinks slowly and pushes away from the headboard. "I just told you—I was fine. I could always take care of myself."

"I know you could," I whisper as he reaches for me, pulling me down to lie beside him as he stretches out on the bed and turns off the light. "But you shouldn't have had to, Peter. No child should've had to."

He doesn't reply, but I know he heard me, because the arm looping around my ribcage tightens, drawing me closer as we lie together in the darkness, feeling each other's warmth and deriving comfort from the steady beating of our hearts.

CHAPTER 32
SARA

After that night, it becomes even harder to resist Peter's efforts to insinuate himself into my mind and heart. I don't know if he thinks his revelations terrified me and is seeking to make up for it, or if he simply senses my resolve wavering, but he becomes impossibly more attentive toward me, pampering and indulging me beyond belief.

Everyone except me has chores. Peter does most of our cooking, and the other guys are in charge of laundry and keeping the house spotlessly clean. I help with the laundry anyway, so I don't feel like a total slug, but Peter doesn't require it from me, and other than that time when I threw the plate, I haven't had to touch a vacuum or do anything else that I don't feel like doing.

On top of that, anything I want is mine—within the confines of my captivity, of course. If I mention a preference for silk pillowcases, Peter gets them for me within a few short days. If I express a desire to go for a walk, he drops whatever he's doing and accompanies me, no longer entrusting that duty to any of his men. Most importantly, though, he does everything he can to ensure I'm not bored.

His dance studio idea is a bust so far—all I use the room for is occasional yoga and some stretching—but I really appreciate the recording equipment he got for me. It's as high-end as anything a professional might use. I can record and edit anything I want, and while I start with the pop songs I love, I soon begin experimenting with variations on those songs and even try composing a couple of my own, setting the lyrics to music mixes I create from different tunes. Mastering the software and the equipment requires a steep learning curve, but I welcome the challenge. It's not only fun, but it consumes a lot of my free time, and when I'm trying to find the words to express the song forming in my mind, I don't think about everything I've lost and the fact that I'm an assassin's captive.

I just focus on the music.

I've also started to perform for the guys. It's an after-dinner ritual now, where Peter asks me to sing as a way of entertaining everyone and I reluctantly (but secretly, quite eagerly) agree to do one song, prefacing each performance with disclaimers about possibly not remembering the words, being unprepared, and so on. Naturally, it's always a song I rehearse in advance, usually a variation on whatever popular hit I played with in the recording studio that day. I'm too shy to share my own songs, but the guys are so enthusiastic about my renditions of pop music that I foresee a day when I might try performing one of my own pieces.

"You have a really good voice," Yan tells me after the first week, his cool green eyes assessing me with some surprise. "Peter was right about that."

I grin at him—praise from our resident psychopath is an exceedingly rare event—and decide to perform two songs next time.

If the guys enjoy it and so do I, why not?

Between the music and my usual activities with Peter, I have enough to occupy my days, but I still miss my old job. Whenever one of the guys gets hurt—which happens with scary frequency during their daily sparring—I get to use my medical skills, but it's not enough. I need the intellectual stimulation of my profession, all the things I learned daily by treating a wide variety of patients and keeping up with the latest studies. Now I feel out of the loop, isolated from new developments in my field, and when I mention it to Peter during one of our walks, he promises to do something about that.

Sure enough, he starts having his hackers send me biweekly compilations of all the cutting-edge medical research happening around the world. Some of the material is obviously public—peer-reviewed studies published in the academic journals I used to subscribe to, et cetera—but a lot of it seems to come straight from the companies' private archives.

"Peter, this is insane," I say after reading about a gene therapy that holds hope for reversing late-stage breast cancer. "Where did your people learn about this? This is huge."

"Is it?" He smiles as he looks up from his laptop.

I nod vigorously. "If this therapy is as effective as these researchers' notes indicate, millions of women's lives will be saved. How did your hackers come across this? I should've at the very least heard rumors about this back home. This is a game changer in cancer treatment. You realize that, right?"

His smile broadens. "What can I say? Our guys are good."

I shake my head and bury myself back in the detailed study analysis. I should feel guilty that I'm essentially stealing some startup's intellectual property, but I'm too fascinated to stop reading. Besides, it's not like I'm going to use this knowledge for financial gain or share it with anyone. My access to the outside world is strictly limited to phone calls with my parents.

It's the one thing Peter won't budge on, no matter how much I beg and plead.

"Come on, what harm would it do to have me browse the news once in a while?" I argue after Peter catches me trying to log on to his laptop—a fruitless attempt, given all the passwords and security he has in place. "You can block certain websites, prevent me from using all email and social media if you want. There are a ton of apps for that, and—"

"No, ptichka." His face is resolute as he takes the laptop away from me. "We can't risk you performing a search that would expose our IP address to the FBI, nor you figuring out some clever way to get in touch with them. Every website has a place to leave a comment nowadays, and you're too smart not to know that."

Frustrated, I give up on accessing the internet and try to think of other escape venues, but none come to mind. The one thing I could try—some kind of coded message to my parents during our brief phone calls—is far too risky. Peter is always with me, listening to every word I say, and I know that if I so much as hint at our location, he'll cut me off from further contact with my family. He's said as much, and I know he means it.

No matter how much he indulges me, I never forget that his obsession has a dark side, that he's willing to do whatever it takes to keep me his.

CHAPTER 33
PETER

As the heated days of summer transition into fall, with the forest bursting into shades of red and yellow, I become increasingly convinced that I did the right thing by taking Sara. Despite our initial rocky start, she's starting to settle in, and I feel certain that one day, she'll adjust completely, accepting and embracing her new life with me.

I love her so much it's like a constant ache in my chest, and though I know she doesn't feel the same, I sometimes catch a glimmer of softness in her gaze, a warmth that spears through my heart and gives me hope. As her anger over the abduction lessens, our arguments grow less frequent, and though neither of us can forget how our relationship began, the past begins to feel more distant, its grip on our present less painful and sharp.

I still think about Pasha and Tamila, and wake up in a cold sweat when I dream about their gruesome deaths. But the nightmares don't come nearly as often, and when they do, Sara is always there. I can reach for her and hold her, hear her steady breathing until the memory of the horror fades.

I can also fuck her. It's the one thing that never fails to soothe me, the single best way to relieve the darkness tormenting me from within.

"Why do you like to hurt me sometimes?" she murmurs one night after I wake her up and take her roughly, fucking her so hard we both end up sore. "Do you have some sadistic inclinations?"

I consider it, then shake my head, though she probably can't see the gesture with the lights off. "Not in the sexual sense—at least not until I met you." I *have* derived pleasure from killing and torturing my enemies, but it was mostly cerebral, a way to feel that violent rush of power and satisfy my sense of justice. At least that's how it was with the guard who boiled Andrey in the showers and, to a lesser extent, with the terrorists I caught for work. I felt no pity for them; their suffering gave me vicious joy. But my dick never got hard from inflicting pain, and during sex, I was always careful and gentle with women, using my knowledge of the human body to pleasure, not to hurt.

It wasn't until Sara that those conflicting impulses—punishment and pleasure, violence and tenderness—somehow merged. I treasure her, love her so much I ache with it, yet sometimes when I touch her, I can't control myself, can't fight the urge to punish her for being what she is.

For belonging to my enemy before she stole my heart.

"So with her… you never?"

The poorly concealed curiosity in Sara's whisper makes me smile, even as a familiar ache constricts my heart. "You mean Tamila?"

"Yes." Her hand splays over my chest, as if sensing the pain within. "You were never rough with her like this?"

"No." I cover that slender hand with my palm, pressing it tighter against my skin. "It wasn't like this with her."

What I felt for Tamila was nothing like the intense, almost violent connection I have with Sara. With my wife, it was a pleasant mix of physical attraction and liking, even a friendship of sorts. I admired her for being brave, in the context of her upbringing, and for being a good mother to Pasha. It didn't hurt that she was beautiful, either, and though we didn't have much in common, I grew to care for her... maybe even love her, I thought. Now, however, I see that I was fooling myself.

My affection for Tamila was just that, a mere echo of the raw emotions Sara evokes in me.

Her hand twitches under my palm, and I hear her swallow. "I see." There's a strange note in Sara's voice, something almost like hurt. "You must've loved her very much," she continues in the same tone, and I smile again as I realize what the issue is.

"Are you jealous?" I ask softly, reaching over to turn on the bedside lamp. Sara blinks at the sudden light, and from the tight set of her pretty mouth, I see that I was right.

She misunderstood my admission, thinking that my gentle treatment of Tamila meant I cared for my wife more than I do for her.

Sara doesn't answer me, just pulls her hand away, and I laugh, feeling peculiarly light despite the dark memories dancing on the fringes of my mind. My ptichka *is* jealous— of a dead woman, no less—and I couldn't be more pleased.

At the sound of my amusement, Sara's expression darkens further, her delicate brows drawing together into a full-fledged scowl. With a barely audible huff, she turns off the light and turns away, giving me a quite literal cold shoulder.

My amusement fades, replaced by the complex tangle of emotions she always elicits in me. Lust and tenderness, anger and possessiveness—it's all part of the madness that is my love for Sara, of this obsession I know I'll never shake.

"Come here, my love." Ignoring her stiff posture, I pull her against me, curving my body around hers from the back. Burying my face in her hair, I breathe in her sweet scent—my favorite fragrance ever—and tighten my embrace, holding her in place as she struggles to move away.

"I do want to hurt you sometimes," I murmur when she stills, her breathing ragged from exertion. "I want to do things to you I've never dreamed of doing to my wife. There are nights when I want to devour you, ptichka, to consume you until there's nothing left… until this addiction fades and I can take a breath without wanting you, without feeling like I need you more than life itself."

Her breathing catches. "What are you saying?"

"I'm saying that I love you, ptichka… and that I hate you. Because it hurts, you see, knowing you still love *him*, still think about *him* when you're with me." My voice roughens, my grip tightening as she again tries to scoot away. "Your husband's killer—that's how you see me, that's *all* you sometimes see. If I could wipe him from your mind, I'd do it in a heartbeat. I'd erase every record of his existence, make him into the nothing that he is. In a different world, you'd have been born mine, but in this one, I had to fight for you… kill for you."

Her entire body stiffens. "For *me*? What are you talking about? It was all about your vengeance, the list that you—"

"Yes, it was… until I met you. Then it became about something else." It's a truth I hadn't admitted to myself until this moment, hadn't known except within the most savage reaches of my soul.

When I stood over George Cobakis's bedside, I hesitated when I thought of Sara, but it wasn't because I wanted to spare him for her. It was because the murder was so pointless, his vegetative state as good as living death.

I ended up pulling the trigger not despite my attraction to Sara but because of it.

Because I wanted her forever free of him.

Because even then, I knew I had to make her mine.

"No." Sara's voice takes on an audible tremor. "You're just saying this. You couldn't have killed George because of some sick interest in me—that's beyond insane."

"Maybe." I'm willing to concede that much. "But in some cultures, what I did makes you mine—my prize of war, my spoils of battle."

"Battle? He was in a coma! You killed a defenseless man. He was no match for you—"

I laugh darkly. "Do you think I'm some kind of noble hero? Do you think I care about a fair fight?"

She freezes, her skin growing clammy where our naked bodies touch as I continue. "I don't, Sara," I tell her. "I don't give a fuck about fairness, because no one else does. The world is inherently unfair. If you want something, you fight for it… you take it. And I wanted you, ptichka. I wanted you from the first moment I held you, when you cried so sweetly in my arms. And you wanted me too—you still want me—because no matter what you say, this is real… far more real than your mirage of a marriage. It wasn't a fairy tale you were living, and Cobakis wasn't your Prince Charming. He was a liar, a weakling who turned to drinking because he couldn't cope with the guilt over the massacre he caused. Even if he hadn't been on my list, I would've killed him if I met you—because I would've wanted you. If ever our paths crossed, I would've made you mine."

She's shivering now, and I know I've been too honest, revealed too much of the beast within. Yet if there's one thing I won't do, it's lie to her.

With me, Sara will always know what she's getting, no matter how ugly it may be.

Pulling the blanket over us, I stroke her arm, hip, and thigh until her trembling stops, and when I hear her breathing slow and deepen, I close my eyes, holding her tight.

This may be wrong in others' eyes, but I have Sara and I'm happy—and I'll do whatever it takes to make her happy too.

CHAPTER 34
SARA

As fall progresses and the weather continues to cool, my life with Peter begins to remind me of an extended honeymoon, albeit one where we share our mountain retreat with other people. His attentiveness shows no signs of lessening, and though I keep reminding myself that I'm not here of my own free will, I can't ignore the fact that Peter is doing his best to ensure my pleasure and comfort. Aside from his profession and the small matter of keeping me captive, Peter Sokolov is everything one could ever wish a husband to be: thoroughly domesticated and so caring I feel like a princess most days.

Every morning now starts with him bringing me breakfast in bed. Like the skilled interrogator that he is, Peter has learned everything I like and dislike when it comes to food, and he indulges me with my favorites daily. Russian-style crepes with raisins and sweet cheese, fluffy omelets, quiches, platters of exotic fruit—I get it all, plus fresh-squeezed orange juice and coffee. For lunch and dinner, I'm equally spoiled, so much so that the guys have taken to begging me to claim their favorites as my own.

"You liked *shashlik* that time, right? Those lamb kebobs Peter made before Nigeria?" Ilya makes a scary-looking attempt at puppy eyes as he corners me in the kitchen.

At my nod, he grins and says, "Then please tell him to make them soon, okay? Just hint that you enjoy lamb in spicy sauce. Please?"

I laugh and promise to do so, as I already promised Anton with apple pie. Despite their role in my abduction, I'm starting to like Peter's men, and I'm pretty sure they're starting to like me. That's a good thing as far as I'm concerned, but Peter seems to be of a different opinion. I've noticed him glaring at the guys when they get particularly friendly, as though he's afraid they might steal me away.

His possessiveness is one of our main problems these days, and one evening, it boils out of control.

"Keep your fucking eyes above her neck," he roars at Anton after I finish singing my variation of Lady Gaga's latest hit. I dressed up for this performance, wearing one of the low-cut party dresses Yan got for me, and as Anton and Peter stand up, glaring at each other, I realize that might've been a mistake.

"Peter, he wasn't doing anything," I say, desperate to diffuse the bristling tension. "I was just singing and he was listening, that's all."

"He was fucking drooling, that's what he was doing."
Peter shoves the chair between them aside. "And it wasn't
the first time, either."

"Fuck you, man." Anton's dark beard quivers with rage
as the two lethal men square off, fists clenched and teeth
bared. "Nobody's doing anything they shouldn't; you're
just too fucking obsessed to see straight."

Peter growls a response in Russian, and Yan says something too, his tone coolly amused as Ilya shakes his head,
grinning. A moment later, Anton storms outside, with
Peter on his heels.

Frustrated, I round on the twins. "Where are they
going?" I hate it when the guys switch to Russian to hide
something from me. "What did you all say?"

"Peter wants to break every bone in Anton's face, and I
suggested he do so outside, so we don't have to make costly
repairs in the house," Yan says, grinning as widely as his
brother. "It seems they listened."

"What? They're going to fight?"

Horrified, I rush outside and am promptly greeted by
the sound of fists striking flesh. Peter and Anton are rolling
on the ground, arms and elbows swinging as they batter
one another. Flecks of blood fly into the air as Peter lands
a particularly brutal hit, and I gasp as I catch a glimpse of
savage fury on his face.

They're not sparring; this fight is for real.

"Stop them, please," I beg Yan and Ilya, who came out
to stand next to me. "They're going to kill each other."

"Nah." Yan waves dismissively. "They'll just break a few bones. We don't have a major job until next month, so it's fine."

"It's not fine!" Gritting my teeth, I turn to Ilya. "If you ever want *shash*-whatever again, you'll stop this right now. If you don't, I'm going to develop a lamb *allergy*." I poke his massive chest with my finger. "Do you hear me?"

Yan bursts into laughter, but Ilya looks suitably worried. "All right, all right," he mutters and starts toward the combatants.

I exhale in relief as he bravely wades into the fray, but neither Peter nor Anton respond well to his attempts to pry them apart. Before long, all three men are rolling on the ground, exchanging brutal blows, and when I turn to Yan, he holds up his hands, palms facing out.

"I'm not going near there," he says, and I know he means it.

I'm on my own.

Desperate, I consider hosing them down with cold water, but decide to go for a more expedient solution.

"Help," I yell at the top of my lungs and bend over, as though in pain. "Owww! Peter, help!"

It works even better than I expected. The men instantly spring apart, and Peter jumps to his feet, the fury on his face transforming into frantic worry as he rushes toward me. "What happened?" he demands, gripping my hands as his eyes scan me from head to toe. "Are you hurt?"

"Yes, by you acting like a barbarian," I snap, trying to pull away as he starts a full-blown pat-down. "Now let me go so I can see how badly you've damaged each other."

His eyebrows pull together as he pauses. "You're not hurt? You just wanted to stop the fight?"

"Of course. How would I get hurt?" I ignore Yan, who's laughing so hard he can't stand up straight, and head toward Anton and Ilya, who look much worse for the wear than Peter. Ilya has a split lip, and Anton's face is already swelling up, his bleeding nose slightly off-center.

"Hey." Peter catches my wrist before I can take more than two steps. "You're going to treat *them* first?" He sounds so outraged I'm tempted to deny it—the last thing I want is to provoke another fight—but some devil makes me nod.

"*They* did not attack themselves." I tug at my wrist in a futile attempt to get free. "And you don't look hurt to me."

If Peter thinks I'm going to reward caveman behavior with tender nursing, he's very much mistaken.

His frown deepens, and he has the gall to look wounded as he releases my wrist. "I *am* hurt. See?" He tugs up his shirt to show me a red spot on his ribcage. "And this." He displays the back of his right hand, where the knuckles are indeed beginning to look swollen.

Despite my anger, my healer's instincts kick in. "Let me see." Carefully, I feel around his torso—it'll be a nasty bruise, but his ribs seem okay—and then turn my attention to his knuckles.

"Does this hurt?" I ask, pressing on the middle knuckle. Peter shakes his head, silver eyes gleaming, so I examine the rest of his hand. To my relief, I don't feel any broken bones.

"You'll be okay," I say, then notice a bleeding scrape by his left ear. I'll have to clean it in the house, where I have medical supplies, but first, I need to see about Anton's nose and make sure Ilya didn't get another concussion.

The guys have already gone inside, so I follow them in, ignoring Peter's dark expression. I don't understand what got into him. I know he's possessive, but Anton is Peter's friend, and as far as I can tell, he's never acted inappropriately toward me. Nor have any of the others, though they're virile, healthy men who've been without female companionship for months.

My bravado lasts until I get into the kitchen and see the extent of damage done to Anton's face. Peter wasn't joking about breaking every bone; he didn't succeed, but he made a very good attempt. With the violence flaring up so suddenly, I didn't have a chance to process the stunning brutality of the fight, but as I work to put Anton's nose back in place, my hands begin to shake, the adrenaline spike aftermath hitting me as hard as if I'd been the one in the fight.

I've become complacent in the last few weeks, let all the domesticity lull me into forgetting what Peter and his men are. This wasn't a drunken brawl at a bar, where someone might land a lucky hit or two. Peter is a trained assassin, and he went after his friend with the intent of inflicting serious damage. If I hadn't broken up the fight, someone could've gotten badly hurt—killed, even.

"I'm sorry," I whisper as Anton winces at the pain of my ministrations. "I'm so sorry about this."

"It's okay." His voice turns nasal as I stuff cotton into his nostrils to stop the bleeding. "Was bound to happen;

bastard's too crazy about you." There's no rancor in his tone; if anything, he sounds amused by his friend's attempt to maim him out of misplaced jealousy.

"That's right," Peter growls, coming to stand next to me. "So do not fucking stare at her. Ever. Got it?"

To my shock, Anton's swollen mouth curves in a bloody smile. "Got it, you crazy fucking asshole."

I stop what I'm doing, my gaze swinging incredulously from one man to the other. Am I hallucinating, or did they just make up?

Sure enough, Peter slaps his friend's shoulder and turns to Ilya, who's perched on a barstool next to us, holding an ice pack against his lip. "Same goes for you and"—he gives Yan, who just joined us, a dark glare—"you."

Both brothers nod, and Ilya says, "Got it. She's all yours."

Ignoring that atavistic statement, I finish taping Anton's broken nose, give him ice packs to apply all over his face, and reach for his shirt to examine his ribcage.

"I'm fine there," he says nasally, stopping me before I can lift the shirt more than an inch. With a wary look at Peter, he adds, "You can take a look at Ilya now, if you want."

I frown but turn to Ilya as suggested. "Let me see this," I say, moving the ice pack away from his lip. "Did you get hit anywhere else in the head?"

"No, just this," Ilya says, wincing as I feel around his swollen jaw.

"All right," I say when I conclude my examination. "You don't have a concussion, but you still have to take it easy. Blows to the head aren't good for your brain—just ask all the NFL players."

"Yes, Dr. Cobakis." Ilya smiles as much as his split lip allows. "I'll be careful."

I smile back at him, ignoring a snort from his brother, and then turn to Peter, who still appears to be in a dark mood.

"Let me see this," I say, tugging him down on another barstool so I can reach the top of his ear. "Looks like you scraped some skin off there."

Peter sits still, letting me clean and bandage the scrape before examining him for more minor injuries. By the time I'm done, my hands are steady again, the familiar work lessening the lingering shock from the explosion of violence.

Unfortunately, my newfound calm doesn't last long. The second I put away all the medical supplies, Peter hops off the barstool and bends down to pick me up. Ignoring my startled squeak and the guys' ribald wolf calls, he lifts me into his arms and claims my mouth with a deep, fiercely hungry kiss.

Then, holding me pressed against his chest like the prize of war he believes me to be, he heads toward the stairs.

CHAPTER 35
PETER

Sara squirms in my arms as I carry her up the stairs, her pale face flushed—presumably with anger and embarrassment. "Let me down," she whispers furiously as soon as we reach the second floor. "Peter, put me down right now."

I don't put her down until we enter our bedroom. I'm still high on bloodlust, the adrenaline from the fight making my heart pump in a hard, furious rhythm. Anger and primal jealousy roil my insides, and underneath it all is a deep, demanding hunger, a need to take and claim her, to make her mine so completely she'll never smile at another man again.

I know what I'm feeling is irrational, verging on pathological, but seeing her tonight in this dress—this red, tight, and way-too-low-cut dress—made me lose whatever semblance of rationality I possessed. Over the past few weeks, I've put up with the guys' occasional glances in her direction, with their mealtime competition for her attention and their not-so-secret food requests. But what I saw in Anton's eyes tonight was a mirror image of my own lust for Sara, and that I could not let slide.

"You are not to wear this dress in public again," I say harshly, reaching around her slender frame for the zipper in the back. "From now on, it's for our bedroom only."

Sara glares up at me, the creamy swells of her upper breasts—exposed by the fucking dress—heaving with her rapid breathing. "You're crazy." Her palms push against my ribcage. "You got this dress for me."

"Yan got it." I yank the zipper down with unnecessary force, the rage still pumping through my veins. "And if there are any other ones like this, you better keep them for my eyes only. The next time I catch another man salivating over you, I'm going to dismember him. Slowly."

I'm not bluffing, and Sara must see that, because some of the color leaves her face. "You're insane," she whispers, her hazel eyes huge as she stares up at me, and I know she's right. I *am* insane, completely crazy over her. I've been doing my best to keep the intensity of my need under control, but I can't do it any longer. I can't pretend that every minute we're apart doesn't feel like an hour, that every time I touch her, I don't want to devour her on the spot. My craving is dark and violent, yet I've been forcing myself to be civilized, to limit myself to acting like a lover when what I want is to strip her down to the bone so I can possess her whole.

I've been fighting a losing battle, and I'm ready to give up the fight.

Some of my thoughts must show, because Sara starts to struggle as I pull down the unzipped dress, exposing her braless breasts and trapping her arms. The contrast of the bright red color with her pale skin brings out the green flecks in her hazel eyes and makes my cock throb with savage need. I want her. Fuck, how much I want her. It's like a sickness, this lust that torments me day and night.

Dropping to my knees, I wrap my arms around her, keeping her arms trapped inside the dress as I take one pink, erect nipple into my mouth. Sara cries out, her struggles intensifying as I suck on the nipple, crushing it against the roof of my mouth with my tongue, but I don't stop. I can't. She tastes like sex and sweet perfection, like every fantasy of mine brought to life. I don't know how I could've lived most of my life without her, because now that I've had her, I need more each time.

I need all of her, and tonight, I'm going to take it.

"Peter, please…" She's panting now, her flat belly quivering as I turn my attention to the other breast. "I just—oh God, please…"

I torment her nipples until the burn inside me reaches fever pitch, and then I yank the dress all the way down, leaving it to pool around her ankles as I stand up and shepherd her toward the bed. She stumbles as the backs of her knees hit the bed, but I catch her and flip her over onto her stomach before climbing on top of her, fully dressed.

"What are you—" She breaks off in a gasp as I remove my belt and capture her wrist, twisting it behind her back and looping the belt around it. Then I repeat the process with her other wrist, ignoring her attempts to buck me off her as I tie her hands together, securing them with the belt behind her back.

"What are you going to do? Please, Peter... what are you going to do?" Her words are muffled against the blanket as I grab a pillow and stuff it under her hips. It's not enough, so I reach for another one, propping her curvy little ass higher. She's wriggling, obviously afraid, so to prevent her escape, I keep most of my weight on her legs as I reach over to the nightstand to get a bottle of lube I keep inside.

Unzipping my jeans, I free my aching cock and lean over her, holding my weight up on one arm as I drizzle the lube over her wriggling ass, letting it drip down into the crack and trickle down to her folds. Sara gasps, struggling harder, and I throw the lube aside before penetrating her pussy with my finger. She's hot and beautifully slick inside, the lube mixing with her own wetness as I push in a second finger, stretching her for me.

As I fuck her with my fingers, I roll my thumb over her clit, and soon, I'm rewarded with helpless little moans, her attempts to get away transforming into squirming movements to enhance her pleasure. Her hips begin to rise toward me, her clit grinding against my thumb with every stroke, and I know she's on the verge. Not wanting her to come yet, I stop and grip my cock, guiding it to the pink, quivering opening of her pussy.

Wet heat engulfs me, slick walls gripping me tight as I penetrate her swollen flesh. My heart thumps heavily, my balls tightening as her inner muscles flex around me, milking me, stroking my cock. The feeling is sublime, and all my senses sharpen, even as my awareness of the outside world fades. She's all I focus on: the sounds she makes, the way her body stretches to admit me... I can smell her arousal on my fingers, and I bring them up to her mouth, ordering hoarsely, "Suck them clean."

She obeys, her agile little tongue circling my fingers as I thrust them into her mouth, and I fuck her with them as I press deeper into her pussy, wrenching a choked gasp out of her throat when the tip of my cock brushes against her cervix. She's small and delicate underneath me, her slender body trembling as her bound hands press against my stomach, and the knowledge that she's completely at my mercy intensifies my lust, my need to dominate and take her.

"Tell me who you belong to," I growl, pulling my fingers out of her mouth to smear the wetness down her chin and neck. Wrapping my hand around her slender throat, I thrust in deep, making her cry out. "Tell me, Sara. Who owns you?"

She's breathing so fast I can feel her rapid exhalations where I grip her neck. "Y-you do." The words are barely audible as they leave her lips, and it's not enough. It's not nearly enough.

Releasing her throat, I reach between her legs, feeling the silky flesh stretching around my cock, the gliding slickness of the lube mixing with her cream. Sara's panting intensifies, her ass arching up as her moans grow louder, and my fingers travel higher, slipping between the pale, firm mounds of her cheeks.

"Peter... wait. Oh God, Peter..." My name comes out a choked gasp as I find the tightness of her other opening and press the tip of my finger in, ignoring the resistance of clenched muscles. It takes all my self-control to go slow, to not take her as violently as my body demands. I don't want to tear her, don't want to hurt her despite the darkness gnawing at my soul. The lube eases my finger's passage as I penetrate her deeper, but she's still too tight and I almost come as I imagine how tight she'll be around my cock, how her ass will grip and squeeze me.

She whimpers at the discomfort of my penetration, but I don't stop until my finger is all the way in and I can feel my cock through the thin inner wall separating her orifices. The sensation is dizzying, surreal in its intensity. It sharpens the hunger inside me, turns it even darker and more feral.

My beautiful caged ptichka.

It's time I fully claimed her.

After tonight, she'll have no doubts that she's mine.

CHAPTER 36

SARA

*O*verwhelmed, I clench my pelvic floor muscles, feeling the impossible girth of his cock and the stinging burn from that invading finger. Even with copious amounts of lube, it didn't go in easily. I feel painfully full, violated and overtaken, and my breath comes in hard pants as I try to adjust to the strange sensation of being penetrated in two places.

To my relief, my tormentor withdraws his finger, only to have it return joined by another. The thick digits work into my ass slowly, stretching the tight ring of muscle with great care, but it still hurts, my body resisting the intrusion.

"Push out, ptichka." His voice is a devil's whisper, seductive and controlled, even as his cock throbs deep inside me. "Relax and let me in. You'll like it."

Panting shallowly, I try to do as he says, fighting the instinctive urge to clench harder. My bound hands flex behind my back, my fingers twitching as they press into my palms. Despite the stinging pain of the invasion, a part of me is curious about this, almost eager in some twisted way. Something about the very discomfort of this—the way my insides cramp and burn, the sensation of being forced and violated—resonates with that strange, submissive streak within me, with the craving for punishment my monster has awakened in me.

If it hurts, it's not a betrayal.

If I have no choice, I'm not falling for the enemy.

"Yes, that's it, my love… Now relax and breathe." The two fingers are inside me now, thick and hard, the edges of his nails abrading tender tissues. It's too much, too over-whelming, the sensations beyond anything I've known. My heart is like a fluttering bird in my chest, my breathing so fast it feels like I'm hurtling into panic. Only his voice keeps me present in the moment, that dark, caressing voice with its subtle accent.

"That's it, my love… Relax…" His free hand strokes over my hip, the calluses on his palm rasping across my skin. "My pretty ptichka, so delicate, so sweet… It'll feel better in a moment, I promise you, my love." Crooning more endearments, he begins to move his cock in slow, shallow thrusts, and my heartbeat picks up further as the rocking movement rubs my clit against the mound of pillows.

The pleasure builds up slowly, maddeningly, the tension rising at a snail's pace. The pressure of the pillow on my clit is far too light, his shallow thrusts too gentle. I'm too aware of the stinging fullness in my ass, and I moan into the mattress in frustration, pushing my hips higher, needing him to go harder, faster. I was on the verge before, and I'm almost there now, but I need more.

I need him to take me all the way and hurl me over, to give me both more pleasure and more pain.

"Peter, please," I beg, but the perverse bastard stops and pulls out of me completely. Only his fingers remain in my ass, and in the next moment, he withdraws them too, leaving me aching and empty, on the edge and frustrated beyond belief.

"Peter," I groan, but then I feel him reach to the side behind me, and more cool lube is squirted between my cheeks.

"Shhh," he soothes as I clench instinctively at the feel of his massive cock pressing against that opening. "It'll be all right, my love, just let me in…" He pushes harder, and the pressure on my sphincter grows more intense, the stinging pain worsening. He's much bigger, much thicker than his fingers, and I can't relax enough to let him in.

"Peter." Growing panicked, I begin to struggle, tugging at the belt binding my wrists behind my back. "Peter, I don't think it's—"

The ring of muscle gives way with a painful pop, letting the broad head inside me, and a wave of dizziness crashes over me as he slides in deeper, the slickness of the lube easing his way. It feels like I've been speared, invaded in the cruelest way, and as he bottoms out inside me, his thick cock stretching me unbearably, I want to scream at him to stop, to end this. The fullness is beyond anything I imagined, and my stomach churns and cramps with nausea, cold sweat trickling down my trembling back.

Why was I so curious about this?

How could I have wanted this in any way?

Yet because I did, I remain silent, sucking in shaking breaths as I wait for the pain to ease. Peter is crooning to me again, stroking my back and hip—praising me for something, even—and soon, the pain does ease, the worst of the discomfort fading. The extreme fullness remains, however, and as his hand slips between my legs to find my clit, I start to tremble with a different kind of tension. It's too much, the twice-thwarted orgasm and the merciless invasion, the feel of him where no man has been before.

"That's it, ptichka," he murmurs as I cry out at his light pinching of my clit. "Now you can have it. Now you can let it go."

He starts to move inside me, carefully and gently, yet each stroke feels like a new invasion, my body wrenched open every time he pulls out and thrusts back in. It hurts and burns, but the steady pace does something, intensifying the throbbing tension in my sex. It begins to feel hypnotic, the rhythmic thrust and drag inside me, the pinching pressure of his fingers on my clit, and as I sink under the spell of the sensations, the tension grows, the pleasure coiling deep within my core.

"Come for me, Sara," he groans, thrusting deep, and to my shock, I do, each muscle in my body spasming in release. The ecstasy is violent, explosive, the burst of tension so strong I scream. With my inner muscles tightening and releasing, the cock inside my ass feels even more invasive, but the pain just sharpens the sensations, makes the pleasure dark and burning hot. He groans, and I feel him jerk inside me, bathing my raw insides with his seed.

In the aftermath, there's just ragged breathing—his and mine—and then he slowly withdraws, removing his belt from around my wrists before disappearing into the bathroom. I move my trembling hands to my sides but remain draped over the pillows, too shaken to get up. After a couple of minutes, Peter returns with a wet towel. I let him wipe the excess lube around my sore opening, and then I take the towel from him, holding it against myself as I get up on unsteady legs and make my way to the bathroom.

I need to wash up. Badly.

Peter considerately gives me a couple of minutes of privacy, then joins me in the shower.

"Are you okay?" he asks softly, blocking the water spray with his back, and I nod, my face burning as I meet his gaze. What just passed between us was so intimate and raw I feel like I've been peeled open. I don't understand what it is about this man that brings out this side of me, why things that should've horrified me—like the streaks of blood on the towel I just used—turn me on instead.

"Good," he murmurs, and in the dark steel of his eyes, I see a reflection of my own confusion, of the conflicting desires that make no sense. How could I want to be free of this man yet feel anxious to get closer? How could he love me yet want to hurt and punish me as well?

"Why?" I ask unsteadily as he frames my face with his large hands, his thumbs gently stroking across my shower-wet cheeks. Reaching up, I wrap my fingers around his thick wrists, feeling the strength of sinew and hard bone. "Peter... why are we like this?"

He doesn't pretend to misunderstand. "Because love isn't always pretty and simple, ptichka," he says softly. "Nor is it with whom you would expect. We don't get to choose our hearts' desires; we can only take them and pervert them, mold them into what we can survive."

"I don't—" My voice cracks as my throat tightens. "I don't love you, Peter. I can't."

To my surprise, his lips curl slightly and he dips his head, dropping a kiss on my forehead before drawing me against him in a hug.

"You can," he murmurs, one hand gently cradling my neck as the other one strokes my spine. "You can and you will. Someday soon, you'll stop fighting, and you'll see. Because it's too late for you, ptichka—you're as deeply ensnared as I am."

PART IV

CHAPTER 37
SARA

*O*ver the next three weeks, I do my best to prove Peter wrong, to distance myself from him, but it's a futile endeavor. Every time I erect any barriers between us, he breaks them down, and the perverse connection between us grows, aided by a physical attraction so strong it rips at the last shreds of my resistance.

Now that he's had me every way, my captor knows no boundaries with my body, and our sex is more intense than ever—and our condom use ever more sporadic. I don't understand how that happens, how my brain just shuts down at his touch, making me miss something so important. I don't want a child with Peter—I dread the mere thought of it—but when he sweeps me up in his embrace, pregnancy is the last thing on my mind.

So far, I've been lucky, with my period coming last week as usual, but I know better than anyone that all it takes is one slip, one careless moment. And I'm not sure that Peter is being careless, exactly. He still uses condoms when I manage to remind him, but there have been no more morning-after pills—not after that one time.

"I've read through all the medical literature on the topic, and I don't want you exposed to those hormones," he stated when I begged him to get the pills for me again. "You're extra sensitive—you said so yourself—and I'm not risking your health on the off-chance we might've gotten pregnant."

And no matter how much I tried to reason with him, pointing out that I'm an Ob-Gyn and can assess the risks myself, he wouldn't budge.

I'm beginning to suspect that Peter *wants* me pregnant, and that, more than anything, is what again turns my mind to escape.

———

This time around, I bide my time, carefully planning every step. I'm almost certain that Peter spoke the truth when he said the mountain is ringed by cliffs, but on our hikes through the forest, I've seen cliffs where the slopes are less sharp and the roots provide convenient handholds. The mountain is definitely inaccessible by car, and going up would be next to impossible, but a hiker who knows what she's doing could possibly get down.

At least I'm hoping that's the case.

I begin by deciding on the provisions and scoping out their locations. I can't stash them in advance without getting caught, but I pay careful attention to where everything is stored. Rope, a sturdy knife, a backpack, nonperishable food, bottles of water—I keep a mental checklist of the essentials so that when the time comes, I can gather everything in a few short minutes. It helps that Peter and his men are neat to the point of OCD; everything in the house has its place, so all I have to do is remember where that is.

I also contemplate stealing a gun. The men are careful around me, stashing their weapons out of sight, but I'm pretty sure I could get my hands on something if I really tried. I haven't tried, though, because by the time I learned where they keep them, I've gotten to know each of my captors and can't imagine hurting them. The healing instinct is too deeply ingrained in me. I could probably pull the trigger under some circumstances—if my life was in danger, let's say—but these men don't pose a mortal threat to me. On the contrary, they're nice to me, each in his own way. And taking the weapon to bluff them into letting me go would be stupid; they'd instantly see through my pathetic threat and take the gun away.

I'm up against elite ex-soldiers, not regular men, after all.

Still, I add the gun to my mental wish list, just in case an opportunity to acquire one arises before my escape. I might not be able to bluff Peter and his men into complying with my demands, but the same can't be said for some Japanese farmer. I'd try the civilized approach at first, of course, but if I'm having trouble gaining access to a phone, I'm not opposed to waving a gun around—unloaded, of course.

As I work on these preparations, I also start keeping an eye on the weather, casually asking the guys for a forecast each day. We haven't had snow yet, but it's already October and winter comes early at this altitude.

The last thing I want is to get caught in another icy storm.

"I don't like the cold," I complain to Peter when we return from a walk one day. "And I especially don't like it when the day starts off at one temperature, and by evening, it's twenty degrees colder."

"Poor baby," he croons, taking off my jacket to rub my arms. "Come, let's take a shower and get you nice and warm."

I let him warm me up with a hot shower and two orgasms, and the next day, I resume complaining about the weather—that way, no one will think it strange if I keep asking for a daily forecast.

As I'm doing all this, the guys are engaged in planning of their own. After a long break to throw the authorities off their scent, the team agreed to take on another job—a highly paid, highly dangerous assassination of a politician in Turkey.

I've been trying not to think about it, because each time I do, I get so anxious I can't eat or sleep. After what happened in Nigeria, just hearing the word "job" raises my blood pressure.

"Why do you have to do this?" I ask Peter in frustration as mid-October—the client's deadline to complete the job—draws nearer. "You said yourself, it's especially dangerous out there for you these days. You got paid millions—*millions*—for that Nigerian banker. You can't have gone through all that money so quickly."

"Of course not, but we have to think ahead," Peter says. "Aside from some of our more expensive toys, our hackers cost a fortune, and we need them to continue evading the authorities—and searching for Henderson."

Shaking my head, I take a breath and head into my recording studio, both to distract myself with music and to avoid another argument. Because if Peter is inflexible about the necessity for these jobs, he's absolutely immovable on the topic of Henderson—the one man still remaining on his list. The one time I cautiously brought up the possibility of forgetting the general and moving on, Peter shot me down so harshly I haven't been inclined to try again.

"He personally issued the order for the Daryevo operation," my captor snarled, his handsome face so twisted with rage it was unrecognizable. "He did this"—he shoved the phone with pictures of the massacre at me—"and I'm not going to rest until he and anyone who's helping him are rotting with the worms, just like the corpses of my wife and son."

I nodded then, backing off, because as much as I'd like to pretend otherwise, I do understand Peter's need for vengeance. I can't imagine losing people I care about in such a horrible way, and I know it had to have been even worse for him. From everything he's told me, those short years with Pasha and Tamila were the only time he's experienced anything resembling family and love.

Last week, for the first time, Peter talked a little bit about his son. It was after he woke up from a nightmare about his family's deaths, his big body shaking and covered with cold sweat. He reached for me then and fucked me, and in the quiet aftermath, he admitted how much he misses his little boy—how acutely he still feels his absence.

"Pasha was… life," he told me raggedly. "I don't even know how to explain it. I'd never met a child who took such joy in the mere act of existing. Birds, insects, trees, the sky and the rocks—everything was new to him, everything was fun. And he had so much energy. Tamila could barely keep up with him. He drove her crazy. And cars…" His powerful chest rose with a deep breath. "He loved cars. He wanted to be a race car driver when he grew up."

"Oh, Peter…" I lay my hand over his. "He sounds wonderful."

"He was," Peter whispered, turning his palm up to squeeze my fingers, and the intensity of pain in those words gutted me to the quick.

For all of his obsession with me, my captor is still grieving the loss of his family—the people he truly loved.

CHAPTER 38
SARA

As mid-October approaches, the men's preparations for the Turkey job ramp up, and I decide that this is going to be my opportunity.

If they do the same thing as the last time, leaving one man to watch over me, I may be able to sneak away unseen—especially if my jailer is going to be as occupied as Yan was during the Nigeria gig.

"So," I casually ask Peter during one of our walks, "what's the plan next week? Is Yan staying behind again?"

To my surprise, Peter shakes his head. "He can't. None of us can this time. The security around the politician is too multi-layered; we'll need all four of us to get to him."

My heartbeat jumps into sudden hope territory. Trying not to sound too eager, I say, "That makes sense. I'll be fine here. There's plenty of food and—"

"No, ptichka." Peter reaches for my hand, settling it in the crook of his elbow. "I'm not leaving you here alone, don't worry."

I swallow my disappointment and attempt to give him a guileless look as we resume walking. "Why? It's not like I can get down, so—"

"Exactly." Peter shoots me a sardonic glance. "You can't get down, but that doesn't mean you won't be tempted to try. Besides, I don't want to leave you stranded here if something happens to us."

"But then what will you do with me?" I ask, genuinely confused. "Are you going to bring me with you on the job?"

"No, of course not, though Yan did propose that. The preppy bastard wants a doctor on hand in case of any injuries," Peter says with a grimace. "No, I'm waiting to hear back from someone, and once I do, I'll let you know what the plan is."

"What?" I frown up at him. "Hear back from whom? About what?"

"Don't worry about it right now," Peter says and holds up a branch to let me pass underneath. "If it doesn't work out, there's a plan B, but Plan A is much better, trust me."

I learn what Plan A is two days before the men are due to fly out.

"You're going to leave me in Cyprus with an illegal arms dealer?" I gape at Peter, so shocked I forget I'm in the middle of taking off my jeans. "And that's better than leaving me here because…?"

Peter sits down on the bed. "Because he and his wife owe me a favor," he explains, pulling off his shirt. "So if anything happens to me, they've promised to return you home. You'll be safe with them until I'm able to retrieve you, and if, for whatever reason, I'm not… Well, you'll get what you say you want, my love. Your old life will be yours again."

Stunned, I finish undressing and sit down on the bed next to him, clad only in my underwear. "But another criminal? How do you know you can trust him? What if he double-crosses you? You did say there's a price on your head…"

Peter shrugs, his eyes roving over my nearly naked body. "Like I said, Lucas Kent owes me a favor, and he doesn't need the reward money. He used to be second-in-command to Julian Esguerra, a powerful weapons dealer, and now he's his boss's partner in some ventures. The reward money doesn't move the needle for him, and neither would whatever favor he could curry with the authorities by turning me in."

"Oh." Something nags at the back of my mind, some tidbit I can't quite recall. Then it comes to me. "Wait, is this Kent the arms dealer you mentioned before? The one who got you your list?"

"No, actually, that was his boss, Esguerra," Peter says, reaching behind my back. "Or technically, Esguerra's wife, as Esguerra had sworn to kill me at that point."

I catch his wrists before he has a chance to unhook my bra. "Kill you? For what?"

Peter sighs. "It's a long story, but suffice it to say that Kent doesn't share Esguerra's hatred of me. I've helped him out of some tight spots, both when we worked together—Esguerra was my employer at one point too—and afterward, when Kent needed to retrieve his wife. In any case, all you need to know is that Kent owes me."

"But this Esguerra—Kent's partner—wants to kill you?" At Peter's nod, I ask in frustration, "Why?"

"Because I saved Esguerra's life, but I had to go against my orders to do so. Specifically, I had to endanger his wife, the woman he entrusted me to protect. It was at her request—she bargained with my list, in fact—but still, he wasn't pleased." Twisting out of my hold with laughable ease, Peter goes for my bra again.

I give up and let him unhook it. "But he and the wife are both okay?"

Peter shrugs again, his heated gaze lowering to my exposed breasts. "Okay is a relative term, but yes, they both survived, and she held up her part of the bargain by getting me the list." His voice is husky as he returns his attention to my face and says, "You don't have to worry about the Esguerras, ptichka. They're in Colombia, far away from Kent's compound in Cyprus. You'll stay with Kent and his wife for the couple of days it takes us to do the job, and then we'll collect you on our way back. Cyprus is right next to Turkey, in case you weren't aware." As he speaks, he cups my breasts, gently squeezing and massaging them.

"Is that why—" I swallow as he flicks my nipple with his thumb, sending a tingle of heat straight to my core. "Is that why you want to stash me there? Because it's convenient?"

"Partially," Peter answers, looking up to meet my gaze. "But mainly because Lucas Kent will keep you safe for me… safe and secure, so when I return, I'll find you there."

And gripping my face between his palms, he kisses me deeply and bears me down to the bed.

CHAPTER 39
PETER

Sara is quiet, almost withdrawn in the two days leading up to the trip, and I know it's because she's worried. Yan told me how anxious she was during our Nigeria job, and while that pleased me at the time, I now regret that I'm causing her such stress.

Whether she wants to admit it or not, my little songbird cares about me.

She cares a lot.

I do my best to distract her from the upcoming trip by letting her talk to her parents daily, taking her on walks, and making love to her every spare minute I have. Unfortunately, I don't have many. There's too much to do, too many scenarios to plan for. The politician—Deniz Arslan—is used to people gunning for him, and his security is top-notch, as good as anything I might've set up for my consulting clients back in the day. There are only a couple of small weaknesses we've been able to uncover so far, and even those could potentially be traps.

This is not going to be an easy job, which is why a Ukrainian oligarch is paying us twenty-five million euros to do it.

The night before the trip, I make us all another nice dinner, but this time, I forbid the guys from discussing anything related to the upcoming danger. We keep the conversation light, recalling amusing stories from our past, and Anton finally succeeds in drawing Sara out of her shell by telling her how we first met.

"So here I am, a twenty-one-year-old army punk recruited into this elite team, all ready to meet my new commander," he says, grinning. "I figured he'd be a seasoned old dog, full of salty tales about Afghanistan and life under communism. And instead, this guy my age"—he waves his fork in my direction—"strides in and starts barking orders. I figured there had to be a misunderstanding and told him to fuck off, only to end up with his knife at my throat."

Sara gasps in shock. "Peter threatened you?"

"If nearly slicing open your carotid artery is a threat, then yes." Anton laughs and shakes his head in remembrance. "It was good, though. Helped us get a sense for what kind of man we were dealing with."

Sara turns to me, her hazel eyes wide. "So you became a team leader when you were only twenty-one?"

I nod, finishing my poached salmon. "At that point, I had four years of experience tracking down and interrogating people, and I was very good at my job."

"I can imagine," Sara says dryly. Glancing at the twins, she asks, "Did all of you start working together at the same time?"

Yan shakes his head. "Ilya and I joined later, after the team was in place for a couple of years. These two"—he nods toward Anton and me—"were pros by then, but we managed to keep up."

"Oh, please." Anton snorts. "What about that time you got stuck in that well near Grozny? How is us having to haul your ass out with a water bucket 'keeping up?'"

Yan shrugs, smiling coolly. "I got a lot of intel on those Chechen rebels by being in that well, and diving in was better than ending up in pieces from the bomb."

Sara pales at the mention of a bomb, and I shoot Yan a dark look. We agreed to keep things light tonight, avoiding whatever might remind Sara about the upcoming trip—and bombs definitely fall into that category.

Realizing his mistake, Yan elbows his brother and says, "Now this one did have some trouble. Remember that hooker who stole his boots?"

Ilya reddens as Yan launches into the tale amidst Anton's guffaws, and I reach for Sara's knee under the table, squeezing her jean-clad leg reassuringly. She smiles at me, and I feel that soft, warm glow in my chest, the one that makes me feel so alive when I'm with her. We're surrounded by my teammates, but we might as well be alone, because she's all I'm aware of, all I hear and see.

My Sara.

I love her so much it hurts.

We finish the dinner with lavish dessert, and then I lead Sara upstairs, where I make love to her until we're worn out and sore.

CHAPTER 40
SARA

It feels strange to walk to the helicopter with Peter and know that I'm leaving the mountain for the first time in four and a half months. For some reason, I didn't do that math before, didn't add up all the days and weeks that have been passing by, but now that I have, I realize it's been a year since Peter came into my life... a year since he broke into my home and tortured me to get to George.

I haven't seen my family in four and a half months, and if I don't escape, I may never see them again.

Unless Peter gets killed, an insidious whisper reminds me, and my heart falters for a beat. Worry for my captor is a constant heavy band around my lungs, unbreakable and suffocating, and no matter how much I reason with myself, I can't make the fear go away.

I don't want my freedom.

Not at this price, at least.

I haven't given up on the idea of escape, but given these new developments, my new plan is to get away in Cyprus. I don't know what kind of security this Lucas Kent has in place, but there's a chance he'll be more careless than Peter and his men, less invested in keeping me away from the internet and phones. He might even have qualms about acting as my jailer, though I'm not counting on that.

Men in Peter's world don't seem to care about a woman's freedom.

As the helicopter takes off, I watch our mountain retreat grow smaller in the window, but instead of hope, all I feel is dread. I should welcome this change, should seize the opportunities it offers, but while I intend to do precisely that, I can't help wishing we weren't going.

I can't help fearing what happens next.

———————————

I don't sleep on the plane this time—I can't—and by the time we land on a private airstrip in Cyprus, my eyes burn from dryness and exhaustion. Peter didn't sleep either, spending most of the thirteen-hour flight going over last-minute logistics with the twins, but he looks as fresh as the moment we stepped on the plane—and so do his men.

If I didn't know better, I'd think all Russians are superhuman.

It's pleasantly warm when we step off the plane, the tropical breeze carrying a hint of salt and sea. A black limo is waiting for us by the air strip, and it takes us on a scenic ride through a sparsely populated area. A couple of times, I even spot what looks like a wild donkey. The drive itself, however, makes me nervous. Not only do we drive on the left side of the road, like in the UK, but the roads are narrow and winding, occasionally stretching alongside some dangerous-looking cliffs.

Finally, we reach an automatic gate, and at the end of a long driveway, I see a Mediterranean-style house on a bluff overlooking the beach—Kent's home, according to Peter. It's large and beautifully maintained but not nearly as ostentatious as I expected from a wealthy arms dealer.

"Don't let the size of the house fool you," Peter says when I mention that to him. "Kent doesn't like to have live-in staff, but he owns all the land as far as the eye can see, including the beach below, and he has extraordinary security measures in place. Right now, there are several dozen guards patrolling the area, and upward of fifty military-grade drones surveilling us. If Kent thought we were in any way a threat, we wouldn't get within a kilometer of his place without getting blown into bits."

"Oh." I glance up, my stomach tightening. Though it's only late afternoon in this timezone, the sky is covered with clouds, and that makes it even more threatening somehow, the fact that something so deadly is hovering above us unseen.

"Don't worry," Yan says, apparently divining my thoughts. He's walking behind me and Peter, carrying a bag slung casually over his shoulder. "If Kent wanted us dead, we wouldn't still be walking."

"Shut it, you idiot," his brother mutters, casting a worried glance at Peter, but his boss is not listening. Instead, he's looking at the tall, broad-shouldered man who just opened the front door and is coming down the steps toward us.

I stare at him too, fascinated by the granite hardness of his features and the iciness of his pale eyes. His light-colored hair is worn short, almost in a buzz cut, and his skin is darkly tanned. Like Peter, he looks to be in his mid-thirties, and like my captor, he must also be former military. I can see it in the way he carries himself and the keen alertness of his gaze.

This is a man used to danger.

No, I realize as he comes closer, a man who *thrives* on danger.

It's not anything specific that gives that impression—he's wearing jeans and a T-shirt, with no weapons or tattoos in sight—but I feel certain of my conclusion. There's just something about men who are intimately acquainted with violence, a kind of fearless ruthlessness that civilized people lack. Peter and his teammates have it in spades, and so does this man.

"Lucas," Peter says in greeting, stopping in front of him. "It's good to see you."

The blond man nods, his smile as hard as his face. "Sokolov." His pale gaze flicks toward me. "And you must be Sara."

I nod warily. "Hello." For some reason, I didn't expect an American accent, but that's precisely what I hear in Lucas Kent's voice as he greets Peter's teammates.

"Congrats on your recent wedding," Peter says as our host leads us up the stairs to the entrance. "Sorry I didn't get a chance to send a gift."

Kent seems amused by that. "It's probably for the best. Esguerra was barely restraining himself as is."

"Ah." Peter grins. "So he still has it in for your bride?"

"You know how he is," Kent says laconically, and Peter laughs.

"Better than most, I'm sure. Where's your new wife, by the way?"

"In the kitchen, cooking up a storm," the arms dealer says, his tone warming slightly for the first time. "You'll meet her in a minute."

I listen quietly as they continue talking, mentioning people and places I don't know. I'm curious what Kent meant when he said that his boss/partner was barely restraining himself. It sounded as if this Esguerra doesn't like Kent's new wife, and if so, I wonder why that is.

When we enter the house, a savory aroma of cooking meat and various spices makes my stomach growl. We ate sandwiches on the plane, but that was hours ago, and I'm starving again. I doubt Mrs. Kent's cooking will come anywhere near Peter's delicious concoctions, but if tonight's dinner tastes half as good as it smells, it'll hit the spot.

Peter and his men are flying out immediately after dinner—they have some scouting to do tonight—so Lucas directs Anton and the twins to a bathroom by the entrance before leading me and Peter to the room where I'll be staying. As we walk through the spacious living room, I note that the interior of Kent's mansion is modern but surprisingly cozy, with overstuffed couches and warm wood finishes softening the sharp lines of Scandinavian-inspired furniture. Floor-to-ceiling windows let in a tremendous amount of light and display gorgeous views of the Mediterranean Sea below, while the walls are covered with pictures of a smiling couple—our host and a beautiful young blonde who must be his wife. A teenage boy frequently appears in those pictures too, his resemblance to Mrs. Kent leading me to think he's her brother.

The gorgeous woman in those photos doesn't look old enough to have a teenage son.

"Here we are," Kent says as we enter a bedroom with an adjoining bathroom and another big window overlooking the sea. "Towels are in the bathroom, and sheets are already on the bed. If you need anything else tonight, talk to Yulia."

"Yulia?" I ask.

"My wife," Kent clarifies as Peter walks over to stand by the window. "She knows where everything is, not me."

"Got it," I say, doing my best to hide my sudden amusement. In Japan, I've become so used to Peter and the guys handling all the domestic chores that I've forgotten most men aren't like that. My dad still asks my mom where he can find the ice cream scooper, and George didn't know how to make anything except barbecue and cheese sandwiches.

At the unexpected recollection, my chest tightens, my mood darkening as I realize that I once again compared my dead husband to his killer. It's something I've caught myself doing more often lately, and each time, I feel ashamed and angry with myself. The comparisons are rarely flattering to George, and that's not fair. What George and I had was a regular relationship, with liking, respect, and a normal kind of attraction. My husband wasn't in any way obsessed with me, and I didn't feel for him even a fraction of the contradictory emotions Peter stirs up in me.

And that was a good thing, I tell myself as I go into the bathroom to freshen up. What I have with Peter is too intense, too overwhelming. What he's willing to do to have me is terrifying, as is my inability to resist him despite the awful things he does. The very idea of us together is wrong on every possible level. And if I needed further proof of that, those photos on the walls today provided it. Even our host, the illegal arms dealer, seems to have a happy marriage—something I'll never have with Peter.

I doubt Lucas Kent was ever cruel enough to keep his beautiful wife captive, much less kill her husband.

When I emerge from the bathroom, Kent is gone, and Peter is sitting on the bed, waiting for me. "Dinner is almost ready," he says, standing up as I approach. "Lucas said to come as soon as you get changed."

"Okay." I grab the bag Peter packed for me and change out of my travel-worn clothes while Peter disappears into the restroom. By the time he returns, I'm dressed in one of my nicer summer dresses and have even managed to swipe on a lipgloss—a recent Yan purchase I remembered to slip into the bag.

"I'm all ready," I say as Peter comes toward me, his metallic gaze oddly intent. "Should we go so they're not—oh!"

Before I can do more than gasp, I find myself bent over the bed, my skirt flipped up, exposing my thong. One hard tug from Peter's fist, and the flimsy piece of fabric tears, leaving me bare to the waist. My heartbeat jumps, my insides clenching with a mix of fear and anticipation, and then Peter is on me, bending over me as his cock presses against my folds.

His entry is rough, borderline violent. One big hand grips my throat, forcing me to arch my back as he thrusts into me, while the other one delves underneath, finding my clit. I'm not wet enough at first, and the savage thrusts burn, his thick cock like a battering ram inside me. Before long, however, his fingers find the right rhythm, and a familiar tension starts to coil in my core. His grip on my throat restricts my breathing, and my nerve endings thrum in agonized pleasure-pain, the lack of oxygen heightening all sensations. It's too much, too intense, and I drag in shallow, gasping breaths, clutching fistfuls of blanket as he continues to hammer into me, fucking me so hard it feels like I might shatter.

And then I do, the tension cresting in a sizzling wave. White-hot pleasure explodes through every muscle in my body, making my heart feel like it's bursting in my chest. Shaking, wheezing for air, I collapse onto the mattress as soon as Peter lets go of my throat, and I hear him groan as he pulses deep inside me in release.

For a minute, I can't think, can only pant weakly into the blanket as he withdraws from me and steps back, but then the significance of the wetness trickling down my thighs dawns on me.

Peter didn't use a condom again.

Scrunching my eyes shut, I silently curse myself, then Peter, and then myself again. Every other time we've slipped up has been at a minimally fertile time, which is why we've avoided consequences so far. Right now, though, I'm just about mid-cycle—and most likely ovulating.

"Can you please hand me a tissue?" I ask stiffly, opening my eyes but not moving lest I mess up the new dress. I only brought a couple of outfits with me for this trip, and I can't afford to get one dirty the first night.

Peter walks toward the nightstand by the bed and returns with a tissue. "Here you go," he murmurs, patting at the wetness between my legs, and I snatch the tissue from him, finishing the job myself before heading to the bathroom again. My sex is swollen and sore, and my legs are not entirely steady, but all I can focus on is that I might've gotten pregnant.

Pregnant with Peter's child.

I wash myself as thoroughly as I can, even though I know it's futile. All it takes is one sperm, not the millions that are still inside me. Fighting the urge to cry, I smooth my hair, make sure my dress still looks presentable, and step out of the bathroom.

"Sara..." Peter gets up from the bed where he was sitting again. His jaw is tight, his eyebrows drawn into a frown as he reaches for me, his fingers gently encircling my upper arms. "Ptichka, are you okay?"

"What do you mean?" I frown up at him.

"Did I hurt you?" he clarifies, his face darkened with concern. "I didn't mean to be so rough. You just looked so beautiful and sexy that I—" He grimaces. "Well, the truth is, I lost control."

OBSESSION MINE

My despair gives way to sudden anger, and furious heat climbs up my cheeks. Beautiful and sexy? Is that his excuse for this?

"Lost control?" Jerkily, I pull out of his hold. "Really? What about every other time you did this? Did you 'lose control' then, too?"

His silver gaze fills with remorse. "I did hurt you. I'm sorry, my love. I was rough, and I didn't mean to be—not tonight, at least."

"You didn't hurt me!" My hands curl at my sides. "I mean you did, but I don't care about that—I came, in case you couldn't tell. I'm talking about the no-condom thing."

His features smooth out, his expression turning carefully opaque. "I see."

"You see what?" I glare up at him, stepping closer until I'm almost treading on his toes. He's a head taller than me, and much, much bigger, but I'm too furious to care. "Just admit it," I hiss. "You're trying to get me pregnant. This was no accident, and neither was every other time we 'forgot.'"

For a moment, I'm certain Peter will deny it, but he captures my hand in his and presses it against his chest, his eyes glittering like dark glass.

"Yes," he says softly. "You're right, Sara. I *am* trying to get you pregnant."

CHAPTER 41
SARA

I don't register anything else about Kent's house as Peter leads me to the dining area, nor do I pay attention to Peter's men as they join us in the living room and follow us to the table. I'm still processing Peter's admission, my anger swiftly transforming into suffocating panic.

This is not a total surprise, of course. I suspected this, knew it on some level. My kidnapper already admitted that he wouldn't mind a child with me, and a man like Peter—someone meticulous enough to plan impossible assassinations and account for dozens of unforeseen variables—wouldn't leave off a condom out of forgetfulness. Not repeatedly, at least.

I was right to want to run. If I don't escape soon, I may never find a way out—and I must. If not for myself, then for my future child.

I can't have a baby with a criminal on the run, a man whose life is steeped in violence and danger.

"There you are. I was beginning to think you decided to take a nap before dinner." The beautiful blonde from the photos—Yulia—greets us with a dazzling smile as we enter the dining area. In person, she's even more stunning, with impossibly long legs, bright blue eyes, and model-perfect features. Like her husband, she's dressed casually, in a pair of jean shorts and a light-colored T-shirt, but the simple outfit only highlights her natural beauty. She looks to be a few years younger than me, somewhere in her early to mid-twenties. Her tall, slender body is curved in all the right places, and her pale skin glows with a golden under-tone that contrasts prettily with the white-blond highlights in her long, thick hair.

If I met her on the street, I would've been sure she was a model or an actress.

Realizing I'm gaping at her as though she's a celeb, I shove all thoughts of Peter and pregnancy aside and give her a warm smile. "Hi. I'm Sara. You must be Yulia?"

I have no idea if Kent's wife knows about my situation or not, but if she doesn't, maybe I can explain my predic-ament to her and recruit her to my cause. First, though, I need to get to know her a bit, get a read on what she's like.

"I am indeed." Beaming, Yulia comes over and gives me a very European kiss on the cheek. "So pleased to meet you." Turning to Peter and his men, she smiles at them. "Hello. Pleasure to meet you all."

As the men introduce themselves, I realize that Kent's wife also speaks perfect American English, with no detectable accent. However, her name makes me think that she's from somewhere in Eastern Europe—a guess that's confirmed when Yan says something to her in Russian and she responds in the same language, grinning widely.

"Yan just asked if the food is going to be as good as at her restaurants," Peter translates for me. "Yulia has three of them so far, and Yan has apparently been to the one in Berlin."

"Oh." I take back my earlier thought; maybe the food *will* taste as good as it smells. "That's wonderful. Congratulations."

"Thank you," Yulia says, her smile brightening even more. "It's a lot of work, but I love it."

"What do you love?" Kent asks, walking in. Going straight to Yulia, he pulls her to him, draping a proprietary arm around her waist. His hard face is expressionless, but his pale eyes glitter dangerously as he surveys Peter and his men, his posture a silent warning to keep their hands—and eyes—off his wife.

"Running my restaurants," she explains, smiling up at her big, dangerous-looking husband without a trace of fear. Reaching up, she smoothes her hand over the back of his short hair. "Yan here has apparently been to my Berlin branch and enjoyed it."

"And why shouldn't he?" Kent's expression softens as he gazes at Yulia. "Your recipes are amazing, sweetheart."

Her color heightens, and for a moment, they seem oblivious to our presence. The look that passes between them is so tender, so intimate that my own face heats up even as a bittersweet ache pierces my heart.

Kent's marriage is indeed a happy one—and I can't help envying that.

"Food?" Anton says plaintively, and we all laugh as a blushing Yulia extricates herself from her husband's hold and hurries into the kitchen. Our host goes after her, and they return a minute later with delicious-smelling dishes that they set on the table. Peter and I go into the kitchen to help them bring out the rest, and a few minutes later, we're sitting down to a gourmet meal that outstrips the fanciest dishes Peter's ever made for me.

"Does everyone in your part of the world cook like this?" I ask, amazed. Not only are there two different kinds of roast chicken and marinated lamb, there's also smoked fish, five different types of salads, puff pastries and crepes stuffed with a variety of mouthwatering toppings, and so many dips and little side dishes I can only hope to have the stomach room to try them all. And everything is arranged so beautifully that each plate resembles a work of art.

"No, you just got lucky with me—and we all got lucky with Yulia," Peter says, smiling. His expression is relaxed, his steely gaze warm as he looks at me. If he didn't tell me five minutes ago that he intends to force a child on me, it would've been easy to pretend that we're a normal couple having a nice dinner with a group of friends.

Everyone digs into the food, complimenting Yulia with every bite, and it's not until we're halfway to being stuffed that the discussion turns to business. As it turns out, Peter knows quite a bit about illegal arms dealing, including all the key players, and I listen in fascination as he and our

host discuss deals in which insane sums of money trade
hands—some to the tune of billions.

I had no idea arms dealing was so lucrative, or that my
own government was sometimes involved.

"Did you ever figure out that manufacturing constraint
with the undetectable explosive?" Peter asks, reaching for a
puff pastry stuffed with a shiitake-camembert mix—one of
the most popular dishes among his men. "That was quite
in demand, as I recall."

"It still is, and no," Kent replies as Yulia ladles a spoon-
ful of crab salad onto his plate. "The base material is so
unstable you have to have highly trained chemists super-
vising the manufacturing process every step of the way.
And even if we could amp up the production, Uncle Sam
doesn't want that. As you can imagine, the Americans are
quite content buying up every batch we produce, whenever
we produce it."

"Of course." Peter snags another pastry for himself
before the Ivanov twins can decimate the entire platter.
"Frank still there for you guys?"

"He retired a few months back," Kent says and reaches
over to play with Yulia's hand, interlacing his big, sun-
browned fingers with her slender ones. "We have a new
CIA contact now—Jeff Traum. He's tough, though. Hates
Esguerra's guts and only works with us under duress."

"How come?" Yan asks, looking keenly interested. "You
guys do something to him?"

Kent shrugs. "Not really. We threw the Israelis a bone
with some intel a couple of times, so I think that played a
role. And that thing with Novak didn't help."

Peter's eyebrows rise. "The Serbian arms dealer?"

"Yeah, that's the one." Kent releases Yulia's hand, his mouth tightening. "He's been interfering with our business, and we had to retaliate. Unfortunately, the CIA was in the middle of a sting operation when we struck, and we blew up a few agents. Not on purpose, mind you. But Traum is still pissed, because that operation was his baby."

"You know, I heard something about that," Peter says thoughtfully. Turning to Anton, he says, "Remind me… the shit show that our hackers were talking about in August—was that in Belgrade?"

"That's right," Anton says, nodding. "Two warehouses full of C-4, fifteen armored trucks, and a factory near that village. Was that your doing, Kent?"

Our host's smile is sharper than a blade. "Indeed. We had to impress our seriousness on Novak. Undercutting us on prices is one thing, but breaking into our Indonesian facility and killing all the staff? *That* crossed a line."

Listening in horrified fascination, I steal a glance at Yulia to see how she's reacting to all this. Could one get used to dinner conversation revolving around staff killings and blowing up of factories?

Sure enough, Kent's wife is eating calmly, seemingly unruffled. She either has no problem with her husband's violent business, or she's an excellent actress. For some reason, I suspect it's a little of both, which makes me wonder about Yulia's background. Has she always been in the restaurant industry, and if not, what did she do before? How did she and her husband meet?

In general, how does one encounter a man from this world if one's husband doesn't have the misfortune to be on an assassin's revenge list?

Driven by curiosity, I get up to help when Yulia starts clearing away the dishes. She tries to wave away my assistance, but I insist on helping her carry everything into the kitchen, leaving the men to discuss whatever went down in Belgrade. It's important that I get close to Kent's wife, and not just because I want to learn more about her.

If I'm to stand a chance of getting away before Peter returns, I'll need her help.

"Where are you from originally?" I ask as she takes several desserts out of a restaurant-sized fridge. "You speak perfect English, but your name…"

"It's Ukrainian," she explains, smiling. "Though it could just as easily be Russian. The name is common in both countries. If it's hard for you to pronounce, you can call me Julia—that would be the English equivalent."

I smile back and start rinsing dirty dishes. "I think I can pronounce the real thing. *Yu-lee-yah*, right?"

She looks pleased. "You got it. Some Americans have trouble, which is why I've been letting them do the Julia bit. Your pronunciation is really good, though—better than most."

"Thank you. It should be—I've had a lot of exposure to the Russian language lately," I say, stacking the rinsed plates in the dishwasher. I'm hoping she'll ask about that, but Yulia merely smiles and carries the first set of desserts out into the dining room before returning to the kitchen for more.

I don't get a chance to talk to her again, because she keeps going back and forth, getting everyone tea and coffee to go along with dessert. Frustrated, I go back to the table, where the men are now discussing the situation in Syria and the continued turmoil in Ukraine. I try to follow their conversation, but they might as well be speaking Russian. Every other word is a place or name I don't know, alongside strange initials like UUR. The only thing I learn is that Kent's business thrives on conflict of all kinds, from small-scale rivalry between drug cartels to full-blown wars between nations.

Every man at this table contributes, in one way or another, to death and suffering around the globe.

By now, I should be used to that—I've been living with a team of assassins for months—but it's still startling to realize how normal this is to them, and how utterly unconcerned they are with such banalities as good and evil. Where I come from, people feel ashamed if they don't recycle or donate their used clothes, much less say or do anything to hurt another. The bad men in my world cheat on their wives, drive drunk, or refuse to give up their seat for a pregnant woman. They don't kill for money or sell weapons that can wipe out entire towns.

That's a whole other level of evil.

Yet even as I tell myself that, I can't help being aware of the treacherous passage of time, of how each minute brings us closer to the end of this meal and Peter's departure. Given everything, it should be a relief to have him leave, but I can't suppress the anxiety simmering underneath my fear and anger.

No matter what, I can't stop worrying about the monster I should hate.

All too soon, the desserts are consumed—most of them by Anton—and the tea is finished. Getting up, Peter and his men thank Yulia, praising the meal in glowing terms, and then Anton and the twins head to the exit, accompanied by our host. Yulia disappears into the kitchen, and I find myself alone with Peter for the first time since his revelation.

Coming up to me, he gently brushes his knuckles across my cheek. "I have to go," he says quietly, and I nod, trying to ignore the painful lump expanding in my throat.

"Okay," I manage to say semi-calmly. "Good luck."

Be careful. Come back to me. I need you. The aching confession is on the tip of my tongue, but I hold the words back, suppressing the urge to step into his embrace and kiss him. He's not my lover going off to war; he's my kidnapper, my captor. By the time he returns, I might be gone, and if I'm not, we'll have the biggest battle on our hands. What Peter wants—to impregnate me against my consent—is worse than kidnapping, more terrible than torture.

It would deprive me of the most basic choice of all and bring an innocent child into the twisted mess of our relationship.

Peter holds my gaze, and I can tell he's waiting. For what, I don't know, but when I continue to stand there silently, his face tightens and he drops his hand.

"I will see you soon," he says grimly, turning away, and I watch, my heart breaking into pieces, as he leaves the room.

CHAPTER 42
PETER

It's just before midnight when we land on a private airstrip near Istanbul, less than five miles from our target's suburban mansion. Our task for tonight is to scope out the area in person, as we've been going by satellite and drone imagery so far.

If all goes well, we'll strike in a few days.

We're all tired and jet-lagged—it's already morning in Japan—so we keep our reconnaissance brief. Anton and Yan drive around the gated community where the mansion is located, noting key landmarks and potential escape routes, while Ilya and I enter the community on foot, using the guard shift change to scale the ten-foot fence near the main gate.

This level of security is designed to keep out ordinary criminals, not former Spetsnaz assassins.

The difficult part will be the security at Arslan's mansion. Though the place masquerades as just another residence in this wealthy community, it's protected with everything from motion detectors to a small army of bodyguards. Retina scanners, weight sensors, silent alarms, backup generators—there are redundancies upon redundancies in the security of the place, and for a good reason.

When you double-cross the ruthless oligarch who put you in power, you know to prepare for the worst.

Once we're inside the gated community, we head toward Arslan's mansion, making sure to keep out of sight of cameras placed strategically at intersections and in front of the majority of the sprawling luxury homes. Our target's neighbors—other crooked politicians and wealthy Turkish businessmen—have enemies too, though none as powerful as the Ukrainian oligarch who is our client.

We don't go up to Arslan's property—the cameras there would be impossible to avoid—but we don't need to. It takes us only a few minutes to disable the alarms on the three-story house on the far end of Arslan's street—the residence of a real estate magnate who's currently vacationing in Thailand. Once the alarms are off, we go up to the roof and set up a long-range camera, so we can observe everything going on at our target's place. We then repeat this process with a mansion on the opposite end of the street, and then two residences a block over, so we have a 360-degree view of Arslan's mansion.

The simplest, and safest, way to kill the politician would be to take him out with a long-range sniper's rifle. Unfortunately, the windows of the mansion are bulletproof, and whenever our target is in the open, he's surrounded by bodyguards. The next best thing would be to wire a bomb into his car, but he switches vehicles regularly and without any detectable pattern—plus the cars are always heavily guarded, even when they're just parked on the street. Every delivery to his place is thoroughly checked too, as is each person entering and leaving the mansion.

At first glance, Arslan's security is impenetrable, but we know better. Home is always where everyone feels safest—and that's a weakness in itself.

Leaving the cameras in place, Ilya and I make our way out of the community and to the intersection where Yan and Anton pick us up. For the remainder of the night, we go to a private house we rented under false identities and organize shifts to watch the footage from the cameras we set up.

Yan is up first, followed by Anton, so I get a solid six hours of sleep before getting up to do my three hours of camera monitoring. Ilya, the lucky bastard, got the long straw this time, with a total of nine hours of shuteye.

It's during the middle of my shift that we notice movement inside the house. Even with the shades on the windows drawn shut, we see the lights come on in the master bedroom on the second floor, followed by more lights downstairs.

Arslan's household is waking up.

He keeps his domestic staff lean, with just a house-keeper, two maids, and one butler/bodyguard living on the premises. Their rooms are downstairs, which works well for our plan. The other guards—all twenty-four of them—are stationed in a guardhouse in the back. To look unobtrusive to the neighbors, they come out in small groups at random intervals to patrol the street and the beautifully landscaped yard surrounding the mansion.

Watching the cameras, I jot down the time and mark the pattern of the lights upstairs. People are creatures of habit, even those who were instructed by their bodyguards to be as unpredictable as possible.

"Keep an eye on his departure time," I tell Ilya when he comes to replace me. "We know he leaves the house at a different time every day, but I want to see how much time passes between those lights coming on and his departure."

Ilya nods and sits down in front of the computer while I go into one of the bedrooms to take a nap. My temples throb with a tension headache, and I need to rest so I'll have my wits about me as we plan this attack.

The moment I close my eyes, however, my mind turns to Sara and our tense parting. I've been trying not to think about it, to focus solely on the job, but I can't help recalling the wounded look on her face when I admitted my intentions... when I confirmed that the forgotten condoms were no accident.

I didn't realize it myself until that moment, didn't know I'd given in to my deepest desires until I heard the words coming out of my mouth. The moment I said it, though, I knew it was the truth. It might not have been a conscious decision to impregnate her, but it wasn't a careless error either. On some primitive, instinctual level, I *chose* to fill her with my seed, to make her mine in the most visceral way possible.

The only time in my life I was careless with contraception was in Daryevo all those years ago, when Tamila seduced me before I woke up.

Opening my eyes, I stare at the ceiling in the unfamiliar bedroom. Despite Sara's reaction, I feel lighter, as if a weight has been lifted off my chest. It's liberating to embrace the worst part of myself, to let go of the last of my moral qualms. I don't know why I resisted for so long, why I tried so hard to fight for her love when she's determined to cling to hate.

It's obvious to me now that no matter what I do, Sara won't let go of the past, and if that's the case, she might as well have another reason to hate me.

Resolved, I close my eyes and force my tense muscles to relax.

When I return, there will be no more condoms. One way or another, Sara is going to have my child.

If she can't love me, she'll love a part of me.

CHAPTER 43
SARA

It takes me several minutes to compose myself after Peter leaves, and by the time I head into the kitchen to talk to Yulia again, Kent returns and politely but firmly ushers me to my room.

"You should get some sleep," he says, and from the implacable look on his face, I can tell he'll use physical force to make me obey if he has to.

He has no intention of helping me, of that I'm certain.

"Thank you for your hospitality," I say evenly when we get to my room, and he nods, his pale gaze inscrutable.

"Good night, Sara," he says, and as he closes the door behind him, I hear the faint click of a turning lock.

I wait thirty seconds, then try the door handle to confirm my suspicions.

Sure enough, I'm locked in.

Taking a breath to calm myself, I walk over to the big window. It looks like the bottom portion should open by sliding up, but no matter how hard I try to push it up, the thick glass doesn't budge. It's either sealed shut or simply too heavy for me to lift. Some kind of bulletproof glass, maybe? That would make sense given Kent's profession.

Either way, opening the window is out.

Next, I explore the small window in the bathroom. It has the same thick glass as the window in the bedroom, and there are two additional problems with it: it's too small for me to crawl through, and there's no opening mechanism as far as I can tell.

Frustrated, I leave the windows alone and go through the closet and the dresser, looking for a forgotten phone or an old tablet. The odds of finding such a device here are slim, but back home, people would leave their electronics everywhere, and it's feasible Kent and his wife might do the same. After all, this is their house, not a place where they regularly keep prisoners.

At least I'm hoping that's the case.

Unsurprisingly, I don't find anything. The closet and the dresser hold what one would usually expect to find in a guest room: extra bedding and towels, along with some unopened toiletries.

Feeling increasingly drained and dispirited, I decide to take a shower and get some rest as Kent suggested.

With some luck, I'll get to talk to Yulia tomorrow.

At this point, she's my best, if not my only, hope.

To my disappointment, I don't see Yulia the next day, nor am I allowed out of my room. Kent himself brings me my meals—a mix of leftovers from dinner and new gourmet concoctions undoubtedly made by his wife—and then he carries away the dishes an hour later. I don't know if he's purposefully trying to keep me away from Yulia, or if it's just an unlucky coincidence, but by evening, I'm going stir crazy, frustration about my predicament mixing with growing worry about Peter. All I have are a few books that Kent brought me around lunchtime, and it's not nearly enough to keep me from dwelling on the dangers Peter's team might be facing at that very moment.

"Have you heard from them? Are they okay?" I ask Kent when he brings me dinner. The hard-faced arms dealer intimidates me, but I'm determined not to show it.

After all, I've been living with four equally dangerous criminals for months.

At my question, Kent looks coolly amused. "You want to know if they're okay?"

I nod, though a flush warms my face. I understand how this appears. Given Kent's treatment of me so far, he obviously knows I'm not here of my own free will. Still, I'd rather he believe I'm suffering from Stockholm Syndrome than continue to remain in the dark and worry about Peter all night.

"They're okay," Kent says, placing the tray on the dresser. His face is expressionless again, though a trace of amusement glimmers in the icy depths of his eyes. "Peter messaged me a couple of hours ago, asking about you. For now, they're just gathering intel for the strike, so I doubt anything will happen tonight. You can rest easy."

I exhale in relief. "Thank you."

He nods and turns to leave, but I decide to push my luck. "Wait, Lucas... where's Yulia? I haven't seen her all day, and I wanted to thank her for these lovely meals."

He gives me an inscrutable look. "I'll convey your thanks to her."

This is my cue to be a good captive and slink away, but I'm not about to give up so easily. "I'd rather do it in person, if you don't mind," I say, pasting a slightly embarrassed smile on my lips. "Is she really busy? There's actually something I wanted to ask her... about some female items, you know..."

"Ah." Kent looks amused again. "Yulia said to tell you that tampons and other girl necessities are in the cabinet under the sink."

"Oh, it's not about that," I say quickly, though that was indeed what I was hinting at. "It's something else."

His eyebrows lift. "Oh? What is it?"

Crap. I was counting on him being like most men and acting embarrassed when confronted with the reality of women's biological functions. Thinking quickly, I say, "It's just a cream for something. It's okay, though; I'm sure it'll go away on its own."

His expression doesn't change. "Just tell me what cream it is, and I'll see if we can get it."

"*Monistat*," I say, looking straight at him as I name a popular treatment for yeast infections. "The generic name is *miconazole*. It's for—"

"Yeast. I know." He doesn't look embarrassed in the least. "We'll get it for you."

I grit my teeth. "Okay, thanks."

He *is* determined to keep me from Yulia, and that makes me want to talk to her even more.

The following day passes in a similar manner, with me locked in my room all day. The only difference is that, at dinner time, Kent voluntarily updates me about Peter.

"They're planning to do it the day after tomorrow, in the morning," he says, placing my food tray on the dresser. "I will let you know if anything changes."

I eye the arms dealer morosely. "Okay, thanks."

It feels like an axe—a very slow-moving axe—is hanging over my head. I dread both the failure of this operation in Turkey and its success. If something goes wrong, I will lose Peter and regain my old life, and if he returns unscathed, I will be tied to him forever, bound by a child he intends to force on me.

The only way out is to escape before Peter returns, and I don't see how that's possible when I'm even more of a prisoner here than I was in Japan.

Kent leaves, and I eat dinner on autopilot, barely tasting the richly flavored food. On the tray, along with covered dishes, is a tube of the cream I requested—something I have absolutely no use for other than as a way to explain my need to talk to Yulia. Now that it's been two days, I'm even more convinced that the beautiful blonde might be sympathetic to my situation—if only I could explain it to her fully.

Finishing my meal, I study the cream, noting dispassionately that it's packaged a little differently from the way I'm used to seeing in the United States. It's not surprising, of course. This is Europe. The Japanese morning-after pill also looked nothing like what I was used to.

The morning-after pill…

Sucking in a breath, I jump up, unable to contain my sudden excitement. I don't know why it didn't occur to me before, but if Kent was willing to get this cream for me, there's a chance he'd agree to get something else—such as the pill I so badly need.

My first instinct is to rush to the door and hammer on it until my jailer comes, so I can implement my plan right away. However, that wouldn't be wise. Acting overeager could make Kent suspicious, maybe even cause him to consult with Peter on the issue.

Taking a calming breath, I force myself to sit and wait for Kent to return for the tray. For this to have the best chance of success, I have to be smart.

I have to pretend this is yet another ploy to talk to Yulia.

The waiting seems interminable, though the clock tells me it's only been an hour. Finally, Kent opens the door, and I implement my plan.

"So," I say casually as he walks in, "is Yulia still busy? I would *really* like to talk to her."

The arms dealer gives me a cool look. "Why? Is it about another female item?"

I try to look embarrassed. "Yes, actually. I'm sorry I forgot to mention it yesterday, but it's something I really need."

"And that is?"

"*Plan B.*" I give him my most innocent face. "Do you know what that is? There are other brands too, like *Next Choice*, *My Way*—"

"Got it. You will have it soon."

And swiftly collecting the tray, he heads out the door.

CHAPTER 44
SARA

That night, I toss and turn, tortured by worry about Peter's upcoming operation and the realization that, despite my little victory this evening, the pill will at most delay the inevitable. Every time I sink into light sleep, I wake up with my heart racing, as if from a panic attack. It reminds me of the first couple of months after Peter's assault in my kitchen, when nightmares about waterboarding and ruthless gray-eyed men were my nightly reality.

Finally, I give up on sleep and get up to use the bathroom. It makes no sense whatsoever, but what I want most right now is Peter. I want his warmth in the darkness and his strong arms around me, holding me tight. I want his deep voice calling me "ptichka" and telling me how much he loves me.

I miss my tormentor, ache for him with every fiber of my being—even as I fear his return.

Walking over to the bathroom counter, I turn on the light, staring at my pale face in the mirror. My eyes are bloodshot and surrounded by dark circles, and my hair is a hot mess. I bet if Peter saw me right now, he wouldn't be so eager to have me.

Of course, that assumes my looks are the reason he's so fixated on me—a big, and likely incorrect, assumption. I know I'm attractive, but I'm nowhere near as beautiful as someone like Yulia. No, whatever it is that draws Peter to me—and vice versa—goes deeper than surface attraction. He knows it, and I know it too. It's something within us that makes us fit together like two pieces of broken china… something dark and perversely needy that calls out to each other's flaws.

I'm about to turn on the faucet to wash my face when a sound reaches my ears.

I freeze, listening intently, and then I hear it again.

A woman's throaty moan, followed by a man's muffled grunt.

My face heats up as I realize what I'm listening to.

This bathroom must be right underneath Lucas and Yulia's bedroom, with the air vent connecting the two floors.

I know I should go back to bed and give them privacy, but my legs refuse to move. If nothing else, this is more entertaining than the thrillers Kent left for me to read. Blushing and feeling like a pervert, I listen as the sounds upstairs grow in volume before culminating in an obvious climax.

When silence reigns again, I turn on the faucet with unsteady hands and splash cold water on my overheated face. This was a bad idea, because not only did I violate my hosts'/jailers' privacy, but I'm now so turned on I will definitely have trouble going back to sleep. My nipples are hard, and my sex is slippery with aching need.

I also miss Peter more than ever.

Groaning silently, I head back to bed. Predictably, I can't fall asleep, so I reach under the blanket and play with myself until I come, thinking of Peter the entire time.

Despite my restless night, I wake up early the next morning, and as I'm getting ready to brush my teeth, I hear footsteps upstairs, followed by tense voices.

It sounds like the Kents are having an argument.

Unbearably curious, I put down the toothbrush and listen.

At first, their voices come across as muffled, as if they're on the other side of the room, but then they come closer to the vent—and my heartbeat accelerates as I realize the topic of their argument.

Me.

"How can you be so sure?" Yulia says heatedly. "She's his enemy's widow. He killed her husband and kidnapped her. How is that not mistreatment? At the very least, he took away all her choices and ruined her career. The woman is a doctor—a *doctor*, Lucas. She's not like you and me. She's never been a part of this world—"

"And now she is," Kent interrupts, his voice hard. "Not that it's any of our business. I owe him a favor, and she is it."

"*She* is a human being, not a favor. At the very least, let me talk to her, find out whether he's mistreating her—"

"Why? So you could do what? Let her go and end up on his hit list? You know the kind of targets his team goes after these days. We don't need to deal with that shit on top of the Novak situation."

"No, of course not." Yulia sounds frustrated. "But she's an innocent civilian, Lucas, and she's a guest in our home. I need to make sure that you're right and she *does* want him—because I can't live with myself otherwise. You understand that, right?"

Her husband is silent for a few moments, and I bite my thumb, my heart hammering as I listen for his reply. I was right to pin my hopes on Yulia; she *is* sympathetic to my plight.

"I understand," he finally says. "But there's still nothing I can do. I will not put your life in danger for this woman."

"But—"

"But nothing. Sokolov asked me to keep her safe for him, and that's precisely what I'm going to do."

"Lucas…" Yulia's voice softens, turning more cajoling. "Just let me talk to her. That's all I ask. I'm not going to do anything without consulting you. I'm not stupid, and I don't want to make an enemy of Peter either. I just want to make sure she's okay… reassure her if she's scared. That wouldn't do any harm, would it? Just a little chat?"

There's no response from Kent, though I hear rustling sounds, followed by something metallic—a belt buckle, maybe?—hitting the floor.

"Yulia…" Kent's voice thickens. "Sweetheart, you don't have to—oh fuck. Motherfucking fuck…" His words end on a groan, and I flush as I realize what I'm listening to again.

Feeling doubly like a pervert, I stay quiet—to see if they mention me again, I tell myself—but when all I hear for the next ten minutes are sex sounds, I force myself to finish brushing my teeth and go back into my room.

Maybe, just maybe, Yulia's persuasion tactic will succeed, and I might find a way out of this predicament.

At least now I have some real hope.

CHAPTER 45
PETER

We spend the day before the strike running through the different versions of the plan, calculating success probabilities and coming up with solutions to potential problems. Our plan is risky, but it has a good chance of working—assuming we get the timing right.

By night, we're as ready as we're ever going to be, and that's a good thing, as our client, the Ukrainian oligarch, is getting impatient. In two days, Arslan is supposed to vote on a bill that will all but decimate our client's business in Turkey, and we have to act before that happens.

As I close my laptop to catch a few hours of shuteye before my shift, Anton calls me over, his tone unusually excited.

"Look at this," he says, and adrenaline floods my veins as I see a new email from our hackers.

Swiftly, I read through it on Anton's screen, and a savage smile spreads across my face.

My adversary has finally made a mistake.

Walter Henderson III's wife, Bonnie, was at a winery in Marlborough, New Zealand—something we learned thanks to a picture posted on Instagram by the clueless winery owner. Our hackers' face recognition program picked it up within hours of it appearing online.

"Get ready," I tell Anton and the twins when I finish reading through the email. "After we're done here tomorrow, we're going to New Zealand."

"What about Sara?" Ilya asks. "Are you going to leave her with Kent?"

I hesitate, then shake my head. "No." I can't bear to be separated from her for even a day longer. "She's coming with us."

And before going to bed, I call Lucas to check up on her.

CHAPTER 46
SARA

I spend the day pacing my room, my anxiety intensifying with each passing hour. By dinnertime, I'm ready to tear my hair out.

In less than twelve hours, Peter's dangerous mission will begin, and Yulia still hasn't come by to talk to me—nor has her husband brought me the promised pill.

"I should have it later today," he told me when he delivered my lunch. "Though it could be tomorrow as well."

By tomorrow, it would be too late, but I kept my mouth shut, not wanting my jailer to know that I truly need that pill. If nothing else, I can stash it away for future use, and pray that my fertile window wasn't so fertile this month.

A quiet knock on the door interrupts my pacing.

"Sara?" a woman's voice asks. "May I come in?"

My pulse leaps with joy. "Yes! Please, come in."

The door opens, and Yulia backs into the room, holding a heavy-looking tray with covered dishes.

"Here, let me help you." I rush toward her, barely containing my excitement as I assist her in setting the tray onto the dresser.

She smiles at me. "Thank you. How is your stay so far?"

"It's good," I answer, beaming back at her. "And obviously, the food is wonderful. Thank you so much for that."

Yulia's blue eyes gleam with pleasure. "You're welcome. And how is everything else? Do you have everything you need? Lucas said you asked for a couple of medicines…"

I nod, then decide to just go for it. With Peter potentially returning tomorrow, I have no time to waste, and I already know Yulia is on my side. "I need the morning-after pill," I say bluntly. "And today is the last day I can take it."

Her beautiful mouth rounds in surprise. "Oh. Wow. Lucas didn't mention anything about that. He sent one of his guards into town today to pick up a few things, but I know that something came up and the guy was distracted. Let me check to see if he got it, okay?"

"Wait." I grab Yulia's slender arm as she turns to leave. "Please. I need your help."

Her expression turns carefully blank. "What do you mean?"

I drop my hand. "I have to leave. Now. Tonight. Before Peter returns. Please, it's very important. I'm not his girlfriend; I'm his captive. He kidnapped me, and now he—"

"Wait, Sara. Please." She lifts her hand, palm out. Though her manner remains calm, I can tell she's distressed. She must not have expected me to plead for help so openly. "Is he abusing you? Has he hurt you?" she asks carefully.

"He cut me with a knife and waterboarded me," I say, and immediately feel a twinge of guilt at the horror on Yulia's face. I should probably mention that the torture took place before our relationship, such as it is, began, but if I'm to get her help, I can't afford to paint my captivity in a rosy light.

As kind and sympathetic as Yulia seems, I can't forget that she's an arms dealer's wife and may have a different view of morality than most people.

"He also wants to force a child on me," I continue, pressing my point while she's still in shock. "That's why I need the morning-after pill today. In another couple of hours, I'll be outside the thirty-six-hour window. Not that the pill would help if I'm still here when Peter returns. He'll do what he wants with me, and nobody will stop him. Please, Yulia"—I catch her arm again—"you don't even have to let me go. Just let me make one phone call or send an email. Nobody would even know it was you who helped me. Please."

She pales more with every word I speak, and I almost feel bad. I understand the impossible position I'm putting her in. Though she seems willing to look the other way when it comes to her husband's deadly business, Yulia is not like him—or at least she possesses enough empathy to put herself in my shoes. At the same time, she knows how dangerous Peter is and what she would be risking by double-crossing him.

"Are you—" She clears her throat. "Are you ever with him willingly? That first night, at dinner, I could feel the tension between the two of you, but the way he looked at you... And then the way you looked when you were saying good-bye... I was in and out of the kitchen, but I thought I saw— Did I get the wrong impression? Is he hurting you? Forcing you every time?"

My face heats with embarrassment at the private question, and I drop my hand again. "That's not— I mean, he kidnapped me. What do you think?"

To my surprise, she looks uncomfortable. "I think it's complicated sometimes," she says after a moment. "Not every relationship follows the same path, and there are times when—" She stops, as if thinking better of it.

Frowning, I stare at her. There's a story there, but whatever it is, I can't afford to focus on it. I have to persuade her to help me before it's too late.

"Yulia, please," I say. "This is my only chance. *You* are my only chance. If he returns and I'm here, I'll never see my parents again, never have any control over my own life... Please. I know you understand my situation. Peter Sokolov killed my husband and tortured me. He stalked and kidnapped me, and he's been keeping me captive for almost five months. I have to leave before he returns, and all you need to do is let me have access to a phone. Just for a second. I could contact the FBI and then—"

"And then we'll have every law enforcement agency targeting our home," Kent says, pushing the door open without knocking. His square jaw is clenched with fury, his pale eyes narrowed into slits as he crosses the room and grabs Yulia's hand in a white-knuckled grip. "Let's go," he tells his wife through gritted teeth, and I watch in growing despair as he drags her out of the room.

"I'm sorry," she mouths before he slams the door, locking me in again, and I know it's over.

My one chance at escape is lost.

I cry for two hours before I finally fall asleep—and promptly sink into a series of nightmares. I don't know why this is happening to me again, but as I wake up, shaking and sweating from another vivid dream about drowning in my kitchen sink, I know I won't be able to sleep tonight.

Throwing off the blanket, I swing my legs over the bed to get up when the lock on the door clicks and the door quietly swings open.

Startled, I grab the blanket to cover myself, but no one enters my room.

Wrapping the blanket around myself, I rush to the door, and at the far end of a hallway, I see a tall, slender figure disappearing around the corner, her blond hair glowing like a beacon in the moonlit darkness.

Yulia.

She came through for me.

I have no idea how she managed to sneak away from her husband, but I don't waste time questioning my good fortune. Quickly throwing on a dress and a pair of flat sandals, I slip into the hallway and head toward the kitchen, being careful not to make any noise.

I need to find a phone or a computer—anything that would let me contact the outside world.

"Here." A pair of keys are suddenly thrust into my hand, and I suppress a squeak as Yulia appears in front of me, seemingly melting out of the wall to my right. With the moonlight streaming through the big windows, her pale face resembles something otherworldly. "The Mercedes is right outside," she whispers urgently before I can recover from my shock. "I disabled the perimeter alarms, opened the automatic gates, and directed the drones to the beach. You have ten minutes, do you understand? There's a gas station seven kilometers to the southwest. Drive straight there, and you'll find a phone."

I nod, my heart racing as I clutch the keys she gave me. "Thank you. Thank you so much."

"Go." Throwing a worried glance behind her, Yulia pushes me toward the front door, and I don't delay a second longer.

Keys in hand, I run out of the house and jump into the car.

CHAPTER 47
PETER

"Five minutes," I whisper into my headpiece. "Get ready."

It's been exactly twenty minutes since the lights appeared on the second floor of Arslan's mansion. That means our target will walk out of his front door and get into his bulletproof car between five and ten minutes from now. As we'd hoped, he's a creature of habit, his morning routine nearly the same every weekday morning. The time he leaves the house varies, as does the route he takes to work and where his bodyguards leave his car, but this—the time he spends at home, feeling safe and secure as he eats his breakfast—is entirely predictable.

In a few short minutes, there will be a small window when he's out in the open with his bodyguards, and that's when we're going to strike.

"The RPG is loaded, and Ilya has the car ready," Yan reports in my headpiece. He's on the roof of the house across the street from the one where Anton and I are.

"Good." I glance over at Anton, who's lying on his stomach next to me, peering into the scope of his sniper's rifle. "You ready?"

He nods without taking his eye off the target. "I'm going for head shots in case they're wearing vests."

"Good." Turning my attention to my own M110, I adjust my scope. Head shots are tricky, especially once your targets start to react, but they're the best way to ensure a professional stays dead.

Body armor is too often concealed under clothing these days.

The seconds tick by, each one stretching longer than the next. It's easy to get impatient at a time like this, so I focus on steadying my breathing and making sure nothing obstructs my line of sight.

This is too important to fuck up.

Unbidden, thoughts of Sara steal into my mind. I wonder what she's doing, if she's still sleeping or if she's already up. As exciting as this is for me—and it *is* exciting, I can't lie—I'd much rather be home in Japan, holding her warm, naked body as she comes awake. In just a few short months, my little songbird has become more important to me than anything else in the world, my passion for her crowding out everything else that once interested me.

The sound of a door opening wrenches me out of my thoughts.

"He's coming," Yan whispers in the headset, and I force myself to focus.

There will be time for Sara later.

If we survive today, that is.

CHAPTER 48
SARA

Ten minutes. The car's tires squeal as I zoom down the long driveway and barrel through the open gates, gripping the wheel so hard my fingers dig into the leather.

I have only ten minutes.

That is, assuming Yulia's estimate was correct. I don't know how she escaped from her lethal-looking husband and disabled all those security measures, but it's entirely possible he's already on my heels.

There are no lights along this one-lane road, no signs—nothing to tell me where I'm going. The moon and my car's headlights are the only sources of illumination. I have no idea which way southwest is, so when I reach a two-lane road, I randomly turn left, going on instinct.

If I just turned the wrong way, I'm screwed.

My heart feels like it's going to hammer through my chest, my breathing loud in my ears. Sweat forms in my armpits and drips down my sides, and my knee trembles as I floor the gas pedal. Driving on the left side of the road, with the wheel on the left side of the car, is beyond confusing for an American like me, but I don't dare slow down.

Eight minutes.

Seven minutes.

I can do it.

I can make it.

Headlights from an oncoming car blind me, sending my adrenaline levels surging. Is it Kent? His guards?

The car passes by without stopping, and I exhale in relief, lifting my foot off the gas pedal as the road curves sharply in front of me. The last thing I need is to lose control of the car and go through the guardrail, like George did that terrible night. As is, even with reduced speed, I'm going 110 kilometers an hour. If the gas station is seven kilometers away, I should make it with time to spare.

Another minute passes before the road curves again, and I see it.

More headlights, this time behind me.

Gripping the wheel tighter, I floor the gas pedal again.

The car behind me accelerates as well.

My stomach climbs into my throat. Out of the corner of my eye, I catch a glimpse of a speed limit sign. It's 50kmh—over sixty, no, *seventy* kilometers less than my current speed. And if that car is catching up to me, it's going even faster.

It's official.

I'm being pursued.

The road twists again, and I hold back a shriek as another oncoming car whooshes by, its headlights blinding me for a crucial second. The side of my car scrapes against the guardrail, sparks flying as metal screeches against metal. Gasping, I take my foot off the gas and veer away from the rail, getting the car closer to the middle of the winding road.

The pursuing headlights gain on me, and as the road curves again, I see two cars behind me, each one large and dark. Two SUVs. My pulse is now a thunderous roar in my ears, my hands so sweaty they slide around on the wheel. Fighting my panic, I press the gas pedal again, but the cars behind me accelerate faster, and as the road curves right, one flanks me on my side while the other one pulls in front of me.

Despair grips me with an icy fist.

It's over.

They got me.

Shaking, I take my foot off the gas.

My one chance at escape, and I blew it.

The SUV in front of me reduces speed as well, and the one on my side moves behind me. They know I have no choice but to comply.

It's officially over.

I've lost.

The SUV in front of me slows further, forcing me to brake. My speedometer shows forty kilometers an hour, then thirty-five... then thirty. I'm practically crawling now, and I realize they're making me stop.

They're going to get me out of this car and drag me back to Kent's house, where I will stay locked up until Peter comes for me.

The future stretches out in front of me, as dark and dangerous as this winding road. Without hope for escape, without choices, I will be Peter's property, and so will our child. I will never see my friends and family again, never help women deliver their babies. As my parents grow older, I won't be there for them, and they'll never know their grandchildren.

All I will have is Peter, and the scariest thing of all is that this doesn't seem unappealing.

I can see it so clearly: the way he'll care for me, the tenderness in his eyes when he'll hold our baby. He'll love me with an intensity that will scorch my soul, and eventually, my own twisted love will grow from its ashes. And after a while, it will all seem normal, from my lack of freedom to the violence of his profession.

We'll be a family, the way he wants, and as I watch the speedometer drop below fifteen, I know I can't let it happen.

I can't give in to the sickest part of me, the one that wants that twisted future.

Another bend in the road, more headlights coming our way. My frantic heartbeat steadies, a strange calm settling over me as I reach over and buckle my seatbelt. I'll have less than a second to act, so I have to make it count.

Easing my foot off the brake, I clutch the wheel as hard as I can, and as the oncoming car whooshes by, its headlights blinding me and my pursuers alike, I yank the wheel all the way to the right, pulling out into the opposite lane as I floor the gas.

The car rips forward, zooming past the SUV blocking me in the front. I can practically hear my pursuers swear as I leave them in the dust again, my sleek Mercedes gaining speed with the throaty roar of a V8 engine. The speedometer jumps to 100... 110... 120... 130...

Sparks fly, metal scraping against metal as I sideswipe the guardrail again, but this time, I don't slow down. I keep my foot steady, correcting just enough to maintain control.

It's a video game, I tell myself. Just a racing video game where I'm driving on the wrong side of the road.

Having recovered from the shock of my sudden maneuver, my pursuers are on my tail again, but I have no intention of making it easy for them. Each time they get close, I veer into the middle of the road, preventing them from going around me. And I maintain my breakneck speed, keeping my foot on the gas even through the steepest turns. Pretending it's a video game helps—I was always good at those as a kid.

One more minute on the road.

Two.

Three.

I can do it.

I can make it.

In the distance, I see lights, and my pulse jumps anew.

It's the gas station. It has to be.

My plan is simple: screech to a stop in front of whatever store is there, jump out, and run in, screaming at the top of my lungs for a phone. With any luck, Kent's people will be too worried about the authorities to grab me in public, but even if they're not, someone—a gas station attendant, other drivers—will see what's happening and call the police.

It's not much of a plan, but it's all I've got.

The gas station looms closer with each second. To my relief, despite the early hour and the wilderness feel of the area, I see a well-lit store with a few people inside, and some cars in the parking lot.

My hope is that Kent won't want to cause trouble so close to his home, and sure enough, the SUVs behind me reduce their speed, allowing me to pull ahead as we approach the gas station.

Triumph floods my veins as I take my foot off the gas, preparing to execute my stop-and-run maneuver.

I'm there.

Even if they catch me before I make it to a phone, my capture won't go unnoticed.

I'm less than two hundred feet from the gas station when it happens.

A dog darts onto the road in front of me.

I react instinctively, swerving as I hit the brakes, and as my car spins into the guardrail, I have one last illogical thought.

I hope Peter and his men return from their job unscathed.

CHAPTER 49
PETER

"Now," I bark into the headset, and Yan fires the RPG as Arslan's bodyguards herd their boss into his car.

Boom!

For a moment, there's nothing but the blinding flash of the missile exploding and the ringing in my ears, but then I see it.

The surviving bodyguards scattering like roaches, with more running out of the guardhouse to confront the threat.

"Do it," I tell Anton, and he starts picking them off one by one, his semi-automatic sniper's rifle firing with deadly efficiency. I join him, and before long, a dozen bodies litter the ground, their heads blown open by our bullets.

"Two o'clock," Yan shouts in the headset, and I spot movement on the ground. A guard is crouched low, using the burning car as a cover. His arm is around a man's back, protecting him.

Fury spikes through me as I recognize the man.

Deniz Arslan.

Our target is still alive.

He's bloodied and covered with dirt, but he's walking—which means his bodyguards are even better than we thought.

"It's Arslan," I snarl into the headset, shifting my position to angle my scope around the obstruction of the burning car.

I have to get this fucker.

He has to die today.

In the distance, sirens wail, and more bodyguards rush into Arslan's yard. We have minutes, if not seconds, to complete our task.

Shutting out the noise and the pounding of my heartbeat in my temples, I concentrate and squeeze the trigger.

Arslan's protector falls, his brains exploding all over the politician as I fire off a second shot.

"Fuck!"

Through training or dumb luck, my target falls and rolls—at the exact right time.

Swearing under my breath, I shoot again, and I hear the staccato roar of Anton's weapon next to mine.

With grim satisfaction, I watch as two of our bullets rip through Arslan's skull, exploding his brain on the way.

It's done.

The corrupt politician is dead.

"Incoming," Yan yells, and I jump to my feet, hearing a helicopter in the distance.

As expected, we're going to have pursuit.

It takes mere seconds for Anton and myself to shimmy down from the neighbor's roof and join Yan below on the street. It's only a few blocks to the community fence from here, and we run as fast as we can as the sirens' wail grows louder. The helicopter is approaching quickly, too.

"Ilya? Tell me you're there," I order, out of breath as I sprint down the street.

"Ready and waiting," he reports. "You guys better hurry. It's about to be a madhouse over here."

Clenching my teeth, I pick up speed, and Yan and Anton do the same as a vehicle squeals out onto the street a block behind us.

Arslan's remaining bodyguards are catching up.

The ten-foot fence looms ahead, with community guards pouring onto the road, armed to the teeth.

"Now," I shout at Yan, and he pulls out a grenade, ripping the pin off with his teeth without slowing down.

The guards scatter as Yan throws the grenade, and Anton and I pull out our guns, firing indiscriminately.

We don't need to kill them all, just get them out of our way.

We're now at the fence, so I jump up, grabbing onto a tree branch to lever myself up. This, here, is why we train so hard, why we have to be stronger than most athletes. My muscles scream as I dangle by one hand, lowering the other arm to pull up Anton, and when Anton scales the top of the fence, he pulls me up before reaching down for Yan as I provide the cover fire.

Another grenade from Yan explodes in a deafening flash, chasing away the guards as we jump down from the fence, and then we're off again, running at top speed.

We need to get to our rendezvous point.

That's the only way we'll make it out.

The helicopter roar intensifies above us, the police sirens screaming ever louder.

"Now, Ilya," I shout into the headset, and his car screeches around the bend, slowing down just enough for us to jump in.

We peel away from Arslan's community, taking the back roads toward a tunnel, and when the sounds of pursuit fade, we switch vehicles and drive directly to our plane.

We made it.

Our target's dead, and no one got hurt.

Elated, I call Lucas as soon as our plane lifts off the ground.

"It's over," I say when he picks up the phone. "We're on our way back, so you can tell Sara to get ready. We're going to pick her up before we make a little detour to New Zealand."

For a moment, all there is silence. Then Lucas speaks.

"Peter…" His tone is grave. "About Sara… I'm afraid there's been an accident."

CHAPTER 50
PETER

*M*y heart turns into a block of ice, my lungs calcifying at Lucas's words. Sara, in an accident—it's impossible, unthinkable.

It's my worst nightmare come true.

Lucas is speaking, telling me something about a car and a dog, but I'm not processing. There is a dull roaring in my ears, and all I can think about is the other time someone gave me news over the phone in that tone.

The stench of death, Tamila's long lashes singed and glued with blood, Pasha's tiny hand curled around a toy car... My vision darkens, all awareness fading as anguish tears through me, decimating everything inside.

Sorting through a pile of bodies, hearing the buzzing of the flies, knowing I wasn't there to save them...

I can't breathe, can't feel anything but gut-wrenching horror.

A car accident. Sara. Her body crushed in crumpled heaps of metal.

The agony is too intense to bear. I can't picture her dead, can't imagine her vital spark extinguished.

Something red and hot trickles down my forearm. Dimly, I realize my fingers are digging into the phone so hard I've torn off a nail. The pain doesn't register, though. Nothing registers except the hollow agony spreading through my chest.

I can't lose Sara.

I won't survive it.

"—so she might have a concussion, but the doctors don't think that—"

"A concussion?" I latch on to the one word that doesn't make sense. My thoughts are disjointed and slow, paralyzed by shock and growing grief. "What are you talking about?"

"The doctors don't think it's too severe," Lucas says, his voice taking on an exasperated edge. "Haven't you been listening? It's a nasty gash on her forehead, but they'll make sure it doesn't leave a scar. And obviously, I'll cover all the bills—it's the least I can do under the circumstances."

"A scar?" It doesn't click for a moment, the despair encasing me too thick, too absolute, but then my synapses start to fire. Dragging in a long-overdue breath, I rasp out, "She's... alive?"

"What?" Lucas sounds confused. "Yes, of course. I told you, she has a dislocated shoulder and a possible concussion. Do you have bad reception there or something? Yes, Sara is obviously alive. Her car slammed into the guardrail, and she cut open her head and hurt her shoulder. We brought her to the clinic in Switzerland—the one Esguerra likes to use, remember? Peter, are you listening?"

I am, but I can't tell him that. My throat muscles have spasmodically locked up, and so has my entire body. The relief is so intense it tears through me like shrapnel from a mine, as painful in its own way as the anguish that choked me before. I don't remember crying when I lost my son, but now I feel that agonizing moisture on my face, the tears leaving scorching trails on what remains of my heart.

I didn't lose Sara.

She's alive.

Injured in my absence but alive.

"Peter? Can you hear me?" Lucas's voice grows in volume. "Fuck, man, can you hear me?"

"I'm on my way," I say thickly, and hanging up, I order Anton to change course for Switzerland.

CHAPTER 51
SARA

I drift in and out of floating darkness, my senses alternating between groggy awareness and total blankness. When I'm coherent enough to think, I'm cognizant of the pain, but I can also latch on to other stimuli... like voices.

"How could you do this? Do you not realize what he's going to do when he returns? We were supposed to keep her *safe*." It's a male voice, harsh and chiding. I know the man the voice belongs to, but the throbbing pain in my temples becomes unbearable whenever I try to think of the name.

"It was *your* guards who chased her. You could've let her go," a female voice objects. The woman sounds upset. I know her name is something foreign and exotic, but I'm too fuzzy to remember what it is. "He was abusing her, Lucas—"

Yes, Lucas, that's it, I recall with relief. Lucas Kent, the arms dealer who lives in Cyprus.

"Abusing her? He fucking worships the ground she stands on. Did you not see the way he looks at her?" Kent sounds like he's on the verge of killing someone. "And I told you—he called about her every day, wanting to know if she's eating, sleeping… if she's fucking *content*. Does that sound like a man who's torturing a woman? And she has been asking about *him*. Would a woman who hates her kidnapper worry about his safety?"

"No, but—"

"But nothing! Even if he waterboards her every night, it's none of our fucking business. I was doing him a favor, and now we'll be lucky if we don't end up on his list."

"Lucas, please." The exotically named woman—Kent's wife, the beautiful blonde, I now recall—sounds even more upset. "It was a freak accident, nothing more. He'll understand. Let me talk to him, explain what happened—"

"No." Kent's voice is grimly resolute. "I don't want him to know you were in any way involved. You're flying back home before he gets here. And I'm going to borrow a few dozen guards from Esguerra until we can hire more of our own."

"But what about you?" Kent's wife asks, her worried tone intensifying the nauseating pain in my head. Wincing, I try to shift into a more comfortable position—and have to choke back a cry as agony explodes in my left shoulder.

"I'm going to stay here until he lands," Kent says as I take shallow breaths to manage the blaze of pain. I want to open my eyes, but something is preventing it, and I don't dare move my arms again to find out what it is.

"What if he tries to kill you?" Kent's wife argues. "If you're right and he won't listen—"

"I'm keeping a dozen guards with me, and besides, he'll have *her* to worry about." I can feel his attention shift to me, and then Kent says, "I think I just saw her move. The painkillers must be wearing off. Get the nurses in here, quickly."

I hear rapid footsteps, and a minute later, I'm floating in fuzzy nothingness again.

The next time I resurface, it's to a soft feminine hand stroking my hair. It feels good, especially since my head feels like a concrete-filled balloon.

"I'm so sorry, Sara," a woman murmurs, and this time, her name comes to me. Yulia—that's what Kent's wife is called. "I have to leave now, but I want you to know how sorry I am. I thought you'd have more time to get away, but Lucas suspected I might try to help you and he set up some additional perimeter alarms. I'm so sorry. I never intended this to happen. I hope you believe me."

I open my mouth to thank her, but I end up coughing painfully instead. My throat is desert dry, and the heavy balloon that is my head throbs with agony. There also seems to be something across my face that's preventing me from opening my eyes. A thick bandage on my forehead, maybe?

"Here. You must be thirsty." A straw touches my lips, and I latch on to it, greedily sucking down the tepid liquid.

"What happened? Where am I?" I croak out when I've drained the cup of water. My voice is weak and hoarse, but at least I can speak again.

"You're in a private clinic in Switzerland," Yulia explains gently. "You were in a car accident. Do you remember?"

I nod and immediately regret it. "Yes," I gasp out when the agonizing wave of pain passes. "There was a dog and—"

"Yes, that's right." She sounds relieved. Is it because I have a head injury? I wonder how bad it is, and then tense, my lungs seizing as I recall something far more important.

Frantically, I ask, "Where's Peter? Is he—"

"I'm afraid so," Yulia says, and my heart crumbles at the genuine regret in her voice. "I'm sorry," she continues in the same tone. "He's on his way back. There was nothing I could do."

My lungs expand on a shaking breath. "You mean he's... all right?" My voice is strained, my extremities tingling from a violent spike of adrenaline. "He didn't get hurt?"

There is a moment of silence. Then Yulia says slowly, "No, he didn't. Sara... did you just ask me this because you're afraid that he *didn't* get hurt—or that he did?" At my confused nonresponse, she clarifies, "Do you have feelings for this man?"

I moisten my cracked lips, aware of an unwelcome creep of guilt. I didn't mean to lie to Yulia or take advantage of her kindness, but that's essentially what I did when I emphasized the negative aspects of my complex relationship with Peter.

Not only did I fail to get away, but I got her into a world of trouble. The worst part, however, is that I'm secretly relieved I failed, glad I wasn't able to escape Peter and the future I both want and dread.

"It's… complicated," I finally say, echoing her words from that day.

She inhales sharply and stands up. "I see."

"Yulia, wait," I say as I hear her footsteps, but it's too late.

She's gone, and before long, the drugs claim me again.

CHAPTER 52
PETER

A dislocated shoulder and a gash on her forehead.

Logically, I know neither of those injuries is life-threatening, but as I look at Sara in the hospital bed, her pale face bruised all over and half-covered by a bandage, fear and rage churn in my chest, defying all attempts at logic.

The four-hour flight to Switzerland was among the longest of my life. Once we changed course, I called Lucas again, demanding more details and explanations, and though he repeatedly assured me that Sara's condition is stable and she's being treated by the best doctors in Europe, I didn't fully believe him until I saw her.

Fate has never been kind to me before.

Sitting down on the edge of her bed, I carefully clasp her hand in both of mine, feeling the fragile warmth of her skin and the delicacy of her slender bones. My own hands are trembling, my emotions too extreme to be controlled.

A dog.

She nearly died because of a fucking dog.

My heart cracks in half again, the pain as intense as when I thought her dead. If the guardrail hadn't been as strong, if the car didn't have airbags, if the shard of glass that sliced her forehead had gone into her eye instead… I shudder, picturing all the cruel ways she could've died and the debilitating injuries she could've suffered.

And it's all because of me.

I can't hide from that brutal reality, can't push away the suffocating guilt.

I wasn't there, and Sara ran.

She stole a car and raced to freedom, so desperate to get away from me she didn't care if she lived or died.

The fury boiling in my chest is only partially for Lucas. He'll pay for his negligence, of course, but I can't pretend he bears the lion's share of blame.

That belongs solely to me.

It was my selfish need to have her, to cage her and possess her, that drove Sara to take that risk. I nearly killed the woman I love, and I don't know how to atone for that.

I don't know if, even now, I can let her go.

Her swollen lips part on a gentle exhalation, and I sink to my knees on the floor, cradling the back of her hand against my stubble-roughened cheek as I close my eyes. Her skin is so soft, her fingers so small compared to mine. My chest squeezes agonizingly. I feel like I'm suffocating, drowning in longing and despair. Why can't she just love me? Why can't she accept that we belong together? There were times when I thought she might, when I was sure that she was getting close.

And maybe she was. Maybe she still might. The monster inside me snarls, demanding that I hold her, that I keep her no matter what it takes... no matter what it ultimately does to her. With time, she'll come around, understand that we are meant to be.

That if she gives me a chance, I'll make her happy... her and the child I so badly crave.

A faint moan jolts me out of my thoughts, and I open my eyes to find Sara's lips moving.

"P-Peter?" she whispers, and a supernova explodes in my chest. Just that one word, and my world is a thousand degrees warmer, a million watts brighter. All the grief and pain are extinguished, the darkness gone instead of sucking at my soul.

"Yes, ptichka," I answer hoarsely, pressing her hand against my lips. "I'm here."

Her slender fingers twitch as I kiss them one by one. "Are you... Did everything go okay?" She sounds groggy from the painkillers. "Did anyone get hurt?"

A pang of agony stabs my chest. "No, my love. Nobody but you."

"That's good." Her lips curve in a small, blissed-out smile. "I'm glad."

I draw in a strained breath, the guilt and anguish overwhelming me again. In some ways, it would be easier if Sara hated me, if all she felt for me was loathing and fear. Then I could walk away, try to curtail my obsession so I could let her live her life while I went back to the cold emptiness of mine. But Sara doesn't simply hate me; it's more complex than that.

She needs me. She's admitted it to me.

"Why did you run?" I ask raggedly, staring at the bruises on her jaw. "Is it because of what I said about the condoms? Do you dread a child with me that much?"

I have to understand what prompted her to do this.

I have to know if there's any hope for us.

Her fingers curl in my hold. "I… yes. I mean, no. I don't know. It's not what I want, but maybe…" She trails off, still high on painkillers.

"But maybe?" I prompt, my heart thumping painfully in my chest.

"But maybe in a different life, I would." Her voice is fading, turning into a cracking whisper. "In a different world, the one where I'd been born yours, it would be different. You wouldn't be a fugitive assassin… you wouldn't have abducted me after killing George. You'd be my husband, and I'd be your loving wife, and we could have a dog behind a picket fence… We'd take our children to the park and celebrate my parents' birthdays… There'd be friends and barbecues and music… and you would love me, really love me… love me so much you wouldn't steal my life."

I squeeze my eyes shut, her words twisting inside me like a killer's blade. It shouldn't hurt, her drugged admission; I should be glad she wants all that with me. But all I can think about is that I'll never truly have her, never give her the life she wants. Even if I succeed in making us a family, even if Sara warms to me more over the years, the past will always lie between us like a chasm, the lifestyle of a fugitive forever a source of strife and stress. There are no barbecues and picket fences in our future, no dogs and children playing in the yard.

She'll love our child, but it won't make her happy.

I could give her everything I have, and it won't be enough.

A monitor beeps softly as Sara's breathing evens out, and I open my eyes to find her asleep again, the painkillers helping her rest and heal.

A shallow breath escapes me, an impossible weight compressing my aching lungs.

I should get up, give my men an update and send them after Henderson, but I can't bring myself to move.

I can't do anything but kneel at Sara's bedside, holding her hand as hollow darkness presses in.

CHAPTER 53
SARA

When I wake up again, this time without the thick bandage across my eyes, Peter is there, sitting on a chair next to my bed with a computer on his lap. He looks exhausted, more weary than I've ever seen him. Dark shadows circle his bloodshot eyes, and his stubble-covered cheeks are hollow, as though he's lost some weight. He's working on the laptop, but the moment I stir, his gaze snaps to mine like metal to a magnet.

"You're awake." His voice is hoarse as he sets his laptop aside and stands. "How are you feeling, ptichka? Do you need anything? Here, drink some water." He picks up a cup with a straw from the table next to my bed and bends over me, helping me to a half-sitting position as he presses the straw against my lips.

I'm still a little woozy from the drugs, and I gratefully suck down most of the water. "How long have I been under?" I croak out when he takes the cup away.

Even after drinking, my throat feels like it's been scraped with sandpaper, my mouth so dry my tongue keeps sticking to my cheeks.

"Three days," Peter answers, sitting down on the edge of my bed. "The doctors thought it would speed your healing."

I run my tongue over my chapped lips, feeling the painful swelling on one side. Now that I'm more awake, I realize there's still a bandage across my forehead—I can feel it pressing down on my eyebrows—and my left shoulder is stiff and sore. "How bad is it?" I ask, wincing as I try to move.

Peter's jaw flexes. "A shard of glass cut a deep gash across your forehead, and you dislocated your left shoulder. Luckily, you had a seatbelt on, and the airbag absorbed most of the impact from the crash. Still, you're bruised all over, including over most of your face." His voice roughens as he speaks, his own face tightening with pain.

Blinking against the sudden sting of tears, I carefully reach up with my right hand, feeling the bandage across my forehead. I should probably worry about how I'll look with an ugly scar, but all I can focus on is the anguish in Peter's silver gaze.

I hurt him, this lethal, indomitable man.

I hurt him when he's been so badly hurt already, when suffering is all he's ever known.

"It won't leave a scar," he says hoarsely, following the movement of my hand. "They have the best plastic surgeons here, and they're going to fix it. I promise you, my love—I'm going to make it right."

I stare at him, my eyes burning with an onslaught of emotions. Maybe it's the aftermath of the painkillers, but I can't stand the pain in his gaze, can't bear the knowledge that I hurt him. Because no matter what I'd like to tell myself, I'm fiercely glad to see him, so relieved he wasn't killed I want to fall to my knees and cry.

If I had to choose between him and my freedom at this moment, I would give up everything to have him in my life.

A knock on the door is followed by two nurses entering the room, and I suck in a ragged breath as Peter rises to his feet.

"Wait!" Ignoring a wave of dizzying pain, I sit up, grabbing his tattooed wrist. "Stay with me… Please, Peter, stay."

He immediately sits down, covering my hand with his big palm. "Of course." His voice is deep and soft, as warm as the dark flame in his gaze. "Anything you wish, my love."

He stays with me while the nurses change the bandage on my head, and when they try to shoo him away, claiming I need rest, I beg him to stay and hold me. I know it makes no sense, but I'm past all attempts at sense and reason. I can't give up on trying to escape—if nothing else, I owe it to my future child and my parents—but right now, I need Peter with me.

I want to crawl into his arms and never leave.

He stays with me throughout the rest of the day and all of the following night, spooning me gently while I sleep, and when I wake up the next morning, I chase away the nurses and he helps me shower before settling me on his lap to watch TV.

I cling to him like that for the next two days, unable to let go, and he lets me, though he must think it strange. There's so much left unsaid between us, so many things still unresolved, but all I care about at the moment is that I have him.

He's mine to love and hate, no matter what.

———

To my annoyance, I heal slowly, the gash on my forehead requiring another surgery to minimize the scar and my shoulder paining me with every move. After another week at the clinic, however, I refuse to stay in my room all day, and Peter nearly kills the doctor who allows me to get up and walk down the hallway unsupervised.

Or at least, unsupervised by him.

I'm not the only one behaving irrationally after the accident. From what the nurses have told me, Peter hasn't let me out of his sight for more than a few minutes since arriving at the clinic. He even tries to accompany me to the bathroom on the pretext that the painkillers make me dizzy. When I categorically refuse, he insists that at least one of the nurses be present, so he can be informed immediately if something goes wrong. He has to know this level of concern is not entirely sane, but like me, he can't seem to help himself.

"I have to know you're safe. I have to see you, touch you at all times," he explains grimly when I assure him that I'm feeling better, and it's okay to leave me for an hour for a business meeting with his men.

"You're losing it," Anton told him in front of me yesterday when Peter put off an important call with a potential client so he could be there for my bandage change. "Sara has eight nurses looking after her, and at least four doctors. Do you really think she needs you there?"

I actually do, but I remained silent, not wanting to add to our mutual madness. I'm pretty sure Peter hasn't been neglecting his responsibilities to the team—whenever I wake up, I find him on his laptop or discussing business with his men—but the nurses have told me that all the Russians' meetings have been held in the room next to mine while I sleep, with Peter looking in on me every ten minutes.

"Your husband is so devoted to you," a young German nurse gushes when Peter leaves her to watch me while he showers. "I wish my fiancé was this crazy about me."

I'm tempted to correct her, to tell her that Peter is my kidnapper, not my husband, but I can't bring myself to burst her bubble. It wouldn't do any good, anyway. The doctors and the nursing staff at this clinic must be paid exceptionally well for their discretion, because no one I've spoken to so far has been willing to call the authorities on my behalf. Not that I've tried all that hard to convince them. Not only am I pathologically incapable of being apart from my captor, but I also feel terrible that I already landed Yulia in hot water.

I desperately hope Peter won't add her or Lucas to his list.

I consider talking to him about it, explaining that they're in no way to blame for my accident, but whenever Peter's men bring up Cyprus or the Kents, he gets such a hard, dangerous look in his eyes that I don't dare press the issue. For the moment, Peter seems focused solely on my health, and I want to keep it that way for as long as possible.

I can't have my dark knight going on another rampage—not when it's all my fault.

In general, we haven't spoken about my escape attempt or the events preceding it. Neither one of us can bear to bring it up. I don't know if Peter still intends to force a child on me, or whether he even knows that himself. Either way, he hasn't touched me—not in any sexual way at least.

I was glad at first—I was definitely in no condition to have sex those first few days—but now that I'm feeling better, I'm starting to wonder. My captor still wants me; I can feel his erection when I lie in his embrace. But he doesn't do anything about it, doesn't so much as kiss me on the lips. Even after I expressly cleared it with the doctors, he abstains, and I know it's because he blames himself for the crash. We might not have talked about what happened, but it's there between us, my injuries a constant reminder of what occurred that night. I see the torment in his eyes when he looks at my fading bruises, the same anguished guilt that consumed me after George's accident.

What happened may have brought us closer, but it's tearing Peter apart inside.

CHAPTER 54

PETER

By the time we've been at the clinic for ten days, Sara insists on walking around on her own, and I let her, though Yan hijacks the hallway cameras so I can watch her on my laptop when she does.

I'm so consumed with Sara it's crowding out everything, even my need for vengeance. I did manage to send my team to New Zealand a few hours after arriving at the clinic, but predictably, by the time they got there, Henderson had figured out his wife's mistake and disappeared again. Normally, that would've enraged me, but I couldn't work up enough energy for that. I still can't. Even Lucas, who prudently flew home as soon as I got to the clinic, isn't currently on my radar for his negligence with Sara. I still intend to make him pay, but for now, all that matters is that she's alive and healing well.

I watch her all the time now, day and night. It's gotten to the point where I barely eat or sleep. I don't know what to do, how to turn off this obsessive fear for her safety. Every time I close my eyes, I dream about Lucas telling me she's hurt, only when I get to the hospital, I find out he lied and she is dying.

It's my new nightmare, and I can't make it stop, any more than I can bring myself to let her go home.

That's what I should do, I know that. Keeping Sara with me will destroy her. I see it now, as clearly as the stitches on her forehead. Even though there were times she seemed content back in Japan, inside, she was torn and bleeding. The separation from her family and the loss of her career are wounds that may never fully heal. Already, here at the clinic, she's trying to help the doctors with the other patients—when she's not asking them to call the FBI, that is.

My little bird hasn't given up on flight, and I'm afraid she never will.

The phone calls with her parents don't help matters. I've let her talk to them every day this week, but that just seems to make things worse. By now, Sara has been gone for five months, and despite her reassurances to the contrary, her family is convinced she's being held against her will.

"Why won't you just come home?" her mother asks in frustration as I listen in on one of those conversations. "If you're just traveling with that man, you should have no problem coming home for a visit. You know they've already replaced you at the hospital, don't you? Your dad and I begged and pleaded for them to wait, but they were swamped. And your friend Marsha—she's been calling every week to ask about you. Why haven't you called her or anyone else from the hospital? They're all worried about you, darling, and so are we. And your dad's heart—" She stops, but not before Sara turns sickly pale underneath her bruises.

"What about Dad's heart?" Her voice takes on a panicked note. "Please, Mom, what's wrong with Dad's heart?"

"Well, he's not getting any younger, and neither am I," Lorna Weisman says, and I hear Sara blow out a relieved breath when she realizes her mother doesn't mean anything specific. My hackers have been keeping an eye on the Weismans' medical records, and I would've told Sara if there'd been any new developments. Still, I can tell this scared her. It's one of Sara's biggest fears: that something could happen to her parents while she's not there... that she would not be able to help the people she loves most because she's my prisoner halfway around the world.

"Please, Mom, don't even talk about such things," she says, forcing a false cheerfulness into her tone. "I'm fine, and I will try to come home for a visit soon."

"When?" her mother demands. "Give us a date."

Sara glances in my direction. "I can't. Not yet."

"Why not? Is it because he won't let you?"

"No, Mom. I already explained. The whole thing with the FBI is a big misunderstanding, but until it's straightened out, Peter can't go—"

"Bullshit." It's her father cutting in; he must've been listening on the loudspeaker all along. "He can't, but you certainly can—and you should. If he's not holding you captive, then come home. Get away from that criminal. You know they think he's killed people? They don't tell us anything, of course, but we overheard them talking and—"

"Dad, I have to go. I'm sorry. We'll talk later in the week, okay? Love you!"

Sara hangs up before her father can say another word, and though her face is carefully blank, I can tell she's on the verge of tears. Quietly, I walk over to her bed, and taking care not to jostle her sore shoulder, I pull her into my lap.

Then I hold her as she cries, my own despair growing as I realize that something's going to have to change.

I can't let her go, but I can't keep her either.

What makes my dilemma worse is that since the accident, something's changed between us. I feel it, and it crushes my nobler impulses whenever they arise. What I've always wanted—for Sara to share my feelings—seems to finally be within my reach. The way she clings to me, the way she looks at me these days—it all adds fuel to my compulsive need to keep her near, to hold her tight and never set her free.

I want to keep her in a gilded cage forever, so I can make sure she's always safe.

I want to protect her from everything, including my own twisted needs.

"The doctors said that it's okay, you know," she murmurs that night, reaching under the blanket to wrap her slender hand around my aching cock. "Let me—"

"No." Grimacing in agony, I carefully guide her hand away, even though every cell in my body weeps at the loss of her willing touch. "Not tonight, ptichka. You're not well yet."

The doctors might've cleared some low-impact sexual activities, but I know myself, and the intensity of my lust for Sara terrifies me. My need for her is too violent, too uncontrolled. I can't risk touching her until she's fully healed, so I force myself to wait until she's better.

Until I can get past my excruciating indecision and figure out what to do.

――――――――――

By the end of the second week, Sara's stitches come out, and the doctors tell us point blank that there's zero reason for us to remain at the clinic. One even dares to point out that in a regular hospital, Sara would have been discharged after the first night. I don't give a fuck about their opinions, of course, but Sara's is a different matter.

She's sick of staying at the clinic and ready to go anywhere, even back to our home in Japan.

"Please, Peter, it's enough. I'm perfectly fine," she insists, and I finally give in, telling Anton to prepare the plane for tomorrow morning.

"About fucking time," he mutters darkly. "We were sure you decided to retire and take up residency at this place."

I fight the urge to snarl at him, because he's absolutely right. Ever since Sara's accident, I've put everything on hold, ignoring the job offers that have been pouring in.

Our fame in the underworld is spreading, and we should capitalize on it.

A few more jobs like the one in Turkey, and my teammates and I will actually be able to retire.

We'll have enough to evade authorities for life.

It's late that evening when I get up to check my email. As usual, my inbox is flooded with messages from clients both current and prospective. Some of the offers coming in are laughable—five hundred thousand dollars to eliminate a local mobster, a million euros to rid someone of a wealthy uncle—but many are worth considering.

I'm almost done reading through the messages when a new email comes in. I open it—and stare in shock at the amount offered.

One hundred million euros.

Four times more than our most lucrative payout to date.

It's from Danilo Novak, the Serbian arms dealer who's making inroads into Kent and Esguerra's business. And if the amount wasn't enough to intrigue me, the name of the target definitely does.

Novak wants me to eliminate Julian Esguerra, my former employer—the man who vowed to kill me for saving his life while endangering his wife.

Stunned, I go through the email again, my mind racing with the implications. Reading between the lines, Novak seems to have some assets in play that would reduce the difficulty of the hit from impossible to impossibly dangerous.

Regardless, if we took this job, Esguerra would be our most challenging target yet.

It's also the only job we'd need to be set financially for life.

As I sit there, staring at my laptop screen, another idea comes to me—one just as dangerous, and infinitely more tempting.

If I handle things just right, this job could indeed be the answer to everything.

I could keep Sara... and give her the life she wants.

Thank you for reading! If you would consider leaving a review, it would be greatly appreciated. Peter & Sara's story continues in *Destiny Mine*. If you'd like to be notified when it's out, please sign up for my new release email list at www.annazaires.com.

If you're enjoying this series, you might like the following books:

- *The Twist Me Trilogy* – Julian & Nora's story, where Peter appears as a secondary character and gets his list
- *The Capture Me Trilogy* – Lucas & Yulia's story
- *The Mia & Korum Trilogy* – A dark sci-fi romance
- *The Krinar Captive* – A standalone sci-fi romance
- *The Krinar Kindle World Stories* – Sci-fi romance stories by other authors, set in the Krinar world

Collaborations with my husband, Dima Zales:
- *Mind Machines* – An action-packed technothriller
- *The Mind Dimensions Series* – Urban fantasy
- *The Last Humans Trilogy* – Dystopian/post-apocalyptic science fiction
- *The Sorcery Code* – Epic fantasy

Additionally, if you like audiobooks, please visit my website to check out this series and our other books in audio.

And now please turn the page for a little taste of *Twist Me*, *Capture Me*, and *The Krinar Captive*.

EXCERPT FROM TWIST ME

Author's Note: *Twist Me* is a dark erotic trilogy about Nora and Julian Esguerra. All three books are now available.

Kidnapped. Taken to a private island.

I never thought this could happen to me. I never imagined one chance meeting on the eve of my eighteenth birthday could change my life so completely.

Now I belong to him. To Julian. To a man who is as ruthless as he is beautiful—a man whose touch makes me burn. A man whose tenderness I find more devastating than his cruelty.

My captor is an enigma. I don't know who he is or why he took me. There is a darkness inside him—a darkness that scares me even as it draws me in.

My name is Nora Leston, and this is my story.

It's evening now. With every minute that passes, I'm starting to get more and more anxious at the thought of seeing my captor again.

The novel that I've been reading can no longer hold my interest. I put it down and walk in circles around the room.

I am dressed in the clothes Beth had given me earlier. It's not what I would've chosen to wear, but it's better than a bathrobe. A sexy pair of white lacy panties and a matching bra for underwear. A pretty blue sundress that buttons in the front. Everything fits me suspiciously well. Has he been stalking me for a while? Learning everything about me, including my clothing size?

The thought makes me sick.

I am trying not to think about what's to come, but it's impossible. I don't know why I'm so sure he'll come to me tonight. It's possible he has an entire harem of women stashed away on this island, and he visits each one only once a week, like sultans used to do.

Yet somehow I know he'll be here soon. Last night had simply whetted his appetite. I know he's not done with me, not by a long shot.

Finally, the door opens.

He walks in like he owns the place. Which, of course, he does.

I am again struck by his masculine beauty. He could've been a model or a movie star, with a face like his. If there was any fairness in the world, he would've been short or had some other imperfection to offset that face.

But he doesn't. His body is tall and muscular, perfectly proportioned. I remember what it feels like to have him inside me, and I feel an unwelcome jolt of arousal.

He's again wearing jeans and a T-shirt. A gray one this time. He seems to favor simple clothing, and he's smart to do so. His looks don't need any enhancement.

He smiles at me. It's his fallen angel smile—dark and seductive at the same time. "Hello, Nora."

I don't know what to say to him, so I blurt out the first thing that pops into my head. "How long are you going to keep me here?"

He cocks his head slightly to the side. "Here in the room? Or on the island?"

"Both."

"Beth will show you around tomorrow, take you swimming if you'd like," he says, approaching me. "You won't be locked in, unless you do something foolish."

"Such as?" I ask, my heart pounding in my chest as he stops next to me and lifts his hand to stroke my hair.

"Trying to harm Beth or yourself." His voice is soft, his gaze hypnotic as he looks down at me. The way he's touching my hair is oddly relaxing.

I blink, trying to break his spell. "And what about on the island? How long will you keep me here?"

His hand caresses my face, curves around my cheek. I catch myself leaning into his touch, like a cat getting petted, and I immediately stiffen.

His lips curl into a knowing smile. The bastard knows the effect he has on me. "A long time, I hope," he says.

For some reason, I'm not surprised. He wouldn't have bothered bringing me all the way here if he just wanted to fuck me a few times. I'm terrified, but I'm not surprised.

I gather my courage and ask the next logical question. "Why did you kidnap me?"

The smile leaves his face. He doesn't answer, just looks at me with an inscrutable blue gaze.

I begin to shake. "Are you going to kill me?"

"No, Nora, I won't kill you."

His denial reassures me, although he could obviously be lying.

"Are you going to sell me?" I can barely get the words out. "Like to be a prostitute or something?"

"No," he says softly. "Never. You're mine and mine alone."

I feel a tiny bit calmer, but there is one more thing I have to know. "Are you going to hurt me?"

For a moment, he doesn't answer again. Something dark briefly flashes in his eyes. "Probably," he says quietly.

And then he leans down and kisses me, his warm lips soft and gentle on mine.

For a second, I stand there frozen, unresponsive. I believe him. I know he's telling the truth when he says he'll hurt me. There's something in him that scares me—that has scared me from the very beginning.

He's nothing like the boys I've gone on dates with. He's capable of anything.

And I'm completely at his mercy.

I think about trying to fight him again. That would be the normal thing to do in my situation. The brave thing to do.

And yet I don't do it.

I can feel the darkness inside him. There's something wrong with him. His outer beauty hides something monstrous underneath.

I don't want to unleash that darkness. I don't know what will happen if I do.

So I stand still in his embrace and let him kiss me. And when he picks me up again and takes me to bed, I don't try to resist in any way.

Instead, I close my eyes and give in to the sensations.

All three books in the *Twist Me* trilogy are now available. Please visit my website at www.annazaires.com to learn more and to sign up for my new release email list.

EXCERPT FROM CAPTURE ME

Author's Note: *Capture Me* is a dark romance trilogy featuring Lucas & Yulia. It parallels some of the events in the *Twist Me* trilogy. All three books are now available.

She fears him from the first moment she sees him.

Yulia Tzakova is no stranger to dangerous men. She grew up with them. She survived them. But when she meets Lucas Kent, she knows the hard ex-soldier may be the most dangerous of them all.

One night—that's all it should be. A chance to make up for a failed assignment and get information on Kent's arms dealer boss. When his plane goes down, it should be the end.

Instead, it's just the beginning.

He wants her from the first moment he sees her.

Lucas Kent has always liked leggy blondes, and Yulia Tzakova is as beautiful as they come. The Russian interpreter might've tried to seduce his boss, but she ends up in Lucas's bed—and he has every intention of seeing her there again.

Then his plane goes down, and he learns the truth.

She betrayed him.

Now she will pay.

———————

He steps into my apartment as soon as the door swings open. No hesitation, no greeting—he just comes in.

Startled, I step back, the short, narrow hallway suddenly stiflingly small. I'd somehow forgotten how big he is, how broad his shoulders are. I'm tall for a woman—tall enough to fake being a model if an assignment calls for it—but he towers a full head above me. With the heavy down jacket he's wearing, he takes up almost the entire hallway.

Still not saying a word, he closes the door behind him and advances toward me. Instinctively, I back away, feeling like cornered prey.

"Hello, Yulia," he murmurs, stopping when we're out of the hallway. His pale gaze is locked on my face. "I wasn't expecting to see you like this."

I swallow, my pulse racing. "I just took a bath." I want to seem calm and confident, but he's got me completely off-balance. "I wasn't expecting visitors."

"No, I can see that." A faint smile appears on his lips, softening the hard line of his mouth. "Yet you let me in. Why?"

"Because I didn't want to continue talking through the door." I take a steadying breath. "Can I offer you some tea?" It's a stupid thing to say, given what he's here for, but I need a few moments to compose myself.

He raises his eyebrows. "Tea? No, thanks."

"Then can I take your jacket?" I can't seem to stop playing the hostess, using politeness to cover my anxiety. "It looks quite warm."

Amusement flickers in his wintry gaze. "Sure." He takes off his down jacket and hands it to me. He's left wearing a black sweater and dark jeans tucked into black winter boots. The jeans hug his legs, revealing muscular thighs and powerful calves, and on his belt, I see a gun sitting in a holster.

Irrationally, my breathing quickens at the sight, and it takes a concerted effort to keep my hands from shaking as I take the jacket and walk over to hang it in my tiny closet. It's not a surprise that he's armed—it would be a shock if he wasn't—but the gun is a stark reminder of who Lucas Kent is.

What he is.

It's no big deal, I tell myself, trying to calm my frayed nerves. I'm used to dangerous men. I was raised among them. This man is not that different. I'll sleep with him, get whatever information I can, and then he'll be out of my life.

Yes, that's it. The sooner I can get it done, the sooner all of this will be over.

Closing the closet door, I paste a practiced smile on my face and turn back to face him, finally ready to resume the role of confident seductress.

Except he's already next to me, having crossed the room without making a sound.

My pulse jumps again, my newfound composure fleeing. He's close enough that I can see the gray striations in his pale blue eyes, close enough that he can touch me.

And a second later, he does touch me.

Lifting his hand, he runs the back of his knuckles over my jaw.

I stare up at him, confused by my body's instant response. My skin warms and my nipples tighten, my breath coming faster. It doesn't make sense for this hard, ruthless stranger to turn me on. His boss is more handsome, more striking, yet it's Kent my body's reacting to. All he's touched thus far is my face. It should be nothing, yet it's intimate somehow.

Intimate and disturbing.

I swallow again. "Mr. Kent—Lucas—are you sure I can't offer you something to drink? Maybe some coffee or—" My words end in a breathless gasp as he reaches for the tie of my robe and tugs on it, as casually as one would unwrap a package.

"No." He watches as the robe falls open, revealing my naked body underneath. "No coffee."

All three books in the *Capture Me* trilogy are now available. If you'd like to find out more, please visit my website at www.annazaires.com.

EXCERPT FROM
THE KRINAR
CAPTIVE

Author's Note: *The Krinar Captive* is a full-length, stand-alone scifi romance that takes place approximately five years before *The Krinar Chronicles* trilogy.

Emily Ross never expected to survive her deadly fall in the Costa Rican jungle, and she certainly never thought she'd wake up in a strangely futuristic dwelling, held captive by the most beautiful man she'd ever seen. A man who seems to be more than human...

Zaron is on Earth to facilitate the Krinar invasion—and to forget the terrible tragedy that ripped apart his life. Yet when he finds the broken body of a human girl, everything changes. For the first time in years, he feels something more than rage and grief, and Emily is the reason for that.

Letting her go would compromise his mission, but keeping her could destroy him all over again.

I don't want to die. I don't want to die. Please, please, please, I don't want to die.

The words kept repeating in her mind, a hopeless prayer that would never be heard. Her fingers slipped another inch on the rough wooden board, her nails breaking as she tried to maintain her grip.

Emily Ross was hanging by her fingernails—literally— off a broken old bridge. Hundreds of feet below, water rushed over the rocks, the mountain stream full from recent rains.

Those rains were partially responsible for her current predicament. If the wood on the bridge had been dry, she might not have slipped, twisting her foot in the process. And she certainly wouldn't have fallen onto the rail that had broken under her weight.

It was only a last-minute desperate grab that had prevented Emily from plummeting to her death below. As she was falling, her right hand had caught a small protrusion on the side of the bridge, leaving her dangling in the air hundreds of feet above the hard rocks.

I don't want to die. I don't want to die. Please, please, please, I don't want to die.

It wasn't fair. It wasn't supposed to happen this way. This was her vacation, her regain-sanity time. How could she die now? She hadn't even begun living yet.

Images of the last two years slid through Emily's brain, like the PowerPoint presentations she'd spent so many hours making. Every late night, every weekend spent in the office—it had all been for nothing. She'd lost her job during the layoffs, and now she was about to lose her life.

No, no!

Emily's legs flailed, her nails digging deeper into the wood. Her other arm reached up, stretching toward the bridge. This wouldn't happen to her. She wouldn't let it. She had worked too hard to let a stupid jungle bridge defeat her.

Blood ran down her arm as the rough wood tore the skin off her fingers, but she ignored the pain. Her only hope of survival lay in trying to grab onto the side of the bridge with her other hand, so she could pull herself up. There was no one around to rescue her, no one to save her if she didn't save herself.

The possibility that she might die alone in the rainforest had not occurred to Emily when she'd embarked on this trip. She was used to hiking, used to camping. And even after the hell of the past two years, she was still in good shape, strong and fit from running and playing sports all through high school and college. Costa Rica was considered a safe destination, with a low crime rate and tourist-friendly population. It was inexpensive too—an important factor for her rapidly dwindling savings account.

She'd booked this trip *before*. Before the market had fallen again, before another round of layoffs that had cost thousands of Wall Street workers their jobs. Before Emily went to work on Monday, bleary-eyed from working all weekend, only to leave the office the same day with all her possessions in a small cardboard box.

Before her four-year relationship had fallen apart.

Her first vacation in two years, and she was going to die.

No, don't think that way. It won't happen.

But Emily knew she was lying to herself. She could feel her fingers slipping farther, her right arm and shoulder burning from the strain of supporting the weight of her entire body. Her left hand was inches away from reaching the side of the bridge, but those inches could've easily been miles. She couldn't get a strong enough grip to lift herself up with one arm.

Do it, Emily! Don't think, just do it!

Gathering all her strength, she swung her legs in the air, using the momentum to bring her body higher for a fraction of a second. Her left hand grabbed onto the protruding board, clutched at it... and the fragile piece of wood snapped, startling her into a terrified scream.

Emily's last thought before her body hit the rocks was the hope that her death would be instant.

———————————

The smell of jungle vegetation, rich and pungent, teased Zaron's nostrils. He inhaled deeply, letting the humid air fill his lungs. It was clean here, in this tiny corner of Earth, almost as unpolluted as on his home planet.

He needed this now. Needed the fresh air, the isolation. For the past six months, he'd tried to run from his thoughts, to exist only in the moment, but he'd failed. Even blood and sex were not enough for him anymore. He could distract himself while fucking, but the pain always came back afterwards, as strong as ever.

Finally, it had gotten to be too much. The dirt, the crowds, the stink of humanity. When he wasn't lost in a fog of ecstasy, he was disgusted, his senses overwhelmed from spending so much time in human cities. It was better here, where he could breathe without inhaling poison, where he could smell life instead of chemicals. In a few years, everything would be different, and he might try living in a human city again, but not yet.

Not until they were fully settled here.

That was Zaron's job: to oversee the settlements. He had been doing research on Earth fauna and flora for decades, and when the Council requested his assistance with the upcoming colonization, he hadn't hesitated. Anything was better than being home, where memories of Larita's presence were everywhere.

There were no memories here. For all of its similarities to Krina, this planet was strange and exotic. Seven billion *Homo sapiens* on Earth—an unthinkable number—and they were multiplying at a dizzying pace. With their short lifespans and the resulting lack of long-term thinking, they were consuming their planet's resources with utter disregard for the future. In some ways, they reminded him of *Schistocerca gregaria*—a species of locusts he'd studied several years ago.

Of course, humans were more intelligent than insects. A few individuals, like Einstein, were even Krinar-like in some aspects of their thinking. It wasn't particularly surprising to Zaron; he had always thought this might be the intent of the Elders' grand experiment.

Walking through the Costa Rican forest, he found himself thinking about the task at hand. This part of the planet was promising; it was easy to picture edible plants from Krina thriving here. He had done extensive tests on the soil, and he had some ideas on how to make it even more hospitable to Krinar flora.

All around him, the forest was lush and green, filled with the fragrance of blooming heliconias and the sounds of rustling leaves and native birds. In the distance, he could hear the cry of an *Alouatta palliata*, a howler monkey native to Costa Rica, and something else.

Frowning, Zaron listened closer, but the sound didn't repeat.

Curious, he headed in that direction, his hunting instincts on alert. For a second, the sound had reminded him of a woman's scream.

Moving through the thick jungle vegetation with ease, Zaron put on a burst of speed, leaping over a small creek and the bushes that stood in his way. Out here, away from human eyes, he could move like a Krinar without worrying about exposure. Within a couple of minutes, he was close enough to pick up the scent. Sharp and coppery, it made his mouth water and his cock stir.

It was blood.

Human blood.

Reaching his destination, Zaron stopped, staring at the sight in front of him.

In front of him was a river, a mountain stream swollen from recent rains. And on the large black rocks in the middle, beneath an old wooden bridge spanning the gorge, was a body.

A broken, twisted body of a human girl.

The Krinar Captive is now available. Please visit my website at www.annazaires.com to learn more and to sign up for my new release email list.

ABOUT THE AUTHOR

Anna Zaires is a *New York Times, USA Today,* and #1 international bestselling author of sci-fi romance and contemporary dark erotic romance. She fell in love with books at the age of five, when her grandmother taught her to read. Since then, she has always lived partially in a fantasy world where the only limits were those of her imagination. Currently residing in Florida, Anna is happily married to Dima Zales (a science fiction and fantasy author) and closely collaborates with him on all their works.

To learn more, please visit www.annazaires.com.

Printed in Great Britain
by Amazon